Krekania

Scarlet Ingstad

Cover Art by Cody Rusk

For my family, who have supported even my wildest ideas and dreams, and without whom I would not be who I am today.

Dear Lydall,

I am not exactly sure where this journey will take us, but right about now I could use a good adventure. What we are about to face will be terrifying…unnerving even. All I know is that we both have some battles to fight, and not all of them are external.

Perhaps the most difficult part of any journey is taking that first step. That's the scariest part of all: beginning. Beginning means you could fail. You could start this grand quest and end up falling flat on your face. Then again, you could also soar higher than the heavens and become someone you never imagined you could be. So, the question is, do we do it? Do we begin?

There are so many stories I have started, and I have quit every single one of them. The stories I have completed were variations of things not my own. I have never once sat down and come up with a world of my own and seen it through until the end. But something tells me, Lydall, that our story will have an ending. I feel it in the depths of my soul. Why? Because I need it. I need to go on this journey, and I need to find what lies at the end. And I think, perhaps, so do you.

We're going to run into roadblocks and moments of indecision. We will also run into people who say we can't do this…or that what we've done just simply isn't good enough. Those will be the hardest fights we will face. In the past I've allowed those things to stop me. But something about you, Lydall, I think will keep me going despite those inevitable struggles.

I've already had so many conversations with you in my head and I haven't even started writing our story yet. I feel as if I know you, despite the fact I created you. In many ways you are more real to me than many people are. I think that is why I believe in you so much…why I believe in us. It's worth the effort. It's worth the risk.

So Lydall…I have but one question for you:

Shall we begin?

Love,

Scarlet

1

Lydall gritted her teeth to keep from swearing as she listened to her parents argue. She adjusted her dress for the millionth time, frustrated with the scratchy material and unnecessary bodice. She knew fighting her mother on her outfits was a lost cause. Ever since she had turned fifteen, Lydall was made to wear dresses with a girdle and shoes with a slight heel. Her hair was plaited daily with small amounts of makeup to compliment her red hair and bright green eyes. In Lydall's opinion, they were the most uncomfortable and undesirable outfits she had ever had the displeasure of wearing. To her despair, those outfits were also almost all she had worn for the past three years.

Her only reprieve from restrictive dresses was when she was permitted to take her riding lessons in the yard. Triton, her pitch-black destrier, was her only friend in all the Kingdom of Histair. Lydall preferred the company of animals to humans anyway, and Triton was her personal favorite. During her time with the stallion, Lydall was also allowed to wear riding pants and a fitted shirt. Those fleeting hours were the only time in her young life when Lydall felt like herself. The freedom of riding Triton through the rolling hills was a stark contrast to her daily life in Histair's castle grounds.

Today, per usual, her parents were arguing over one of the many issues that Lydall's existence presented them with. However, this particular issue was the most taxing and abhorrent to Lydall: the marriage alliance. For generations, the

Kingdom of Histair wed their first born to the offspring of the Kingdom of Westland. This marriage served as a pact between the two kingdoms and had prevented confrontation. Prior to the treaty, the two kingdoms had warred themselves to near mutual destruction, costing many innocent civilians their lives.

The Earl and Lady of Westland had two children: a son only a couple months older than Lydall, and an eleven year old daughter. Since the Westland's son was slightly older, it was Lydall who would have to move to their kingdom when the marriage took place.

Lydall highly resented being the first born. Her younger brother would have a much easier life. Angus would be allowed to grow up in his own kingdom and become the next ruling Lord and be allowed to marry whomever he chose. The very notion of marrying and leaving Histair disgusted Lydall to her core. Marriage alone caused her to wrinkle her nose in displeasure, but the thought of marrying a stranger from a kingdom not her own was something else entirely. Her complaints and refusals over the past year had fallen on the deaf ears of her parents as they battled out the best way to force her into the marriage.

"I won't marry him!" shouted Lydall, finally having heard enough of the discussion, "I don't understand what it is you both cannot comprehend. It is *not* happening."

"You have no say in the matter!" roared Earl Oliver Barron, his large face growing red, "You are our daughter and you will do as we say! It's for the benefit of the entire kingdom…"

"And what about my benefit?" snarled Lydall, eyes flashing defiantly, "Did no one stop to think if this would be in *my* benefit?"

"That kind of thinking will destroy our entire

kingdom!" said Lady Amelia Barron, feeling rather faint as she dabbed at the sweat gleaming on her forehead, "It is selfish of you, Lydall to even say such a thing. I married your father when I was only sixteen. I moved here from Westland and began a new life in a new world. If I could accomplish this task than so can you."

Lydall glowered up at her mother, "You wanted to. You loved Father. You met years before you were to be married! I don't even know who the first-born son of Westland is! And why do we have to keep doing this? There must be someother way to keep the peace between ourselves and the Kingdom of Westland. Hasn't this tradition gone on for long enough?"

"You don't know what you're saying," sighed the Earl, forcing himself to calm down, "To break tradition is to surely instigate a war. Our peace exists only because of the marriage alliance, and I certainly will not go down as the Earl responsible for breaking tradition and destroying the entire kingdom."

"How do you know?" asked Lydall, face flushed and eyes stinging from tears that threatened to spill down her cheeks, "Have you even spoken to the Earl of Westland? Have you even asked him if we have to do this?"

"You don't understand," said Lady Amelia, "And it's hopeless to even begin explaining the same thing to you that we have for the past three years! This was always your destiny, child. Embrace it! Be proud that your marriage vows are the reason our alliance will hold strong in the years to come."

Lydall growled in frustration and stormed out of the throne room. She had never felt so trapped in all her life. The pressure of maintaining the peace for the entire kingdom rested on her young shoulders, and the cost was her very freedom.

Her chest felt as if a mule were sitting on top of her as she ran down the long, wide staircase and shoved open the massive doors of the castle. Lydall instantly felt her spirit lift as the fresh morning air filled her lungs. The smell of grass, morning dew, and crisp air renewed her spirit as she continued her flight toward the horse paddock.

A loud whinny from the stalls made her heart skip a beat as she rounded the corner. A large, black destrier was throwing his head joyously as he watched her run toward the stable.

"I'm here, Triton!" cried Lydall as she ran inside and threw open the wooden stall door, "I need to get out of here. Want to go with me?" she asked her horse fondly.

Triton threw back his head and let out a snort of excitement as Lydall flung herself onto his back and gave him a slight kick, urging him to hurry. The feeling of riding bareback, just her and her stallion, made the anger and sadness in Lydall's heart ease a bit. Together, horse and girl flew from the stalls and into the sprawling green landscape of Histair, leaving the castle and its walls far behind them.

…

Lydall smiled as she listened to Triton's hooves thunder across the vast green valley. The destrier ran at full speed for several long moments until Lydall was sure they had escaped without detection. She gently pulled back on the reigns, slowing Triton down to a brisk walk as they neared the main village on the outskirts of the kingdom.

Lydall frowned slightly when she realized she was still in her royal clothing. The villagers would recognize her instantly as the Earl and Lady's daughter and she knew she wouldn't be able to stay in town for very long. They were sure to report her travelling without her required escorts. Lydall was never permitted to leave the castle grounds without her armed guards and if reporting such a thing to the Earl had even the slightest chance of garnering favor, the villagers would not hesitate to do so. Lydall had snuck out dozens of times in the past couple years and suffered the stern lectures of her parents, but after the latest argument she worried what her parents' reaction would be this time around.

"I suppose any amount of time out of that place is worth it though," muttered Lydall, accepting the inevitable.

Triton snorted and shook his head as if he understood her words. Lydall smiled slightly as they walked down the cobblestone main street of the village. Peddlers moved about the streets, hands outstretched as they begged, while street vendors called out for her to purchase their various products. A group of children playing tag paused for a moment and gazed up in awe at the massive black destrier and its royal rider as they walked by. Lydall gave the young ones a friendly wave, laughing as she watched them giggle and shrink away shyly.

"Isn't that the daughter of the Earl?" muttered an older woman as she purchased a loaf of bread from one of the street sellers.

"Aye, it is," said the man as he packaged her bread, "Lydall. The red-head. She's a spit-fire that one. Doesn't look like she has her guards though," he added, eyes narrowed slightly, "That's rather odd isn't it?"

The woman turned and stared at Lydall, suspicion and interest glittering in her gaze.

Lydall frowned and gave Triton a nudge with her boots, "Come on, boy," she said quietly, "Let's get out of here."

Lydall and Triton moved away from the old woman and the bread maker, continuing on down the main street of the village. She moved on ahead toward an old, ramshackle shop with stacks of books in the windows.

"Whoa, boy," murmured Lydall as she and Triton slowed down in front of the store.

Lydall smiled to herself as she stared at the shop, memories of her childhood flooding back, as an elderly man and young boy opened the door and stepped outside.

"Good day, Lady Lydall!" called the older man as he gave her a quick bow, "A gift to you from my humble shop," he announced as he pushed the young boy forward.

The boy nervously held a book up toward Lydall, his little arms trembling under the weight of it as he strained to reach her atop her horse.

"Oh, you don't need to do that," said Lydall, as she held the leather book, "I must repay you!"

"No, no," he replied as the man put his hands out, refusing her offer, "It's been an absolute honor to have you in my store so frequently over the years. You always were an imaginative one...reading all those books about magic."

Lydall smirked, "Thank you Randall. Although, they were mostly for my brother, but I enjoyed them a bit, yes," she added as she remembered all the late-night reading sessions full of tales with faeries, elves, unicorns and dragons. Angus was fond of the topic, so she frequently obliged her younger brother.

Lydall smiled as she read the cover of the large tome: *Dragons and Their Origins*. Angus was going to love the next few nights of bedtime stories. If she was being honest with herself, she was going to enjoy the tales as well. Despite their silliness and illogical characters, fantasy stories did have a way of drawing one into their depths.

"You will be missed greatly, Lady Lydall," said Randall, a sad gleam in his eye as he gazed up at her, "Consider this a parting gift. Take it with you to Westland...may it remind you of simpler times and the joy of magic, for no matter where you end up, you must *never* forget its power. You never know when you may need to call upon it."

Lydall gave the old man an indulgent smile, "Thank you, Randall. I will do just that. I better go. It won't be long before my father sends out the royal guard…not all the villagers are as kind and understanding as you are," she added, smiling fondly at the man and the young boy by his side.

"Ah yes, they will have reported your unescorted presence I'm sure," said Randall, shaking his head, "A shame, really. Well my apprentice and I must return to our work. Lots of books to bind you know. Take care, Lady Lydall."

Lydall waved goodbye as she gave Triton a gently kick. The stallion tossed his head before he plunged forward at a brisk trot down the cobblestone street. Soon, they found a side road that led them back out onto the open grassy valleys that made up the majority of Histair's land. Lydall squeezed her legs a bit more and together horse and girl flew through the hills back toward the castle.

She smiled a little to herself and shook her head. Crazy old man. He always rambled about magic and fantasy and bizarre creatures. She supposed that's what happened with age: one reverts back to the simpler, more fanciful things. Lydall laughed to herself as she realized that if her younger brother weren't careful, he'd end up the village's next "Randall."

…

Lydall arrived back at the castle well into the afternoon, much to her parents' distress. They had greeted her at the castle gates, arms crossed in anger. Clearly the villagers had sent word back to the castle that she'd been hanging around the village again without an escort. Lydall grimaced as she thought back to the bread maker and the woman in the marketplace.

Her mother forced the maids to scrub Lydall down, re-dress her, and fix her hair and makeup. Lydall scowled through the entire process, unsure as to why her parents were so insistent that she look perfect all the time. It was such a chore having to dress as royalty especially right after ridingher stallion.

She endured the ordeal and quickly slipped away to her brother's room once the maids let her be. Angus' face lit up with excitement as Lydall presented him with the book from Randall.

"Dragons!" breathed Angus, his eyes wide with wonder as he stroked the leather cover.

The look on her brother's face made Lydall smile, "I suppose me running off sometimes has its perks, eh little brother?"

Angus smirked at Lydall before his face turned more serious, "You shouldn't do that you know," he said, "You worry them, then anger them, and then things are worse for you than they were before. Why do you do it?"

Lydall sighed and stroked her brother's short blonde hair, "Sometimes...I just need to feel free. Even if it's just for a short time. I just...need it."

Angus frowned a bit, but nodded sagely. His serious countenance made Lydall laugh.

"Come on, we better not be late for supper," she said with a smirk, "Wouldn't want to upset Mother and Father again, now would I?"

Angus gave her a doubtful glance and tried to suppress a grin, "I don't know, Lydall. Sometimes I think you enjoy it."

...

"Finally," grumbled the Earl as he glanced up at his children.

Lydall tried to stifle her desire to roll her eyes as she settled on her side of the large table. Angus sat across from her and smiled at their parents as they passed around a bowl of warm bread.

"Now that we are all here," began the Earl, "We can discuss tomorrow's event."

Lydall raised an eyebrow at that, green eyes shining with interest, "An event?" she asked, curiously.

"Yes," said her father, as he paused to take a swig of wine from his chalice, "The Earl and Lady from Westland and their charming young son, Victor, will be visiting our land to share a meal with us. We will also be discussing the marital arrangements between Victor and yourself, Lydall," he added.

Lydall felt her heart shatter at the thought. In her father's words she heard her freedom dissipate like a cloud of dust on a windy day. She knew this day was coming, but it still felt so sudden that it took her breath away like a blow to the stomach.

"How could you?" she asked, her voice in a whisper of shock, "I told you this isn't what I want! I don't want to marry him, or anyone for that matter!"

"And we have told you time and time again that it is not up for discussion!" countered her father, face turning red with frustration, "This is beyond your own trivial desires, Lydall, it's for the good of the kingdom. You have a great destiny, far more than just playing with your horse all day long."

Lydall knew from experience that continuing the argument was a useless venture. Ever since she had turned fifteen three years ago, she and her parents had battled constantly, only to reach the same conclusion: Lydall would marry the Lord of Westland.

. . .

Lydall grimaced and shut her eyes against the sudden bright light that flooded her room as her mother threw open the curtains.

"Now," said Lady Barron, "Let's go get you cleaned up for our guests. They'll be here in a few hours and we cannot have you looking like…well, like *you*," she added as she eyed Lydall's frizzy hair and wrinkled nightgown.

Sighing in resignation, Lydall forced herself out of bed and followed her mother up a sweeping spiral staircase to her bathing room, her heart heavy with despair. Her naturally curly hair would be pulled back and braided and her face hidden behind swaths of heavy makeup reserved only for special occasions. The maids would surely lace her up into another one of those stiff dresses and only then would she be declared suitable for their special guests.

The entire process made Lydall weary just thinking about it. With another sigh she sat down in front of her mirror and watched the maids in its reflection as they began their work, her eyes dull and miserable. It was going to be a long day.

. . .

"Maybe it won't be so bad," whispered Angus as he walked with Lydall down the main corridor to the Great Hall early that evening, "Maybe he'll be handsome? Like those warriors who rode dragons!"

Lydall smiled sadly down into her brother's blue eyes.

"I guess you've been reading that book from Randall then?" she asked.

Angus beamed, "Oh of course. I'll give it back when you—when you have to leave of course, but it is truly fascinating. I wish the dragons still lived."

Lydall smirked, "Well perhaps you're right. Maybe my betrothed will be a handsome dragon rider with a fierce gleam in his eye," she said indulgently.

Angus' smile only widened, eyes growing distant as his imagination took over.

"Alright, let's get this over with," said Lydall under her breath as she pushed open the large, golden doors that led to the Great Hall.

"Ah, there they are now!" announced Earl Barron,

standing as his children entered the Great Hall, "Children, come take a seat. Please allow me to introduce the Earl and Lady O'Connor of Westland and their son, Victor O'Connor."

It took every ounce of Lydall's royal training to not react. The Earl and Lady of Westland were large people, bellies stressing the seams of their clothing, and large faces grinning up at her. Their son, on the other hand, was a lanky, dull-looking, brown-haired boy. His eyelids hung halfway down his eyes as if he hadn't slept in months. He was so skinny that Lydall briefly pondered whether his parents regularly ate his portions at the dinner table back in Westland. His awkward countenance immediately made Lydall sick to her stomach. How could her parents expect her to marry and fall in love with someone like this?

"I don't think he's a dragon rider," murmured Angus with a frown of disappointment as they took their seats.

Lydall felt her heart plummet as she tried to hide her revulsion at the pathetic looking young man across from her.

"It is lovely to meet you, Lady Lydall," mumbled Victor, looking as glum as Lydall felt.

"Likewise," she managed to choke out, forcing a smile as she sat down and smoothed out her yellow dress, feigning excessive interest in her own attire to avoid making eye-contact with the young Lord.

"Now," began her father, "Let us discuss the arrangements, shall we?"

"Ah yes," agreed Earl O'Connor, his mouth already full from taking a large chunk of meat out of a turkey leg "I do believe we previously decided that the wedding will take place in Westland, seeing as how Lady Lydall will be residing there right after the wedding?"

Lydall felt her appetite disappear instantly. Couldn't they have waited at least a little while before starting in on this discussion? She forced a pleasant smile on her face and attempted to look interested. Angus kept shooting glares of dislike in Victor's direction as the adults talked.

"Ah, yes," said Earl Barron, "Quite right. I believe we can agree to that. The wedding should take place where Lydall will be living, I agree. As for the date, I propose next month's time? That should give Lydall and her mother plenty of time to prepare her attire and pack her belongings."

Earl O'Connor glanced at his wife, seeking her approval before he replied, "We concur. Next month our kingdoms will be united by the next generation, our children, and so our alliance shall continue for many years to come!"

The Earls and Ladies lifted their chalices in a toast to good health and peace between their kingdoms. Lydall, Angus, and Victor joined in half-heartedly on the toast, each of them trying to hide their true feelings on the matter.

"May I ask one question?" said Lydall in a small voice, gathering her courage.

Earl Barron shot his daughter a warning glare, willing her to not say anything that would compromise the alliance.

Lady O'Connor nodded kindly in Lydall's direction, her long dark hair spilling onto the table, "Why yes dear, go on."

Lydall cleared her throat, tossing her long braid over her shoulder before she spoke.

"Well…could I perhaps take my destrier, Triton with me to Westland? He's my best friend and…"

Immediately Earl O'Connor gave a loud chuckle of amusement, "That black beast in the stalls? Oh heavens, no child. Our steeds in Westland are far superior to your mixed breed horses out here—no offence of course, Earl and Lady Barron, but Westland prides itself on the purest lineage of destriers in all the land. You'll find a much more suitable one once you're settled."

Lydall felt the color rush to her cheeks as her rage boiled up to the surface, threatening to overtake her, "With all due respect, Earl O'Connor," she said, teeth clinched in anger, "Triton may not be as *pure* as your horses, but he is my best friend and there is no replacing him. I would like for him to go with me to Westland so that I might have a piece of Histair with me when I am forced to leave my home."

Earl O'Connor's good-natured laugh halted abruptly as he glared down the table at Lydall, "How dare you speak to me in such a manner, you insolent child!"

"Earl O'Connor, I apologize for my daughter," said Earl Barron as sweat began to form across his forehead, "Clearly she has forgotten all her manners," he added as he glared at Lydall.

"That is rather evident!" stated Earl O'Connor, "The insolence! And to think this is what our son must marry. You, child," he stated as he pointed a finger at Lydall, "You will leave that beast in Histair where it belongs and learn to ride a horse worthy of a Lady of Westland. Is that understood?"

Lydall stood abruptly, knocking her high-backed chair onto the marble floor, "I will do no such thing, Earl O'Connor," she said, voice trembling with fear and anger, "I asked for one thing to comfort me while I move away from my homeland and you have refused me. I will not forget it."

"I am giving you my wife's throne upon our passing!" stated Earl O'Conner, sputtering in disbelief, "What more could you possibly want?"

"I don't want your stupid throne!" shouted Lydall, fists clenched at her sides as she glowered down the table, "You're taking me from my family and you won't even allow me to bring my best friend? You're taking my entire life from me!"

"Lydall, that is quite enough," interrupted her father as he rose to his feet, "You have your mother in hysterics and you've angered our guests. Do try to be reasonable. Triton will be fine here, and you'll be able to visit us during the summer and winter festivals."

Lydall felt her heart racing in her chest as she looked around the Great Room. Only seeing her family twice a year, living among strangers, marrying the odd-looking boy, and never riding Triton again. It was all too much for her to bear.

Lydall turned and fled from the Great Hall as tears began to fall down her cheeks, the voices of her family and the Earl and Lady O'Connor fading behind her as she urged her legs to move faster. She could hear Angus crying and felt her heart crack, but she couldn't stay and let their family tear her life apart for the sake of some ancient treaty. She had no other choice.

Lydall was running away.

Lydall flew out of the castle and tore off down the long, winding slope that led to the stables. Her heart pounding in her chest, she flung open the stable doors and ran inside.

Triton whinnied in surprise from his stall as Lydall ran over and quickly unlatched the door.

"Come on, boy," she said, tears streaming down her face, "We have to go now. I can't lose you too."

Quickly, Lydall climbed onto her horse and urged him forward. Triton, sensing her urgency, flew out of the stable and into the bright light of the setting sun. His long, silky mane streamed out behind him as he and Lydall tore off into the emerald-green valley and away from the castle of Histair.

...

Lydall felt as if she had been riding Triton for hours. Her anger and heartache pressed her to continue on, despite her fatigue. She replayed the events in the Great Hall over and over again in her mind. The realization that she would never see her family again nearly broke her heart, but she knew that returning would mean the end of her dreams and the loss of Triton. No matter what decision she had made, Lydall would lose someone forever. At least with Triton and her freedom she could find a semblance of a life for herself, one of her own choosing.

"If only we can figure out what to do now," she muttered to herself, looking around at the unfamiliar hills and valleys,

"Oh Triton…where do we go from here?"

Lydall slowed Triton down to a walk. His hide was covered in sweat from the long journey and Lydall felt a sting of guilt for not paying more attention to her stallion's condition.

"I'm sorry boy," she murmured, "Let's find you some water, shall we? We'll figure out what to do once we've rested."

In the distance, Lydall could see moonlight flickering on a small pond of water with a thin stream leading to it. She clicked her tongue and directed Triton toward the pool. The destrier eagerly lowered his head to take a long drink while Lydall climbed off his back and crouched down next to the stream, taking long gulps of the fresh, cool water herself. The chirps and calls of nighttime creatures made Lydall's skin crawl. She shuddered slightly as she gazed around them, the pale moon light the only thing guiding their way.

"I guess I didn't have the time to think this through properly," she said to Triton, who nickered quietly as she stood back up, "I don't even know where we are—or what's out there. We have to find people. There has to be some kind of village nearby. Father always said where there is a fresh source of water, people gather. This stream and the pond aren't very big, but maybe there is a small village nearby? We could disappear into a small village—no one will know who we are."

Lydall began to take her hair out of the carefully done plait, "Well, as soon as I take off all this nonsense they won't," she said as she began to take off her dress and bodice. She stripped down to the thin, white underdress and sighed in relief, "There. That's better. Now I just look like a poor girl in a white gown."

Lydall frowned at her own statement, "I suppose a

white gown is not what a poor girl wears," she muttered to herself as she walked back toward the pool of water.

Triton whinnied in surprise as Lydall laid down in the mud near the water and began to roll around, laughing at her stallion's reaction, "It's alright, boy. I can't look all perfectly clean walking into a village with a white dress or braided hair now can I? They'd know right away I was royalty, or at least from a wealthy family."

Triton shook out his mane in disapproval at Lydall's antics and looked away, snorting and stomping his hoof.

Lydall laughed as she got up from the ground, her hair tangled and dirty and her white dress covered in splotches of mud.

"Perfect."

...

As Triton and Lydall continued to wander through the open landscape, the distant sound of a howling wolf startled them. Lydall had been so sure they would have found a village of some sort by now. Instead, miles and miles of brilliant-green valleys and copses of trees dotted the landscape without any sign of civilization.

"Triton," whispered Lydall in despair, "What are we going to do?"

Lydall began to think that running away had not been such a good idea after all. She had no idea what direction they were traveling in and no way to know how to get back home even if she wanted to.

As they crested another ridge, Lydall spotted what looked like a giant stone in the center of a large valley. She tilted her head curiously as she urged Triton toward the bizarre object. How strange that in all this wide, sweeping grassland there was a gigantic rock sprouting straight from the earth. It looked so out of place that it almost unnerved her. Lydall had never seen anything like it.

As they drew closer, she felt a suddenly pull—as if the stone were calling to her. It was a peculiar sensation and it was clear that Triton felt it too. Her horse's ears shot forward as he stared in interest at the stone. Whickering impatiently, Triton picked up the pace. Lydall's instinct was to pull her horse back from approaching the odd object so quickly, but the magnetic force drawing him to the stone had overtaken her as well. All she knew was that, for some reason, she had to get to it as quickly as possible. It was calling to her, silently, urgently.

As they drew up alongside the rock, Lydall's mouth hung open in awe. The stone was easily twenty feet high and covered in strange markings. They circled it, staring in wonder. Near the top the words "An Chloch" were inscribed. Lydall recognized the old Gaelic language and realized that the words meant "The Stone." Her parents had taught her and Angus to read old Gaelic since many of their ancient manuscripts had yet to be translated to the modern tongue. For the first time in her life, Lydall felt a slight bit of gratitude for the lessons.

Beneath "An Chloch" was the word "Krekania." Lydall frowned slightly as she said the word out-loud, wondering what it could mean.

"What is this thing?" she whispered to Triton, her heart hammering in her chest, "I can feel it calling to me—like a pull. You feel it too, don't you boy?" she asked, noticing that Triton had yet to take his eyes off the stone as they circled it.

After a moment, the siren call of this "An Chloch" overwhelmed Lydall. Taking a deep breath, she reached out, cautiously, with one hand and touched the stone.

Instantly Lydall's world spun out of control. It felt like her insides had leapt up into her throat and everything was upside down. Bright lights and loud screeching sounds overwhelmed her senses. She briefly heard Triton whinny in panic as the multitude of sensations overtook them both.

After what felt like an eternity the spinning and flashing lights finally stopped. Lydall felt herself hit the ground hard, knocking the air from her lungs. After a few moments, she hesitantly opened her eyes and found herself staring up at a brilliant night sky. The stars were so close she felt as if she could reach up and pluck one out of the sky. She had never seen something so magical in all her life.

Grunting with effort Lydall sat up slowly, testing each limb for damage. Triton was standing near her looking as bewildered as she felt. He whinnied and stomped his feet anxiously as he tried to take in this sudden change of surroundings.

Lydall gazed around in awe. Everything around her seemed to be exceptionally rich with color. The trees and flowers looked exotic and almost foreign as they shimmered and hummed with life. Even though it was nighttime, most of the foliage appeared to glow in the dark and was casting a gentle light on the ground beneath it. Everything around her seemed to have a vibrant aura. The luminescent undergrowth and oddly shaped flowers gave the place an unearthly feel.

"What is this place?" whispered Lydall, her breath catching in her throat.

She turned to look at Triton and gasped in shock. Two large and feathered wings had sprouted from her destrier's back. Triton seemed to have discovered this new development himself as he gave a shrill cry of surprise and whirled around in a circle, trying to look at his newly acquired limbs. He stretched the wings slowly and snorted in astonishment asthey moved on command.

Lydall felt faint. Certainly she must be hallucinating? Perhaps this was a result of their long ride? She was dehydrated and hungry. This must be some kind of vision or a trick of her mind. This could not be real—could it? It just simply was not possible. Glowing plants? Her horse sprouting wings?

Lydall shook her head, trying to clear the foggy feeling from her mind. As she slowly stood up from the glowing grass, she heard a rustling from the forest to her left. Her heart skipped a beat in panic. What kind of creatures called this strange place home?

"Triton," she murmured as she slowly backed up, feeling for her horse.

Triton gave a snort of panic as he tossed his black head and began to side-step away from the trees.

The crunching of underbrush grew steadily louder as whoever, or whatever, it was drew closer and closer to the wood line.

Lydall felt her hands brush against Triton's side as she backed into him, "It's okay boy," she murmured, trying to convince herself as much as Triton, "It's going to be okay…"

3

A figure stepped out of the gloom and Lydall felt her heart race in fear.

"Who are you?" she demanded, feigning bravery.

An amused laugh answered her shout as the figure stepped fully out of the shadows. A tall and muscular man, not much older than Lydall approached her, his dark-brown eyes gleaming with laughter.

"You're asking me who I am? In my land?" he asked with a smirk, "Well, you have courage I'll give you that much. But you're lucky it's me you ran into. Not everything in these woods is quite so friendly," he added as he furtively glanced around the clearing.

Lydall swallowed nervously as she studied the strange man. She noticed he had scars along the side of his face that looked like claw marks and his ears came to a point at the top in a very peculiar way. He was athletically built and carried himself much in the same manner that a Histair soldier would. He struck Lydall as one who had been through a lot in his short life and she found that both intriguing and intimidating at once.

"I—where am I?" she asked, her voice trembling slightly, betraying her fear. She tried to steady her voice and lift her head a little in an attempt to hide her uncertainty, "The plants here…they're glowing. I've never seen any flowers or trees like this back home."

The man tilted his head, his eyes narrowing in interest as he listened to Lydall, "So…you are a human then?"

Lydall looked startled by the question, "What? Oh, yes, I mean of course I'm a human. Why would you ask that? Aren't you also—human?" she said, glancing at his bizarrely shaped ears.

The man laughed at that and shook his head, his eyes sparkling, "No…I'm an elf. One of the last of my kind actually. Although I suppose these days every being in Krekania is one of the last of their kind," he added, glancing away as his eyes flashed with a myriad of emotions.

Lydall felt faint, "An—an elf?" she choked out, "How? Elves aren't real. They're just in the stories and fairytales I tell my brother. Who are you really?" she demanded, her voice taking on an edge as she felt herself begin to panic. An elf? Could it be? His ears…they looked just like the pictures in Angus' books.

"Easy there," said the elf as he reached out a hand to steady her, "We are very much real—the few of us who remain at least. This is Krekania, the last land of magic. The Dark Sorceress has destroyed the old lands so the Krekanians moved here and banded together to fight her.I lead the Army of Spellbinders. We're building our forces so we can bring war to her dark army."

Lydall's mouth dropped open as she listened to the strange man and his story. Magic? Spellbinders? Dark Sorceress? What in all the kingdoms was he blabbering about?

"This has to be some kind of joke," she said, looking around her, "Magic isn't real. I mean, there are the true stories of the dragons, but they died centuries ago. The rest…the rest are just myth and fables."

"Ah, the dragons," murmured Jasper, smiling at the

memory, "I've heard similar tales as well. A shame that they were wiped from our world…and yours as well. But we must go now. The Sorceress' dark army enjoys prowling about in the cover of darkness and they'll sense our magic soonenough so it's best we get a move on."

Lydall took a step back, staring intently at the elf, "*Our* magic?" she repeated, "What are you talking about?"

"Yes, *our* magic," replied the elf as he closed his eyes and furrowed his brow in concentration.

Lydall raised an eyebrow, "What are you doing?"

Whoever this man was, he was very odd. Part of Lydall resisted accepting that something beyond logical explanation was happening here, but the other part of her, the part that secretly wished for Angus' stories to be true, was celebrating. Was this really happening? Could more creatures from the fairy tales exist? Maybe her world had it all wrong. They had always been taught that dragons were just a species that had died off many years ago and that the other stories weresimply just, well, stories. But every story always holds a bit oftruth…

Suddenly a great gust of wind caused Lydall to cry out in surprise, jolting her from her thoughts. Triton jumped back, startled as a large creature fell from the sky and landed next to the elf, flattening the glowing grass around them. Another wave of disbelief washed over Lydall as she stared at the winged creature. It had a head like an eagle, a body like a lion, and wings like Triton's, but unlike Triton's dark black coat, this creature was solid white. Lydall watched as it nuzzled the elf affectionately. She gaped in astonishment, staring openly at the long, ugly scars along the side of the beast's flank. Clearly both creature and elf had fought terrible battles at some point in their lives…but what could have caused such devastating injuries?

"What…what is…?"

The elf shook his head at Lydall, turning away for a

moment as he hugged the beast, "He's a griffon. His name is Dionysus. Now, enough talking. We're going to take you to the Queen of Krekania. She can explain more once we're safely in the walls of the Castle. Mount your pegasus and follow me," he instructed as he gripped Dionysus' fur and hauled himself onto the griffon's back.

"Mount my pegasus?" repeated Lydall, looking back at Triton, "You mean Triton? And wait, I don't even know who you are and I'm just supposed to follow you and—and—that thing?"

The griffon gave a screech of indignation, giving Lydall the impression that he had understood her words. She stared at Dionysus with wide eyes as she slid closer to Triton, trying to hide behind the destrier while the griffon flapped his wings irritably.

"Oh for the love of all magic you have a lot to learn human," said the elf shaking his head, "Your beast there is a pegasus. I presume the wings are a new addition since you arrived in Krekania? No matter. Just hop on and follow Dionysus. As for me, I suppose you'll just have to trust me for the time being. Unless of course you prefer to take your chances out here alone at night?"

Lydall shook her head in bewilderment as she climbed awkwardly onto Triton. She found herself having to adjust her normal position on his back to accommodate her destrier's new wings.

Her destrier. She supposed he was her 'pegasus' now. She shifted her weight until she felt comfortable and threaded Triton's mane through her fingers.

"I don't think he knows how to fly!" she called over to the elf, "It's not like we've done it before."

The elf smiled, "Just trust me. Give him a little kick. He'll figure it out. He'll see Dionysus flying and work it out for himself."

"Just trust me he says. Unbelievable," muttered Lydall, her bafflement briefly replaced by annoyance, "Like my horse is supposed to suddenly know how to fly the moment he sprouts wings. Wait, what am I even saying?" she asked, shaking her head as she watched the griffon take to the sky, "Well…here goes nothing, Triton. Let's follow a strange elf and his griffon into the unknown. Sounds like a splendid idea!"

Lydall had a moment where she thought about what her parents would have to say about her running off with a strange man in foreign land. The image of their fuming faces made her smirk, her eyes glittering rebelliously.

With a gently kick, Lydall urged Triton forward. He whinnied in surprise as he watched the griffon take flight. Slowly, Triton began to mimic the griffon and began flapping his wings as he ran through the glowing grass. Lydall cheered him on, willing Triton to figure out how to use his new limbs.

With a snort of excitement, Triton flapped harder as hefelt his hooves begin to leave the ground. He whinnied in surprise as he felt himself lift up into the air. Lydall felt an odd, swooping sensation in her stomach and a rush of adrenalin as her horse-turned-pegasus took to the night sky and began to fly among the stars.

. . .

Lydall gazed down in amazement at the world beneath her. Everything was luminescent and brilliantly colored. Whatever this magic was, it was certainly beautiful. She had never seen anything like it. The stars were now so close she felt as if they may accidently run into one as they flew by. Everything felt so alive. She closed her eyes briefly, letting the feeling of energy and life flow through her.

"You can feel it," remarked the elf, flashing her a grin of satisfaction, "That's a good sign."

"Feel what?" asked Lydall, eyes snapping open. She felt her face flush with embarrassment as she realized the elf had caught her having a private moment.

"The magic," he said, laughing, "You can feel it flowing through you. It's a good thing…it'll make things a lot easier."

Lydall frowned and shook her head, not even bothering to try and decipher what the elf meant. All of this was so confusing to her, and yet somehow her fear had evaporated, replaced with a feeling of wonder and excitement. She no longer felt as if she were in danger, but instead felt something she never had before: belonging. None of it made any sense, but it felt *right*.

"Earlier," said Lydall, cautiously, "You mentioned a Dark Sorceress and that it isn't safe here anymore. Why is that?"

"It's probably best to let the Queen explain," said the elf as he leaned back to stretch across his griffon's back, the muscles in his face tensing slightly, "It will all make sense soon enough."

Lydall sighed impatiently, "Fine. Well, will you tell me your name at least? Please tell me you actually have one."

The elf laughed loudly at that, "Of course I have a name! I'm not some wild beast you know."

Dionysus cawed in annoyance at the elf's statement and bucked irritably.

"Whoa!" laughed the elf as he gripped the griffon's fur, "Easy there, Dionysus. I wasn't referring to you. You're no wild beast; you're a civilized magical creature of course."

Dionysus gave a noncommittal grunt as he flew on, eyes narrowed as he glanced back at the elf.

"Don't mind him," said the elf as he leaned toward Lydall and Triton, "He's a bit sensitive about such things. Most griffons are indeed wild beasts, but Dionysus is much too intelligent to just be a simplistic creature living on the land," he added, patting the griffon affectionately, "And my name is Jasper. Your name would be…?"

"Lydall. Lydall Barron of the Kingdom of Histair, daughter of the Earl and Lady to be exact—but you can call me Lydall," she replied, glancing away uncomfortably as her mind drifted back to her family and the life she'd been destined for in Histair.

It also didn't help that this Jasper fellow was rather attractive. The way he confidently lounged on his griffon's back, muscles taut beneath his cloth and leather clothing made her squirm a bit. She wondered briefly what his story was and what had caused the scarring on his face and Dionysus' flank.

"Quite the title you have there," said Jasper as he ran a hand through his long, black hair, "So you were royalty back in your world then?"

Lydall frowned at Jasper's use of the word "were."

"Yes, I *am*," she corrected, "I'm the only daughter of the ruling Earl and Lady of Histair," she added, straightening up slightly, "I was about to become the Lady of Westland…after I marry their *charming* son. But I ran away before that could happen. They were going to make me leave Triton behind," she said quietly as she stroked her pegasus' mane, "It might sound silly, but…he's my best friend. I can't imagine a day without him much less… forever."

Jasper gave her a knowing smile as he ran his hands through Dionysus' feathered neck, "I understand better than you realize. I'd be lost without my griffon."

Dionysus made a purring noise in response, his lion-like tale waving appreciatively.

"So I'm guessing after you ran away with Triton, you two got yourselves lost?"

Lydall tilted her head, giving Jasper an inquiring look, "Yes…how'd you know?"

Jasper gave her a lazy side smile, "No human can find Krekania unless they are lost. That is part of the magic of An Chloch, the stone that brought you here. Of course there is also the matter of the prophecy as well, which was clearly about you."

Lydall felt her heart begin to race, "Prophecy? About me?"

"Like I said, it's a matter for the Queen to address when we get to the Castle," said Jasper with a yawn, "And after a good breakfast. I'm sure you are just as hungry as I am. It'll be morning by the time we greet the Queen."

Lydall felt her stomach growl in response to Jasper's mention of food. She felt slightly alarmed that morning was so near. She had left Histair through An Chloch a couple hours before the sun had set. Had the journey through the stone taken that long? Perhaps the time in Histair and the time in Krekania differed. Anything was possible with this strange land. Lydall already it felt as if she had been gone from Histair for months. Her old life was beginning to feel very far away.

"Yes, food would be good," said Lydall distractedly as she peered down into the pale light from the glowing forest ahead of them. She soon caught sight of a large glowing object in the distance, shining brightly against the night sky, "Jasper, what is that—over there?" she asked, pointing toward the glowing white object.

Jasper smiled slightly, his eyes dancing with excitement, "That, Lydall of Histair, is the Castle of Krekania."

Triton snorted as he flapped his wings harder, eager to get closer to the gently glowing object in the distance. Lydall felt the pull too. It was a similar feeling to when she first saw An Chloch in the middle of the field.

"That's the magic isn't it?" asked Lydall, in awe as she glanced back over at Jasper, "That feeling? It's like—it wants me to come closer."

"You're truly meant to be here, Lydall," murmured Jasper as he gazed at her, a flicker of fear and understanding in his eyes.

Lydall felt uneasy under the handsome elf's scrutiny. It was obvious that Jasper knew more about what was to come than she did, and she found that rather unnerving. She felt oddly safe here, but something told her there was a lot more to come that she didn't yet know. Something that had the power to change everything. Part of her felt excited at such a prospect, but another part of her wondered if her quest for freedom and a life of her own would also come at a heavier price than she realized.

As they approached the Castle, Lydall found herself squinting against it's bright glow. It seemed to radiate with magic and Lydall could feel a pulsing vibration like the beat of a loud drum in her chest. The large white structure seemed to suddenly loom up in front of them as Triton and Dionysus landed gently on the cobblestone road.

Triton tossed his head and stamped his hooves with excitement, ears pricked toward the Castle. Even the more-reserved Dionysus struggled to refrain himself from reacting to the magic as Jasper led them down the path.

Lydall's mouth dropped open at the sheer beauty of the shimmering structure in front of her. She had never seen a castle this large or quite this beautiful before. Without explanation, she knew with every fiber of her being that this was the heart of all magic. Nothing felt as compelling or intense as the pulsating power that emanated from the tall palace before her. Even An Chloch's magic could not compare to the pull of the Castle.

A long cobblestone bridge hovered over a massive lagoon that shimmered in the early morning light. Several small waterfalls cascaded from beneath the overpass while one roaring waterfall poured down from a section of the Castle separate from the main structure. Lydall could feel her heart thudding loudly but the sound was quickly drowned out by the roar of the waterfalls as they walked across the bridge.

Soon, they approached two enormous golden doors that seemed to reach all the way up to the heavens. Next to the towering castle doors stood two monstrous white wolves. The great beasts were nearly as large as Triton and were as white as the walls of the Castle. They had large wings that spread open wide as they stood to confront the newcomers. Their muzzles curled back, revealing their long, flashing fangs as they took an aggressive step forward.

Dionysus screeched in fury at the two massive wolves while Triton reared back in fear, nearly throwing Lydall from his back. Lydall cried out and clung to her pegasus' long mane, her eyes wide in panic.

"*Mac tire! STAD!*" shouted Jasper as he leapt down from Dionysus, his face thunderous with rage.

Instantly the advancing wolves froze, ears flicking up in surprise as they quickly recognized Jasper's command.

"Don't mind them," called Jasper over his shoulder, "They only know the old language. They know me but they didn't recognize you or Triton, so they went on high alert."

Lydall took several deep, steadying breaths as she slid from Triton's back. Triton snorted uneasily as she slowly walked up behind Jasper, shielding herself behind his broad form as she glanced hesitantly up at the wolves.

"What are they? Why did they do that?" she asked, eyes wide.

"Meet Akira and Logan. They're a very rare breed of winged-wolves and serve as the Guardians of the Castle," replied Jasper as he walked over to stand between the large beasts and began petting them affectionately.

The wolves let their tongues loll happily from their jaws as Jasper stroked their fur, tails wagging in pleasure.

"So…do all the animals in Krekania have wings?" asked Lydall, raising an eyebrow as she watched the exchange.

Jasper laughed heartily at that, "It would seem that way I suppose, but no they don't all have wings. Several species do, but there are other magical creatures who have other traits. You'll see some of them today."

Lydall felt a thrill of excitement at that notion. What other creatures resided in such a majestic and magical place?

"Can I…can I pet them?" asked Lydall as she slowly approached the shimmering wolves.

Jasper gave her an encouraging nod as he stepped aside, allowing Lydall to move closer to the animals.

Akira and Logan studied Lydall and sniffed her carefully as she approached them. Then, with a quick wag of their tails, they lowered their heads in a friendly gesture, tongues out and ears relaxed with wolfish grins on their faces.

Lydall smiled as she ran her hands through their thick, silky fur. She could feel a tingling sensation running through her arms as their magic seemed to skate across her skin. The wolves whined with glee as they rubbed gently against Lydall. She laughed as she found herself trapped between the friendly creatures.

"They're amazing!" she exclaimed, looking over at Jasper with pure joy written on her face, "This entire place—it's perfect!"

"Oh, Lydall," said Jasper, that sad, knowing look crossing his face again, sending chills through Lydall's veins, "You have no idea. Come. Let's get inside."

Lydall gave the winged-wolves a final pat on their broad heads before she returned to her spooked pegasus, "Come on now Triton," she murmured in his ear, "We have to get used to this. I have a feeling there are many more strange creatures we're going to meet here."

Triton flicked his ears nervously, almost as if he understood her words. Lydall gently guided the destrier through the towering white and gold doors of the Castle. She kept one hand on Triton's neck, steadying both the stallion and herself, as they walked inside together.

The interior of the Castle was vastly different than the outside of the colossal structure. Lydall felt a rush of wonder as she gazed around at the various plants and small streams, and heard the sounds of creatures flitting about the cavernous main room.

"Welcome to the Castle of Krekania!" announced Jasper with a wide grin, "Beautiful, is it not? This place is where many of the magical creatures in our world call home. It serves as a sanctuary for them."

"This is amazing," whispered Lydall, wide-eyed as she ran a hand through her tangled hair, "It's unbelievable."

The flora that decked the walls, floors, and even the ceiling glowed with the same magical aura as the plants back in the forest. The magic hummed softly around them, making the plants feel as alive as any flesh and blood being. It was like a tropical paradise from another planet.

"This way," urged Jasper as he and Dionysus walked toward another large interior door, "The Queen will want to see you immediately."

Lydall instantly felt self-conscious and anxious. The Queen. What was she like? Would she like her? Would she banish her and Triton from Krekania? What would they do then? Wander around aimlessly as they had before shetouched An Chloch? She had grown accustomed to adults not approving of her, so why should this Queen be any different?

These awful scenarios clouded Lydall's mind as she and Triton passed through the large oak doors, following Jasper and Dionysus.

The doors led to another large room, filled with the same

magical flora and a small stream that led to a pond. Early morning light began to filter down from a skylight in the ceiling and shimmered on the water. A wooden throne stood on the far side of the glade. It glowed softly, much like the foliage around it, making Lydall wonder if it was made from the wood of the magical trees in the forest.

Near the edge of the pond, a small creature was bent over, lapping eagerly at the water. To Lydall's horror, the creature appeared to be on fire.

"Jasper! Look!" she cried, her voice shrill with panic, "We have to help it!"

Jasper gave Lydall a quizzical look, "Help it? Oh it's alright the pond is shallow. And besides, firefoxes are very careful to not fall into bodies of water. It takes a long time for them to get their flames back to normal after one of those incidents."

"Firefoxes?" breathed Lydall, shaking her head, "Oh. I, um, never heard of…those," she said as she studied the little flaming creature.

The firefox gazed back at them, eyes narrowed in annoyance. He sniffed the air and gave a quick bark before vanishing into the undergrowth.

"Don't mind him," said a strong female voice from the shadows, "He isn't as friendly as the rest of his kin."

Lydall whirled around and came face to face with a tall woman clothed in a white dress made of several different layers of silk and lace. Her hair was as black as night and glistened in the early morning rays. Her dark eyes studied Lydall carefully before she turned to face Jasper.

"And who is this?" she asked him, one dark eyebrow raised with interest.

Jasper bowed low before he answered, his black hair sweeping over his eyes as he straightened himself, "My

Queen, this is Lydall from the land known as Histair. She is…she is a *human*."

The Queen's eyes widened and flashed with alarm as she quickly turned back to Lydall, "You are a human?" she asked, eyes moving quickly over to Lydall's ears. The Queen's gaze flickered slightly as she realized that Lydall's ears were rounded and not pointed like Jasper's.

Lydall took a step back at the sudden fervor in the intimidating woman's eyes, "Yes. Um, I mean yes, *Queen*."

"Where did you find her?" she demanded as she whirled around, her face pressed close to Jasper's.

"In the forest, the wildlands," answered Jasper, swallowing nervously, "I was on patrol watching the place we spoke about before. It's her, Queen. She's the one—the one from the prophecy."

Lydall's heart kicked up a few notches as Jasper mentioned the prophecy again. They had been watching the spot where she'd appeared in Krekania? But why?

The Queen seemed to shudder as she fought to get control of her emotions before turning back to Lydall, "Has he told you the prophecy then?"

Lydall shook her head, hands shaking slightly as she leaned on Triton for support, "No, Queen. He said I had to wait until you could tell me yourself."

The woman nodded slowly, "Very well. That is probably best," she murmured as she turned away and began to pace, muttering to herself.

Lydall glanced over at Jasper with a worried look as the Queen continued to pace around in front of the large wooden throne.

"Alright!" announced the Queen firmly as she came to an abrupt halt, "First things first. I suppose you are both hungry then?"

Lydall and Jasper exchanged another glance before they nodded earnestly. Lydall felt her mind spinning in confusion, but the pain in her empty stomach overrode her uneasiness at the Queen's reaction to her arrival.

"Yes, my Queen," answered Jasper, "I believe it has been a long time since our guest has eaten anything."

"Very well," said the Queen as she clapped her hands.

Two young winged-wolves scampered into the throne room, yipping in excitement as they skid to a halt in front of the throne.

"Fetch our guests some food, young ones," said the Queen kindly, the air around her mouth shimmering oddly as she spoke.

The young wolves curled their front legs beneath them in the semblance of a bow before they disappeared back into the gloom.

Lydall shifted awkwardly on her feet, unsure of what to do in the sudden silence. Jasper, on the other hand, was calmly smoothing his griffon's ruffled, wind-blown feathers and fur. Lydall mimicked the elf and began to tidy Triton's flowing mane as the Queen watched, her eyes distant. For a moment it looked as if the Queen wasstaring right through her. Lydall swallowed uncomfortably.

Soon the wolves returned, balancing a large silver tray on their backs. As Lydall watched them approach, she realized that the tray was tied down across two harnesses strapped to the small wolves' backs. The plates were brimming with slices of hot bread with a variety of jams and jellies. They knelt before Jasper and Lydall, offering the visitors the tray. Jasper untied it from between their harnesses and sat it on the floor. He gave the youngwolves grateful pats on their heads before they took off out of the throne room and back into the wooded area beyond.

"As soon as you're done eating," said the Queen as

Lydall began to eagerly tuck into the steaming bread, "I must give you the grand tour of the Castle and the grounds. I want you to meet the creatures that reside here so you can have an appreciation for the things I have to tell you later."

Something about the way the Queen had worded her last statement made Lydall even more uneasy than she already was. What could she possibly have to tell her that required an entire tour beforehand? At least she wasn't being banished out of the Castle and into this strange, magical world, especially after what Jasper had said about it no longer being safe. With her deepest fears abated, Lydall watched as the Queen grabbed a long, dark robe from behind the throne and put it on over her lacey dress. She reached over to one side of the throne and picked up a long walking stick with a glowing sapphire on the end.

"Quickly now," she said as she strode past them, "No time to waste. We have much to discuss after your tour and I don't live in a small Castle. You may leave your riding-beasts here, they'll be fine."

Lydall quickly stuffed another slice of thick bread into her mouth. Jasper smirked as he calmly nibbled on another slice before he turned to follow the Queen. Lydall nearly choked on her food as she scrambled back up to her feet to follow Jasper. The Queen of Krekania was not one for dillydallying so it seemed.

Lydall glanced up at Triton and gave him a quick hug, "Stay here, boy," she murmured quietly, "I'll be back soon. Be good, okay?"

Triton whinnied in displeasure at the sudden turn of events and stomped his foot irritably, black wings flapping in frustration. He glanced over at Dionysus who was giving him a less-than-pleased look. The griffon narrowed his eyes at the pegasus and sniffed in disdain.

"I don't think they like each other much," said Lydall

quietly, glancing over her shoulder at the two creatures as she walked next to Jasper.

Jasper smirked, "Different species learn to get along in time," he said, giving her a quick wink, "Lock them away in a room together long enough, or put them in a perilous situation and they will find a way to get along."

Lydall felt her face flush and turned away before Jasper could see her reaction. The elf was as charming as he was handsome, but the secrets he was keeping from Lydall frustrated her to no end. She felt completely lost in aworld that was not her own. But this was what she had wanted, was it not? To escape the world she had been living in and to find freedom. However, in this land called Krekania, Lydall felt nearly as dazed and confused as she had in Histair. She silently hoped that the Queen would be more forthcoming after her grand tour of the Castle. As beautiful as Krekania was, Lydall felt that there was something she wasn't being told—something big.

5

The Queen moved through the winding corridors at a rapid pace, forcing Lydall and Jasper to jog to keep up.

"We'll start at the heart of my kingdom," she called over her shoulder, "This is where the majority of the magical creatures gather throughout the day to socialize. I'll introduce you to them so you'll see why this place is so important to me."

Lydall glanced over at Jasper who, unlike herself, had a relaxed and slightly excited look on his face. It was clear that Jasper had been here many times before and enjoyed the experience. Those thoughts put her more at ease as she tried to forget the fact that after this grand tour was over, shewould be told why she had been transported to Krekania and what this prophecy stated.

Soon the winding corridor opened up into an expansive room full of light. The sun was beginning to rise and its rays flickered about the room in a cheerful way. Like the main entryway and the throne room, this room also had magical flora covering the ground, walls, and even the ceiling. The exotic flowers and mushrooms gave the space a very other-worldly feel. Several smalls streams trickled lazily down into what looked like a larger version of the pool in the Queen's throne room. Near this pool were several creatures Lydall had only ever heard of in the books she had received from Randall.

Splashing in the middle of the pool were two beautiful white horses with long horns that grew from their foreheads.

The horns glimmered as the two creatures whinnied with glee, kicking water at one another playfully.

"This is beautiful," breathed Lydall in awe.

The Queen gave her an approving nod, "Yes, it is. This is the heart of Krekania and the heart of all magic. The creatures come here for sanctuary and peace from the dangers of our world. It is here that I protect and care for each and every one of them," she added as she glanced over at the frolicking ponies, "Those are unicorns. There are several in the Castle, the grounds, and even in the wildlands beyond. They are carriers of magic as you can see from their glowing horns. They use the magic within them only when absolutely necessary to protect the innocent from harm."

"Unicorns," said Lydall with a quiet laugh, "Who would have thought such things could ever exist?"

The Queen gave her a quizzical look, one dark eyebrow raised as she leaned on her scepter.

Lydall swallowed nervously, wondering if she had said the wrong thing, "Where I come from, creatures like unicorns exist only in fairy tales. They're not in Histair."

The Queen smirked in amusement, "Ah yes I have heard the land of humans is rather dull. My parents came from your land many years ago and told us stories. But here, the magic is real and so are the creatures who harbor it. Come. We must travel through the glade to get to the next part of our tour."

Jasper gave Lydall an encouraging nod as they followed the Queen further into the magical sanctuary.

As they walked forward, winged creatures of various colors flew around the domed room, making noises Lydall had never heard before. One in particular looked seemed to be on fire, just like the firefox she had seen at the pool in the throne room. The fiery bird screeched and dove right above their heads. Lydall ducked, feeling the heat from the creature's feathers as it soared upward.

"That was a phoenix," explained Jasper as he stood back up, "Similar to the firefox. Both use fire magic bestowed upon them by Krekania itself. Powerful creatures, but water can weaken them. It takes a long time for a phoenix to regain their magic after a good rain storm."

Lydall stared up at the domed ceiling and watched the colorful, strange birds flying around and calling to one another from the tops of the trees. She felt herself groan inwardly when she glanced back down and saw that the Queen and Jasper had started walking away already. She could have stayed in this spot watching these beautiful birds for hours.

As they walked through the glade, the trio came upon a small pack of winged-wolves near the edge of the tree line. While they looked very similar to Akira and Logan, these wolves were about half their size and grey in color.

"No doubt you met my two guardians when you approached my Castle?" inquired the Queen, "Well those two are of the rare giant breed of winged-wolves. Most are gone from this world, like so many of the giant magical beasts. These wolves here are the more common breed. There is a rather large pack of them that live outside the Castle grounds as well. Many of their members have also joined Jasper's Army."

Lydall paused for a moment to watch two winged-wolf pups wrestling in the soft glowing grass. Their parents watched with warmth in their eyes. Lydall smiled at the happy scene as she turned to glance back at Jasper.

"They're very intelligent beasts," he said as he met her gaze, "Arguably the most intelligent of the land, aside from griffons of course."

Lydall noticed the gleam of amusement in Jasper's eyes and realized he was slightly biased because of Dionysus. She rolled her eyes, "Oh but of course. What could possibly beat the intelligence of the lion-hawk you ride?"

"Lion-hawk?" asked Jasper with a bewildered look.

Lydall laughed, "Never mind."

Jasper gave her an odd look as they continued on the path that led around the large domed structure. Lydall noticed several multi-colored owl-like creatures that hooted and craned their necks to get a better look at her from holes in the trees. She watched as they blended into their surroundings, changing colors quickly as they hopped from branch to branch.

"Those are strigs," explained the Queen, noticing Lydall watching the strange birds, "They are able to change both color and texture at will. Clever little creatures."

One of the strigs hooted a reply as they continued on through the sanctuary. Up ahead, Lydall saw a small group of griffons eagerly eating glowing fruit from some unusual looking trees. More winged-wolves darted between the trees and a couple of pegasi, who looked just like Triton, galloped through a small clearing.

Suddenly, movement in the undergrowth near the edge of the magical forest caused Lydall to jump in alarm. Something that looked like a tangle of sticks scuttled out onto the path and chirped at the group before it scrambled back into the forest.

"Nothing to worry about," assured the Queen, "Those would be the wood nymphs. They're the caretakers of the flora and the library. They are very curious beings, but also extremely shy. They'll keep to their woods. The open areas tend to cause them some anxiety I'm afraid."

Lydall watched as a small group of wood nymphs near the edge of the trees giggled and ran deeper into the undergrowth. They were strange looking little creatures made from bits of twigs and leaves, and somehow magically strewn together into tiny human-like figures. Lydall thought they were both bizarre and wonderful at once. She stared into the gloom and watched them dive into the brush, disappearing deep into the woods.

"The only creatures you won't find in my sanctuary are the sabretooth cats," said the Queen as she led them down a path and through another set of double doors, "There are very few of them left and the ones who do exist have chosen to live among Jasper's Army of Spellbinders. You'll learn more about the Army soon enough. For now, I want to show you my lagoon."

Lydall's head was spinning with information as she tried to absorb everything she was being shown. She and Jasper continued to follow the Queen through more winding hallways. The sounds of creatures that had only existed in Lydall's fairytales echoed down the corridor, adding to the aura of magic that embodied this strange place.

It was hard to believe that any of this was real. Lydall half expected to wake up at any moment and find herself once again in her chambers in Histair, waiting to be taken to Westland to marry the scrawny Lord Victor. She shuddered at the thought. As strange and somewhat scary as this world was, she much preferred it to her old life. At least here there were mysteries and magical creatures. In her old world, Lydall's life was mapped out for her in a series of tedious and monotonous events. In Krekania she had no idea what was in store for her future and as terrifying as that was, it was also rather thrilling.

The hallway opened up into another section of the Castle. Lydall instantly recognized it as the portion that had the large waterfall cascading from it. It sat separate from the rest of the Castle and was connected to the main structure by a covered bridge. As they walked across the bridge, Lydall looked up in wonder. The pathway glowed with multiple shades of blue and the sound of rushing water surrounded her, almost overwhelmingly, as they entered into another domed room.

"This is the Lagoon," announced the Queen, her eyes lighting up with pride as she gazed out at her creation, "It is the sanctuary for the mer-folk. I designed this myself a couple of years ago."

Lydall's mouth dropped open, "Mer-folk? You mean, like mermaids?"

The Queen nodded, tucking a stray strand of black hair behind her ear, "Yes, the mermaids and mermen reside here."

Lydall thought that description was quite an understatement. Similar to the colossal woodland room, this area was also domed, but the majority of the space beneath it contained mostly water. The only sections of land that existed were the small section they were all standing on, a thin pathway that ran around the Lagoon, and a complex rock structure in the center. The water itself was a perfect shade of blue and crystal clear. Magical water flora decorated the bottom of the Lagoon creating a tropical effect as it glowed softly, lighting even the deepest sections.

On the large rock at the center sat three merfolk, two mermaids and one merman, lounging lazily in the bright morning light. One mermaid had short red hair with adeep green fish-like tail. The other mermaid had long blonde hair and a light blue tail that sparkled in the light and resembled that of a dolphin. The merman had brown hair and a deep burgundy tale that stood out sharply against the light blue water. All three merfolk were exceptionally beautiful in a startling way. They gave them all a friendly wave and Lydall waved back, numb from disbelief that these beautiful beings actually existed.

"Their old home was poisoned," said the Queen quietly, her eyes glimmering with unpleasant memories, "Most of them died. So, I saved some of the ones who survived and moved them here—where no one could harm them again. There are others in a lake out in the forest, but not very many."

Lydall frowned, "Who poisoned them?"

The Queen flinched slightly, "That is part of the story I must tell you when we return to my throne room."

Lydall felt her heart clench in sympathy as she turned her gaze back to the mermaids. They were stunning and mesmerizing. She could not imagine what kind of person would want to harm something so beautiful.

The Queen smiled at the look of rapt awe on Lydall's face, "Come, I will show you my library and the apothecary before we return."

As they left the Lagoon, the Queen took a sharp left, leading them through a tunnel that looked as if it were made out of the roots of the neighboring trees. Lydall and Jasper ducked under the lower hanging roots as they tried to keep up with the light-footed woman.

The Queen stopped and nodded to an opening off to their right, "Here is my enchanted library. Every book you could ever imagine is here. All the research we have conducted, the information that has been revealed—it's all gathered and bound here."

Lydall watched, fascinated as several little wood nymphs moved deftly about the large room, gathering papers and slapping glue onto bindings. The entrance was a rather small hole that made the enormity of the room beyond it that much more astounding. Floor to ceiling shelves lined every inch of the walls, filled to the brim with books. Several wood nymphs scaled long ladders and sorted the books with great care.

"The wood nymphs take great pride in their work here, almost as much pride as they take in their work in the woods," said the Queen with a satisfied smile, "For paper comes from wood which comes from their trees. They find the sacrifice of their trees to impart knowledge a very sacred ritual. They're some of the most important living things in Krekania," she added, nodding in approval to a couple of nymphs who paused in their work to give her brief bows of respect, "Without them, our woods would fall to ruin and magic would suffer as a result. Let's continue to the apothecary. We're nearing the end of our journey."

Lydall glanced at Jasper who was beginning to look more and more grim as time went on.

"What I'm going to learn about this place," she whispered as they walked a small distance behind the Queen, "Is it...is it that terrible?"

Jasper looked away quickly and gave her a subtle nod, "Yes. It is. But allow her to explain when the time comes. It isn't my place to tell you."

Lydall stared at Jasper's tense face and swallowed nervously. She bit her lower lip as anxiety began to creep in. Whatever Krekania's secrets were, they seemed rather upsetting to both the Queen and Jasper. Uneasy, Lydall grew quiet as she continued following the dark-haired woman.

After a few more winding turns, the Queen halted in front of another small hole on the left side of the root-tunnel. Like the library, beyond the small entrance was a cavernous room. This room, however, was filled with bottles, boxes, and containers filled with various liquids, powders, and plants. A litany of different scents assaulted Lydall's nose, overwhelming her senses.

"This is where we store our medicine," explained the Queen, "Even magical creatures need assistance— especially when the wounds are grievous."

Lydall looked up in alarm at the change in the Queen's tone. Jasper turned away and seemed to be breathing rather deeply as if trying to control his emotions.

"And now that you have had a taste of what magic is,"

said the Queen, "We must return to my throne. There are some things you need to be told. You have now seen a lot of Krekania, the best parts of it in fact, but now it's time to hear the rest of our story."

The pit of dread settled again in Lydall's stomach. Whatever the secrets were about Krekania, the prophecy, and her role in all of this, was about to be revealed. Part of her wondered if she was going to be able to accept all of it, or if she would realize that running away from home was the biggest mistake of her life.

6

The Queen led Jasper and Lydall back through the halls and into her throne room. Lydall glanced over at Jasper, seeking reassurance, but the elf's mouth was set in a firm line, his eyes dark and glittering with barely suppressed rage. Whatever Lydall was about to be told must be even worse than she imagined.

Triton whinnied excitedly when he saw Lydall emerge from behind the Queen. He and Dionysus were on opposite sides of the throne room, eyeing one another skeptically. Dionysus cast a withering glance over at Triton as he watched the pegasus trot around and toss his head with joy. The display seemed to disgust the stoic griffon as he calmly approached Jasper and briefly nuzzled him in a more formal greeting.

The Queen walked swiftly to her throne and sat down with a great sweep of her long black cloak. She tossed her hair over her shoulder and sat up tall and proud.

Lydall looked at Jasper again before she approached the throne, bracing herself for what was to come. Wooden chairs seemed to form before their very eyes as tiny wood nymphs scurried about the floor. Jasper sat down in one of the chairs, his back rigid and his jaw clinched. Lydall settled next to him and fidgeted nervously with her hair as she watched the nymphs chirp to one another and scuttle across the floor, running back into the trees behind the throne.

"You have now seen what Krekania should be," began the Queen, her voice low, "You have seen magic in its truest form. You have seen creatures in the condition they should always be. However, you have not yet seen the dark side of Krekania—the dark side of magic. Are you prepared? If you are afraid speak now and we will send you back to your world through the standing stone."

Lydall felt a shudder creep up her spine at the Queen's ominous words. Steadying herself, she straightened her back and looked at the Queen, "I'm ready. I don't want to go back there. I left Histair for a reason. I want to make this place my home. It's beautiful here and…whatever it is that's harming or threatening this place—I'd like to try and help stop it if I can."

As she said the words, Lydall knew in her heart this is where she was meant to be. She could not properly explain why she felt so strongly about Krekania, but she knew, down to the marrow of her bones, that this land was where she was destined to make her home.

The Queen smiled slightly at Lydall's response, giving her an appreciative nod before she continued.

"You have spirit, I will give you that," said the Queen as she took a deep breath, "Now, as you know, only humans can find Krekania under the circumstances that they are both lost and Krekania requires their presence. I've had Jasper patrolling the area where humans have traditionally arrived in Krekania through An Chloch. We knew you were coming soon because of the prophecy. Whenever a human has come to this land it's because Krekania knows it is either in need of a new ruler or will be in need of one soon. Humans have always ruled Krekania, and Krekania chooses for itself which humans will rule."

Lydall's eyebrows shot up in surprise, "R…rule it?" she stammered, looking quickly between Jasper and the Queen, "But…you are the Queen? Why would I—how could I? I barely even know this place…I just got here!"

The Queen held up a hand to stop Lydall, "Do not trouble yourself over these things," she said with a small smile, "You will know when the time to rule arises. Such things can take many years, and I do not intend to leave my home or die anytime soon."

Lydall relaxed slightly as she noted the gleam of humor in the Queen's eyes.

"Now," she continued, "Your arrival in Krekania has brought a certain level of concern to my subjects. It is no secret that Krekania is in dire straits, but your arrival has signaled that perhaps we are in more danger than we ever realized. However, before we come to that, I need to explain to you the history of our world—or at least the relevant history as it pertains to us today.

"As far as we know, Krekania has existed since the dawn of time. Many years ago it was a sprawling, vast world full of creatures and magical castles, much like my own, with multiple rulers and villages all around. Now, Krekania has been reduced to my small kingdom here. Magic is dying and those who once ruled saw the downsizing of this world as a good thing. To them it meant there would be less to care for, less to worry about, and so they allowed it to continue. They turned a blind eye to the fading away of magic, choosing instead to enjoy the lessened responsibility their thrones now had.

"But as magic died...so did they. Now, there is a single ruler of Krekania rather than many lords and ladies undera King or Queen. Even before I began ruling about five years ago, the land was nearly double what it is today...but that I am afraid, is my fault."

The Queen looked away, her pale white cheeks turning red from shame and her eyes filling with unshed tears.

"My parents were the previous rulers of this world. They were chosen to come into Krekania shortly before the current ruler died. At this point in time, magic saw fit to have two rulers rather than just the one as is the normal tradition. My parents reigned over this world for many years and had two children: myself and my sister."

Lydall blinked in astonishment, "Your sister?" she asked, green eyes narrowed in confusion, "Where is she?"

The Queen sighed before replying, "My sister's name is Caillic, which in our world means 'one who is old.' She was born with white hair, much like that of an old woman: as white as the snow in winter. My name is Fenelia, which means 'one who is beautiful and wise.' I suppose this is where our rivalry began," she added wistfully, "My sister was always envious of my name and angered with our parents for her name. Our parents did not name her Caillic to be cruel, mind you, it was just because of her unusual hair. But I suppose my sister, when comparing her name to mine, saw it as something else entirely.

"When we were sixteen years old, our parents held the naming ceremony for us. This ceremony only occurs when the current rulers have had offspring, so it is extremely rare. As far as we know there has only been one other time in Krekania's history where such an event occurred.

"Since our parents did not have any boys to naturally assume the throne, it came down to either myself or my sister. My sister and I are twins, however I was the first one to be born and thus my parents selected me to reign after they died.

"As I am sure you can already imagine, my sister was enraged. Our entire childhood she tried to compete with mein every way and now, in front of all the denizens of Krekania, I was named to rule over her. In Caillic's mind it was yet another slight against her and one that she had no control over. She was always second to me and now it was beingmade an official decree. I had never seen such rage in another beings' eyes as I saw in my own sister's that day."

Fenelia swallowed, clearing her throat and steeling herself

against the ugly memories of her past.

Lydall stared at Fenelia, seeing her in an entirely new light. Her first impression of the Queen had been that of a slightly eccentric woman with a passion for magical creatures, possibly even a collector of them. She would have never guessed that there was so much more to her story.

"It was shortly after I was named Queen-in-waiting that it happened," continued Fenelia, exhaustion and sadness filling her gaze, "Select denizens of Krekania inherit magical abilities unusual to their own kind. They are rare abilities and typically given to those who are destined to rule. My sister and I were both chosen by magic to have our own. Caillic's magical ability is to create ice and mold it to her will. She could create the most beautiful ice sculptures for parties and even form bridges of ice when we were young for us to play on.

"The problem with Caillic is that she also had a fascination with dark creatures, the ones who have bent magic into something twisted and evil. Her obsession with such things further separated us for I have no toleration for such beasts. Her passion for them disgusted me, but we had that one thing in common: our love of her ice art. We used to skate together on her good days out on frozen lakes of her own creation. She was so creative and talented in her art…"

Fenelia's voice shook as she tried to conceal the depth of emotion that revisiting these horrible memories stirred up in her soul.

"That day, however, she used her given-powers to kill," she said, looking directly at Lydall, "My sister, full of rage and envy, unleashed her full power on the guests at the party…and our parents. She struck them down…she sent spears of ice out from the palms of her hands and they sliced right through our own parents—right in front of my own eyes. I had to stand there, helpless, as our parents bled on the floor of the grand staircase that leads up to this Castle. She lashed out at our guests and killed many of the creatures and elves who were in attendance. She had to be stopped.

"However, my magical ability is nothing like Caillic's. I was given the ability to speak to animals and communicate with every creature in the land, no matter what language they speak. I can guide, persuade, and understand all living beings in ways that no one else can. I have no fighting ability or way to stop someone such as her. So, I did the only thing I knew how to do…I talked to her. I begged her to stop, I begged her to not kill me, for she had turned her wrath on me as well. She hesitated long enough for one of my dearest friends, a grey winged-wolf, to rescue me from her assault. Once the wolf, Zarius, had lifted me to safety outside of the Castle, he turned and asked me for permission to slay my sister. He wanted to rip her throat out and let her bleed as my parents had bled. "

Fenelia shuddered and she stared at the stone floor for a long moment, gathering her courage to finish the bloody tale.

Lydall's mouth was hanging open in disbelief as she tried to absorb what she was hearing. This beautiful place had seen bloodshed? And, from what it sounded like, Lydall had a feeling it had seen even more since the day of Caillic's attack.

"I told him no," Fenelia said, her voice barely above a whisper as she lifted her head to face Lydall's gaze, "I could not bare to see my sister dead, despite what she had just done to our family. However, she could not continue killing Krekanians and she could certainly not take over the kingdom."

Fenelia stared intently at a spot over Lydall's head as she confessed the decisions she had made on that terrible day, unable to continue making eye-contact with Lydall or Jasperas she spoke.

"Krekania had just fallen into my hands upon the death of

our parents. So, I had Zarius summon the creatures of the woods with one of his gathering-howls and we led a counter-attack on my sister. We drove her from the castle. Zarius, however, did not survive the battle. My sister made sure he died the moment she realized she was losing the fight.

"I told her she was banished from Krekanian land for all of eternity for what she had done. I told her she was no longer my sister but a sworn enemy of the throne. I even told her that should she return to Krekania, I would have her struck down in the most gruesome way possible. She swore to me, to my face, that she would indeed return and lay waste to what I loved. Caillic said that she would one day rule Krekania and that the dark creatures she loved more than anything, and anyone, would one day command these lands.

"That was five years ago. Since then, my sister has gathered her dark creatures and multiplied them tenfold. She resides in a deep cavern on the side of a mountain many miles from here. My scouts and spies have located it and have told me that the army she began to build the day I banished her is substantially larger than the denizens of Krekania who are capable of defending this land. I know this is why you are here—because Krekania has never needed help more than it does right now."

Lydall gritted her teeth and shook her head, "But how?" she asked, green eyes wide in bewilderment, "I'm only eighteen…I've never fought in a battle and I don't even have any of this—magic—that you all have. What can I possibly do? I mean, I want to help and I certainly do not want to go back to Histair. This place is beautiful and I would be willing to do whatever you need to help save it…I just don't know what *I* could do that could possibly change the fate of this *entire* world. How could someone like *me* face someone like your sister?"

Fenelia smiled a little, the darkness in her eyes lifting briefly, "Well, I have a friend who may shed some light on that. Remember I mentioned a prophecy? It's a prophecy about one who is destined to find Krekania and save us all from this impending doom. But I am not the one who should be telling you this. There is one far more powerful and far more in touch with the magic of Krekania who should be sharing this with you."

As Fenelia spoke, a creature walked out from the tangle of brush behind the throne. Lydall was convinced that, of all the creatures she had seen in Krekania thus far, this was by far the strangest.

The creature had a tan face resembling that of a dog with a long snout and long, black, feathery ears that hung down on either side of its head. A slender, muscular neck connected to a body that was a cross between a deer and a wolf, ending with a long, foxlike tail that swished back and forth as the animal settled down next to the throne. Tall antlers protruded from the top of its head and were adorned with various baubles that glowed in the evening gloom. It had a talisman around its neck that looked like the small skull of a bird tied on with a leather cord. Along its black body were streaks of tan, the same color as its face, and it had four tall, tan legs. The front legs ended with paws that looked like that of a raccoon, while the back legs had hooves like an elk.

"This," said Fenelia, her eyes glowing with pride, "Is the Seer. He has visions given to him by the magic of Krekania. Krekania has chosen him to be our Seer, our guide, and the Hand of the Queen. He is connected to the magic of Krekania in ways that most of us could only dream of. He's truly the greatest of all the creatures and the most valuable. But more than that, he is my truest friend."

The Seer bowed his head at the Queen's gracious words, "You are too kind to me, my Queen."

Lydall nearly fell over backwards when she heard the Seer

speak, "You can talk?" she exclaimed.

Jasper smirked at Lydall's reaction, eyes twinkling in amusement as the tension in his stiff, silent form eased for a brief moment.

"Yes, Lydall," he laughed, "The Seer can speak every language in Krekania. He is the one creature, aside from the Queen, who can communicate with all of us, which adds to his invaluable contribution to our world."

The Seer looked kindly upon Lydall, "So you are the one who is promised," he said, his voice gravely and deep, "You look exactly as I had pictured you, wild one."

The Seer stood and walked toward Lydall until he was standing directly in front of her. He sat back on his haunches and studied her, staring directly into Lydall's emerald eyes.

"You have a fighter's spirit, a true warrior at heart," he stated, "I can see it in your very soul, Lydall of Histair. Your heart is pure and full of a fierce passion for life. You are truly what the magic of Krekania promised us."

Lydall felt her heart begin to beat against her chest at the Seer's proclamation. She was flattered, yet taken aback by the gravity of his words.

"There is a prophecy that came to me in a vision not long ago," he said, his bright golden eyes trained on Lydall, "I will recite it now. Commit it to memory, young Lydall, for it will guide you as your journey begins:

"'*Upon the day that darkness rises once more, the Woman of Fire shall appear. A decision will alter the future. A war will ravage the land. A powerful love will unite or divide. The fate of magic rests on The Woman of Fire. She alone holds the power to save and to destroy, for power is not held by the darkness, but by those who control the light. In the end the Woman of Fire shall rise, or darkness shall reign for all eternity.*'"

The Seer's voice turned into a growl with the final words of the prophecy, his various baubles glowing brightly as the words reverberated in the throne room.

"Good luck, and magic be with you, Woman of Fire. I am sure this will not be the last time we see one another."

The Seer stood abruptly and turned away from Lydall. He walked in long, graceful strides toward the throne where he bowed to Fenelia before disappearing back into the shadows.

Lydall's chest felt as if it were on fire. She realized she had stopped breathing as she listened to the Seer and quickly took a gulp of air. She panted as if she had just run a mile through the wilderness, her heart beating heavy and loud as she gazed up at Fenelia.

"I...I am the Woman of Fire?" she whispered, fear and disbelief overwhelming her as she tried to understand what all of this meant, "How am I the Woman of *Fire*? I don't even know what that means..."

Fenelia nodded, giving Lydall an encouraging smile, "We are not sure what it means precisely. However, it is unmistakably you," said the Queen as she stared at Lydall's vibrant red hair, "You are the Woman of Fire who has come to save us from the darkness. Prophecies aren't meant to be understood directly. Many are revealed to us in time and through new experiences. Do not fear this prophecy. I hesitated to tell you when you first stepped foot inside my Castle because I worried it would scare you. However, I feel as if it would only be right to be honest with you about the land you have found...and what it could mean for your future."

"There is more to understand about the battle that is to come. But for that, I believe, Jasper is more capable of explaining it, seeing as how he is the Captain of the Army of Spellbinders."

Jasper stood proudly at this and bowed low, "Yes my Queen. I will take her to Catha and show her the Army. She has a lot to learn."

Lydall observed the exchange in shocked silence.

Everything was becoming rather overwhelming. Somehow, she was this Woman of Fire in a prophecy and destined to save the last land of magic from utter darkness and destruction. And yet, she was merely a young girl from a far- off land who was to be married to a lord of another kingdom. All she had ever known was how to act like a lady, sit properly, walk correctly, eat politely and dress accordingly. She knew nothing of battles or wars or fighting or anything that would be necessary to fulfill the prophecy the strange Seer spoke of.

Lydall felt her head spinning with all the information she had been exposed to in such a short amount of time. This was a lot to take in at once, but it also felt right somehow. She took a deep, steadying breath. In time this would all make sense. That's what Fenelia herself had said: they would understand the prophecy and her role in it as time went on. She didn't have to figure everything out now. One step at a time.

Fenelia gave Jasper a small, sad smile, "I am afraid that she does still have quite a bit to learn about our world. Before you both leave, there is one last place Lydall must see. I avoided it during our tour because I felt it more appropriate that you saw the beautiful side of Krekania before you saw—the other side of it—what my sister has done to our world."

Lydall swallowed nervously. What else could there possibly be? What had Caillic done? The look on Jasper's face told her that this would by far be the worst part of her experience here at the Castle. Jasper had gone rigid and an emotion flickered through his eyes that Lydall could not quite put words to. Whatever this was, it was going to cause him pain to see it.

Lydall was beginning to realize that there was a lot more to the elf that had not yet been revealed to her. It was almost as if, with every new piece of information she received, she realized there were only more questions and more layers to peel back in this complex new world.

Despite how overwhelming everything about this land was, Lydall felt as if she were ready. It felt right. She felt as if she was meant to be here. Hearing the Queen's story and learning that this magical world was in imminent danger, Lydall wanted nothing more than to do her part in protecting it—whatever that part might be.

7

The Queen led Lydall and Jasper through a dark tunnel that opened up on the far side of the room. Lydall was struck, yet again, by how large the Castle and the grounds were. There were dozens of tunnels leading to numerous coves, fields, and sanctuaries for magical creatures, yet this tunnel felt very different than the ones they had been through before. This tunnel had smooth walls of stone with no vegetation and no sign or feel of magic anywhere.

Lydall realized how unnerving the lack of magic felt. She had only been in Krekania for a single day and yet she already could feel the loss of it as they walked farther and farther away from where magic so freely flowed in the heart of the Castle.

"It's not much farther now," said Fenelia, as if she could sense Lydall's unease, "This area must be as sanitary as possible, so we could not allow the magical flora to grow here. The flora and the creatures of Krekania hold the magic, so that is the loss you are probably feeling now, as both are absent. I feel it too."

Lydall felt relieved at the Queen's words and tried to relax as she followed her through the winding passageway. Jasper had once again gone silent, his face grim and his jaw clenched with unspoken tension as they approached a large doorway.

"This," said Fenelia, with sadness in her eyes, "Is our infirmary. It's where the magical creatures of Krekania reside when they are injured after battling my sister's beasts."

Lydall felt her heart sink into her stomach, finally understanding why both Fenelia and Jasper were reacting the way they were. What she was about to see in here must be the worst part of this world. The very thought of magical creatures in pain mortified Lydall to her very core.

"This is difficult to see," said the Queen quietly as she placed a hand on the door, "Brace yourself, Lydall. The suffering you will witness in here—I only share it with you so that you will fully understand what we are fighting to save— and what we are fighting to prevent. These magic beings are why I fight every day; they are why Jasper has given all of who he is to lead the Army of Spellbinders. They are more precious to us than anything else in our world, for they, along with the flora, are the harborers of magic. Without them magic dies…and so does Krekania."

The gravity of Fenelia's message struck Lydall as if she had been slapped across the face. Some of the creatures in this room were dying, and with their deaths their magic would die too. The Queen's sister was murdering not only these beautiful beasts but magic itself. Lydall was about to witness the direct impact of Caillic's hateful vengeance.

As Fenelia cracked open the door, Lydall could feel asense of deep sadness and pain creep across her skin, as if the suffering of the creatures inside was a living and tangible entity. She shuddered as she stepped through the door and into the rectangular room.

The sight that greeted her made Lydall stop in her tracks. Her heart felt as if it had frozen in her chest. Lying on beds that lined all four walls were many of the creatures Lydall had just encountered in the Castle-sanctuary of Krekania. Some of the creatures cried out in despair and others whimpered quietly in pain. All of their coloring was muted, as if all the magic had been drained from their bodies. The absence of magic felt sharper here, more palpable and it made Lydall queasy.

A pegasus cried out with anguish as it flapped its broken, useless wings. A dull-colored mermaid floated idly in a large tank. A griffon lay on a bed near the back, his head low and his eyes filled with sadness, large scars tracing patters across his shoulders. Wood nymphs in various stages of disarray lay scattered about the large room. Two winged-wolves curled around one another, their light grey coats dingy and limp with deep, freshly healed wounds along their sides.

Lydall whirled around to Fenelia, her green eyes flashing, "You have magic…fix them," she said, her voice cracking with emotion, "How can you just stand there and let them suffer like this?"

Jasper gave Lydall a startled look as he turned to Fenelia, "My Queen, apologies for the human—she didn't mean…"

Fenelia raised her hand to stop him, "No need. It is a fair question. I am, after all, the ruling Queen of these creatures. I should be able to stop this," she said, her eyes misting over, "And yet…I cannot. These creatures are victims of Caillic's attacks. She has damaged their spirits and taken their magic. Where Caillic lives, there is no magic. In order to gather it for her own dark purposes, she invades our land and destroys the plants and the animals of Krekania, sucking the magic out of their souls."

Lydall felt as if she was going to be sick. She clutched her stomach with one hand and steadied herself against the wall with the other.

"These creatures," continued Fenelia, "They survived the attacks. However, enough magic was stolen from them that they cannot recover fully. We—we don't know how to restore the magic that was taken from them."

Lydall leaned against the wall and closed her eyes

briefly, trying to fight off the sudden wave of nausea.

"How did she do it?" she whispered, her eyes blazing with fury as she slowly opened them again and glared at Fenelia, "How did your sister do this?"

Fenelia flinched slightly at Lydall's tone, guilt weighing heavily in her hunched shoulders, "She launches attacks on villages throughout Krekania and either takes captives or she drains them of their magic on the spot. She has a scepter that she uses to pull the magic from them and then takes it back to the land she was exiled to. Then she uses the magic she steals to make her beasts larger and more powerful. When she is interrupted in her attempts to drain a creature of magic, the creature falls weak and we take them here where we care for them to the best of our ability."

"When the magic is gone," said Lydall, "Can it be replaced? If we were to find Caillic and her scepter…?"

Fenelia shook her head sadly, "The magic is transferred to her creatures and it dies when they die. We captured some of her minions before and tried to pull the magic from them with my own scepter, but the magic was tainted, evil. When it was transferred to the creatures of Krekania it corrupted them, making them evil as well. It changed them completely and there was nothing we could do to restore them to what they once were."

Lydall shook her head in frustration, "Fine, then what else creates magic? Can new magic be created somehow and be given to them?"

Fenelia sighed, "That is what we have been trying to discover. We have tried every species of flora there is. The Seer can use healing magic but it drains him so terribly. He's only able to use it on rare occasions because his strength must remain at its height so he can commune with Krekania itself and receive the visions. It seems as if the only other way to restore their magic…is to do so with another dying

Krekanian."

Lydall looked up sharply, horror flooding her vision. Jasper's jaw was clenched tight again and he refused to meet Lydall's bewildered stare.

"A dying Krekanian?" repeated Lydall, "So…you're saying that we have to wait until a creature is dying after one of Caillic's attacks, bring them here, and transfer their remaining magic into one of these creatures? We have to sacrifice one for another?"

Fenelia nodded sadly, the color drained from her face. The Queen appeared to age a couple of decades by the time she was done explaining the horrendous situation to Lydall. The weight of her sister's crimes, and her own personal guilt, showed in her pained and hollowed expression

"I'm afraid that is all we have found so far. All we can do is make them comfortable. Some of the weaker ones— they don't last long. The stronger ones last a few months at best, but we gradually lose them too. The ones who are mere inches from death are the ones whose magic we take and use to try and save those who stand a chance at recovering. In this way, their deaths at least have meaning and purpose."

Lydall felt as if the world were spinning out of control around her. In the short time she had been here she had felt magic course through her veins, skate over her skin, and touch her very soul. She had seen what beautiful creatures and brilliant flora filled with magic were. The beauty of what Krekania was, and should be, was life-altering. Now, standing here, Lydall felt as hopeless as Jasper and Fenelia looked. Who could possibly stop this unbelievable tragedy in front of them from continuing? If Fenelia and Jasper, with their Army of Spellbinders, massive Castle, and magic could not stop Caillic and her demonic creatures, what was she expected to do?

Just then, a small creature pawed at Lydall's leg, just below the hem of her thin, dirty gown. She looked down and saw a firefox, or what had once been a firefox, looking beseechingly up at her. Its large brown eyes were wide and glossy with sadness and her once flaming coat of fire had been reduced to wisps of grey ash with a pale blue flame faintly glowing on the end of her tail.

Lydall, feeling her heart break at the sight, bent down to pick up the bedraggled creature. With tears in her eyes, she held and stroked the pitiful fox, lifting her gaze to look fiercely up at Fenelia.

"With all do respect, *Queen*," she growled, "I cannot accept this. I know I am new here, but I feel it in my very bones that I was meant to be here—that I was meant for somethingmore than the life I had in Histair. I don't know what it is I am meant to do to save these creatures, but I am telling you now that this…what you have shown me here, is unacceptable," she said, sweeping the room with her hand, "This cannot be the fate of Krekania. I need to be taken to where the fighting is. I need to do something other than stand around here and stare at pretty things. This has been wonderful, Queen, but this isn't helping anything at all.

"This Army of Spellbinders," continued Lydall as she turned toward Jasper, "What are they? Where are they? Can they train me? I know I'm a human without any magic, but I cannot continue to stand here and accept what I'm seeing. Will you teach me, Jasper? Let me join your Army. Show me what I can do to help."

Fenelia looked appraisingly upon Lydall, "The Seer was right. You are a fighter, deep inside your soul. You are finding your inner warrior, Lydall. Perhaps there is more to you than meets the eye. More than you even know."

Fenelia turned back to Jasper. The elf was standing solemn and rigid a few feet away, carefully avoiding looking around the room of suffering creatures. He kept his tortured gaze on

Lydall, her green eyes blazing with emotion.

"Jasper," said Fenelia quietly as she placed a hand on the elf's shoulder, "She is yours now. Take her to your home…show her the Army."

Jasper nodded curtly, his jaw still tightly clenched and his arms crossed tightly over his chest.

Lydall felt a trimmer of fear course through her,cutting into the sudden rage of injustice that had overtaken her just moments before. She hoped beyond all hope that she could find a way to fulfill the prophecy the Seer had spoke of earlier. There had to be more to this world, and to her, than she realized. Lydall felt as if she were missing a vital piece, one that she knew she would not find sitting in the secluded, protective walls of the Castle. She needed to go into the land of Krekania and be with the creatures that were fighting for their lives against the Queen's vengeful sister.

Fenelia lifted her hand and indicated that they should leave the room. Lydall gave the pitiful firefox one last stroke and sat her gently on a nearby bed. She turned, with tears in her eyes, and walked away.

As she and Jasper followed the Queen out of the infirmary, Fenelia looked over her shoulder, directly into Lydall's eyes.

"Fear not, young Lydall. You are ready. I know it in my soul. By all magic, you are the one who was promised. I believe in the Seer and in the magic of Krekania. If the prophecy says you are the chosen one, then you will truly save us all…Woman of Fire.

8

Jasper and Lydall returned to the Queen's throne room and mounted their winged creatures. Jasper seemed to come alive as they prepared to leave the Castle and journey to his village. The furious glint in his eyes had turned into an excited gleam and the tension seemed to melt off his shoulders. Even his griffon, Dionysus, appeared to look less stoic as he hopped from one foot to the other, eager to take flight.

"Take care, Woman of Fire" whispered Fenelia as she stood next to Triton and gazed up at Lydall, "There is still much to understand about this world and the danger we all face. I have faith in you, and now you must have faith in yourself."

Lydall felt a twinge of annoyance with the Queen as she adjusted her position on Triton's back. While she understood that Caillic was Fenelia's sister, she still had a difficult time accepting that the Queen just let the vile woman leave Krekania freely. Because of that decision, creatures, like the whimpering firefox in the infirmary, were suffering and dying.

Lydall nodded curtly to the Queen, forcing herself to show respect despite her feelings on the matter, and turned to Jasper. She locked eyes with the handsome elf and gave him a confident smile.

"Take me to your Army, Captain," she said, eyes flashing with determination, "We have a world to save."

Jasper smirked at her confidence, "It's only been one day

and the frightened little girl I found in the woods has already fashioned herself into a warrior, eh?" he asked with a wicked grin.

Lydall narrowed her eyes in a playful manner as she gave Triton a firm squeeze with her legs. Her heart was racing with excitement at the thought of the adventure that lay ahead.

Triton whinnied and pawed the ground before he took off at a steady canter toward the main doors, wings flapping as he prepared to take flight.

"Quite the handful, that human," murmured Jasper to Dionysus, "I suppose we should catch up, seeing as how neither she nor the pegasus know where they are going."

The griffon grunted in annoyance, miffed at not being the first creature to take to the skies and lead the way back home.

Jasper turned around and gave Fenelia a quick salute before Dionysus began to charge down the long bridgeway. The griffon spread his wings and took off into the bright light of the morning sun.

…

"How much farther?" asked Lydall for the fifth time that afternoon.

Jasper narrowed his eyes as he turned around to look at her, "Must you always ask the same question?"

"Must you always give the same answer?" retorted Lydall, "I feel as if we have been flying for days."

Jasper shook his head, "Humans," he muttered, much to Dionysus' amusement, "Come on," he said, louder so Lydall could hear, "Follow us. Right down this way."

The white griffon gave a loud screech as he turned mid-air and glided down toward the ground. Lydall quickly guided Triton around to follow the swift bird-like creature.

The black pegasus folded his wings in tight to his side, pummeling down to the ground at a rapid speed. Lydall felt a thrill of fear and adrenalin course through her veins as the ground rose up to meet them. At the last second, Triton spread his wings and slowed their descent, landing gently on all four hooves.

Lydall was still gripping Triton's mane as if her life depended on it long after they had landed, her hands white and shaking as she tried to steady herself.

"Was that entirely necessary?" she muttered to her pegasus as she slid off his back.

Triton snorted and tossed his head, looking rather pleased with himself.

Jasper hurried over to Lydall and reached for her arm, grabbing her lightly and pulling her forward in his excitement, "Welcome to my home," he said with a broad grin, "This is the home of the Army of the Spellbinders. We call it Catha. It's the ancient word for 'battlefield.'"

Lydall gazed around her. They were in a rather large clearing in the center of the magical woodland of Krekania. A large wooden fence, topped with sharp spikes, surrounded the open area. Two massive grey winged-wolves pushed open the gates as they approached, tails wagging as they caught Jasper's scent on the breeze. They were nearly as large as Akira and Logan, the Queens guardian wolves back at the Castle.

Inside the gates Lydall could see homes of various shapes, sizes, and colors. Some of the thatched roof structures were high up in the three robust trees that grew around the clearing, while others were jumbled about on the ground. One section of the village looked like a marketplace with a small garden filled with growing vegetables. Off to the other side was a smooth, grassy space with various weapons strewn about the ground. A myriad of creatures ran around freely and greeted one another, pausing to bow their heads to Jasper as they continued on their way.

"This place," breathed Lydall, "It's…it's brilliant!"

Jasper smiled, pleased at Lydall's reaction, "Well it certainly isn't as grand as the Castle, but it is full of life. These are the creatures who have chosen to fight back against the Sorceress and her army. They have both the capability to fight as well as the unrelenting desire to avenge those they have lost. Most of them have that same warrior spirit you have," he added, glancing back at Lydall as they walked down the main pathway.

Lydall felt herself blush under Jasper's praise. He was rather attractive, for an elf, even more so in the way he moved through Catha. His entire demeaner exuded confidence, strength, and love for the creatures around him. This was Jasper's true home, that much was evident. The ruggedness of Catha suited the warrior-elf much more than the grandeur of the Castle.

Lydall gazed around at the creatures milling about them: winged-wolves, griffons, pegasi, unicorns, owls, multi-colored birds, firefoxes, and even a sabretooth cat.

"Are there other elves here?" she asked, looking around, "I've seen just about every creatureimaginable, but I haven't seen anyone else like you."

A look of sadness and anger crossed Jasper's face,but he quickly masked it, "Yes. There are five of us left. The rest were killed by Caillic and her army."

Lydall felt that now all-too-familiar pang in her stomach as she let this latest revelation sink in. There were only five of Jasper's kind left? This Sorceress had murdered nearly all his species. What kind of monstress being could be capable of unleashing so much death and pain?

Jasper noted Lydall's reaction and reached out to her, "Come. I'll tell you my story then you can meet the others.

Their stories are very similar to mine, but I have an easier time telling it. I've had to rehash that day many times. I've grown more used to it I suppose," he said as he gently took Lydall's elbow and guided her to a large tree to the left of the clearing. A small house sat among the branches about halfway up the trunk, nestled securely among the leaves.

"Leave Triton and Dionysus here," he said as they neared his house, "They'll be fine inside the walls of Catha."

Lydall murmured quietly to Triton, explaining that he had to stay behind once again. Triton snorted and flapped his wings in discontent as he eyed Dionysus. The griffon screeched at the pegasus and stalked away into the brush, clearly not interested in spending anymore alone time with the black Destrier.

"Go make new friends," said Lydall as she watched the griffon slink away, "He's a bit too grumpy for you anyway."

Triton whinnied in agreement as he turned to explore the open grassy area on the other side of the encampment. Several magical creatures were grazing and lounging about, looking rather content as Triton trotted over to join them.

Jasper smiled slightly and began to climb up a wooden ladder attached to the tree, gesturing for Lydall to do the same. Lydall followed, the hollow feeling in her stomach reminding her that it had now been several hours since their rushed breakfast at the Castle.

Jasper pivoted deftly as he pulled himself into the house. He turned and reached down to help pull Lydall up the last few feet.

"Welcome to my little piece of Catha," he said with a satisfied smile as he gestured to his little home.

Lydall looked around in surprise. Jasper's thatched home was well-outfitted for something built into the branches of a tree. He had a small living quarters with a bed on the far wall and a kitchenette off to the other side of the house. There were several windows, letting in plenty of light and fresh air. Covering most of the floor was a large fur rug that caught Lydall's attention.

"I'll start making us some porridge," said Jasper as he began to fiddle around in his makeshift kitchen. He lit the small fireplace in the corner and placed a pot inside the flames, "Should only be a few minutes now," he said as he gestured for Lydall to settle down on the rug.

Lydall sat down and felt the rug with her hands. It was soft to the touch and gave the room a warm and cozy feeling.

"What is this rug made out of?" she asked, curiously as Jasper joined her.

"The pelt of the dark winged-wolf who killed my family," replied Jasper, matter-of-factly.

Lydall's jaw dropped open and her emerald eyes widened in shock as she stared at Jasper. The calm and simple way in which he made such a heavy statement unnerved her.

Jasper sighed, "I suppose this is the part where I begin my story," he said glancing back at the porridge cooking in the fire, "My father, mother, and sister were all killed by one of Caillic's dark wolves a couple years ago. We were out scouting for a new home after our village had been destroyed in one of Caillic's raids. What we didn't know was that Caillic had sent her dark wolves out to hunt down any *strays*, as she called them—anyone who had escaped the initial attack. This wolf just so happened to have found my family.

"It was quick. There wasn't much to it. The dark wolf was smart; he had clearly struck down many other Krekanians before that day. He killed my father immediately upon landing on the path in front of us, then struck down my mother and sister in a single move, and then he turned to face me."

Lydall felt a cold shiver run down her spine at the look in Jasper's brown eyes. What he must have endured that day was unimaginable. She had willingly left her family to escape an arranged marriage, while the elf before her had been forced to watch his entire family be slaughtered in front of his eyes.

"The wolf lunged at me and I knew I was dead," continued Jasper, "There was no escaping those jaws. I felt his claws rake across my face," he said, gesturing at the long scars on one cheek, "And I hit the ground hard. I remembered feeling the wolf's breath on me one instant and then the next, he was just gone.

"I remember looking up and seeing this great white griffon gripping the wolf in his talons and slashing through the thick fur, blood splattering everywhere. I remember the wolf's death cries as the griffon struck again and again. It was a short battle and the griffon won. He carried the dead wolf in his talons and dropped him in front of me. I will never forget the look on Dionysus' face that day. He looked mortified and grief stricken. He bowed to me and I knew that day he and I would fight together forever.

"I will never know why he risked his life for me and my family. I believe some creatures are just pure of heart and willing to die for the innocent. Dionysus is the bravest and purest creature I have ever known. I would be dead today if it were not for his decision to rescue me."

Lydall shook her head in astonishment, "That is why you two are so bonded then," she said quietly, "Dionysus is a true hero."

Jasper nodded, "That he is. That day I swore to avenge my family's death. I would do anything to stop the Sorceress. Dionysus and I tended to our wounds and then flew out to meet Fenelia, the Queen. I told her my story and swore my life to her and all Krekania. We spoke for hours and began to form our plans for creating the Army of Spellbinders. She made me their Captain and together, we all built this little city in the center of the magical wood."

Jasper paused his story for a moment to retrieve the porridge from the flames. Grasping the kettle with a long pair of metal tongs, he gently poured it into two large bowls. He carefully brought the bowls over to Lydall and settled back down on the wolf-pelt.

"So far we have managed to build quite the Army," he said as they began to eat, "Unfortunately, so has Caillic. She is relentless. We have lost a good number of creatures to her attacks. She steals their magic and harbors it for her own use, like the Queen mentioned before."

"That's what I don't understand.I thought Caillic hated Krekania and magic?" asked Lydall, looking perplexed as she blew on a spoonful of porridge, "Even if she is taking it and manipulating it to her will, why would she use the very thing she despises?"

Jasper smirked, "You're a smart one aren't you?"

Lydall felt her cheeks flush again under his praise as she glanced quickly down at her bowl.

"Well," he continued, "You are correct: she hates Krekania and she hates *Krekanian* magic. But she is rather fond of dark magic. She hates the Krekanian magic because she blames its existence for all the bad things that have happened to her in this life, and since the Darkness is Krekania's age-old enemy, dark magic pleases her. Anything and anyone who stands against Krekania brings her joy.

"You see, shortly after the Queen banished Caillicfrom Krekania, the Sorceress sought out the Pool of Darkness. Dark magic is fueled by hate, greed, and jealousy. The more such things exist, the larger the Pool becomes. It's somewhere deep in the dark woods far from Krekanian land and Caillic sought it on purpose to sell her very soul in exchange for a heaping of dark magical power. Think of it as if...the Darkness itself now owns her."

"How did the Darkness come to Krekania?" asked Lydall, furrowing her brow in confusion, "Has it just...always been?"

"In a way it has always existed...at least as far back as anyone can remember and what the recorded histories have told us," answered Jasper as he dipped his spoon back into the porridge, "The Darkness is Krekania's ancient enemy. Its deepest desire is to destroy all the magic that makes Krekania what it is so that it can reform the magical world for its own purposes. The Darkness emerged many centuries ago in the form of a Dark Wizard who sought to overthrow the founder of Krekania, his brother. A great battle was waged, and after many years of fighting, the Dark Wizard was defeated. However, the Dark Wizard had introduced a contorted version of magic to the world, and there is no way to permanently be rid of it. So, the Dark Wizard's brother, the First King of Krekania, banished the magic to the Dark Pool and cast many spells to contain it forever. Until Caillic, the Darkness remained in the Pool.

"We believe that the magic can escape through someone who gives their soul over to the Darkness, much in the same way the Dark Wizard did. No one has ever tried to do so...until now. Once committed to the Darkness, there is no going back. So even if Caillic had a change of heart, she is forever bound to the desire of the Darkness."

Lydall nodded slowly, "So Darkness can walk among the rest of us now because Caillic possesses it inside ofherself."

Jasper nodded, pleased that she was catching onquickly, "Exactly. And it exists inside her sadistic creatures."

Lydall frowned as she ate more of the porridge, "And Caillic was the only being to actually go to the Pool? The only one who actually sold their soul to the Darkness?"

Jasper flinched at Lydall's question. He took a deep breath and sighed before he answered.

"I'm afraid there was one other being who may have done the same thing…although no one has heard from him since the day he fled into the dark woods."

Lydall's eyes widened with interest, "Who?" she asked, leaning forward.

"My brother.

9

Lydall's eyes widened in shock, the spoon in her hand frozen halfway to her mouth.

"Your…your brother?" she stammered, her voice barely above a whisper.

She watched Jasper's face tighten as he glanced away, "It's a part of my story I still have a hard time talking about, but you need to know the truth…even the ugliest parts, if you're truly going to join my Army."

Lydall nervously ate her porridge, her eyes fixed on Jasper's face as he readied himself to continue.

"About a year before Caillic became the Dark Sorceress and turned on her own family, my brother turned on ours," began Jasper, his voice low and gravely, "There was a girl, a young and pretty elf named Tiela. She had dark red hair, stunning green eyes, and, well, she actually looked a bit like you, Lydall."

Lydall blinked in surprise, "Oh?"

Jasper smiled sadly, "Yes. She was quite the beauty."

Lydall's face grew warm as she realized Jasper was indirectly calling her a 'beauty.' She quickly dipped her head back down into her porridge bowl, trying to hide her face.

"She caught my eye a long time ago," continued Jasper, oblivious to Lydall's reaction, "We began courting and I quickly fell in love with her. She was not just a rare beauty, but also one of the most intelligent elves I had ever met. She was everything I could have ever wanted. Unfortunately, my brother, Archer, felt the same way. He made his feelings known one night. Archer found Tiela wandering around the woods one evening, as she often did, and approached her. He confessed his love for Tiela and pledged himself to her.

"Tiela did not respond well to my brother's aggressive advances and lashed out at him. She struck him across the face before she ran back to the village. She came to me in my family's home and told me what Archer had said. I was enraged. My own brother was trying to take the girl I loved from behind my back. I sent Tiela home to her family and waited for my brother to get back to the house.

"He didn't get back until late that night. I confronted him the moment he set foot in the doorway. We got into a heated argument. He swore that he loved Tiela since the day he set eyes on her and that I had stolen her love from him. He claimed that she had wanted him long before I noticed her and that I was keeping him from having true happiness. This was all a lie of course, but the fool stuck to his story. He swore by all magic that Tiela was meant to be his betrothed and not mine and that he would do whatever it took to make sure that happened.

"Our parents separated us before the disagreement became violent. I was enraged beyond words at that point. Several days later, Archer approached Tiela again before a Gathering, when the elves of the village all came together for a meeting. He professed his undying love for her again and Tiela told him to stay away and to never approach her again. Archer begged her to reconsider his offer and at least talk to him about it later. At this point Archer was beginning to create a scene, so in an effort to avoid further attention, Teila told him she would join him for a walk in the woods after the Gathering.

"Tiela told me of the exchange and her decision. I urged her to not go, but she was a stubborn one," Jasper gritted his teeth and squeezed his eyes shut as a wave of emotion threatened to overwhelm him, "She insisted that she could put an end to all of this—that she knew she could talk sense into my stupid brother. I listened to her. I trusted her judgement and figured she would know what was best—she always did after all. She was persuasive and well-known for solving even the most difficult problem without an argument. And my brother and I never got along well. We were always at odds over one thing or another. Our personalities were too much alike, and he had a fascination with the darker side of magic that I found rather alarming, so we stayed out of each other's way as much as possible. I thought that perhaps Tiela dealing with him would be the best way to fix this entire thing and put it behind us before it got out of hand.

"So, after the Gathering, Tiela and Archer went off onto the main trail through the woods around our village. The rest of this story is mostly guess work, as we never truly found out what had happened that day. All we know is that they went into the woods, and neither of them ever came back."

Lydall shivered and pulled her knees to her chest, wrapping her arms around them as she gazed at Jasper. The pain in his eyes was enough to break her own heart.

"We found Tiela several hours later after we rallied a search party. He left her body in the middle of the woods, her throat cut and her eyes still open, staring at the sky. As for Archer…we had no idea where he went. My parents were in denial that Archer could have killed Tiela, but there was no doubt in my mind. My brother's fascination with the darkness and the magic that was tied to it along with his jealousy and rage—I knew what had happened. He had probably begged and pleaded with Tiela to choose him over me, Tiela most likely refused, an argument ensued, and eventually it became violent. I have a feeling that Archer tried to force her decision and she fought back, and in one of his moments of rage, he killed her. I always knew he had a temper and that his rage often overtook him…but until that day I had no idea he would be capable of killing. He must have panicked and ran away instead of dealing with the consequences he knew would follow.

"It was not until much later that we found out my brother had given himself over to the dark magic. I saw him the day our village was raided by Caillic's Dark Army. He was riding a winged-wolf, black as night, and had a large sword in his hand. I watched him strike down several of the elves in our village…the place that raised him. He murdered his own kind, just like he murdered Tiela. The most I can guess is that when he fled that night, he went straight to the dark woods. There he must have found the Dark Pool, like Caillic did, and drank from it and traded his soul for the powers of dark magic…the thing he always loved more than the rest of us anyway.

"It was that or he found somewhere else to live until Caillic found him and led him to the Pool. They are together now, he and Caillic. Their mutual love of the darkness, their sworn allegiance to it, and their thirst for power and revenge brought them together in an unholy union. Now he is the captain of her army as I am the captain of the Queen's. Brother against brother. It's poetic almost," said Jasper with a slight sneer, "And so we stand on opposite sides of the War. He wants to help Caillic destroy Krekanian magic and take over the land in the name of the Darkness, and I want to stop them—and to avenge Tiela's death."

Lydall felt her breath come out in a shaky gasp as Jasper ended his tale, "I'm…I don't know what to say. You've been through so much—and yet you are still here, fighting."

Jasper smiled sadly, "What else can I do? I have lost

everything. Now I must fight for what is left of the land I love and the world I am part of…and for the remaining elves who survived the raids. They are all that is left of my kind."

"It must get lonely sometimes," said Lydall quietly.

Jasper looked away for a moment, "Yes…it can be."

Lydall looked into Jasper's sad eyes and felt her heart begin to beat in an unsteady rhythm. Jasper slowly leaned forward toward her, mesmerized by her bright green gaze. The heat rushed into Lydall's cheeks as she realized what was happening when suddenly, a high-pitched voice interrupted them. Lydall looked over to the door of the house quickly, breaking eye-contact with Jasper. The elf sighed in resignation as he looked between the door and Lydall.

"You're a unique human, Lydall," he murmured quietly, "I'm looking forward to getting to know you better."

Lydall smiled, blushing fiercely now, as Jasper stood and walked over to the door. He opened it and looked down toward the roots of the massive tree.

"It's Effie," he said with a smirk as he glanced back at Lydall, "She's one of the last elves. Come on. It's about time for the Gathering anyway. Might as well go and meet everyone."

Lydall urged her beating heart to calm down as she nodded to Jasper and followed him out of the tree-house. The intense emotion that had flooded through her body as she listened to Jasper's story was overwhelming. This elf had been through things she could never imagine. To survive such loss took a level of courage she had never seen before. It also didn't hurt that he was rather easy on the eyes.

A startled gasp from below broke Lydall's train of thought and almost caused her to lose her footing on the ladder as she made her way down the tree.

A young, small elf gazed up at her, light-brown eyes wide

in astonishment as she openly stared at Lydall.

"That's…that's a human!"

10

The tiny elf gazed up at Jasper and Lydall, her mouth gaping open in shock as she absentmindedly ran a hand through her short brown hair.

"It's alright, Effie," said Jasper as he let go of the ladder and let himself fall the final few feet to the ground, "She's with me. This is Lydall."

Lydall eased her way down the ladder and jumped down next to Jasper.

"Hello," she said with a smile, doing her best to not appear intimidating to the much-smaller elf.

"H—hello," stammered Effie, glancing back and forth between Lydall and Jasper, her large eyes wide.

"You'll have to excuse Effie," said Jasper with a smirk, "Your arrival in Krekania is going to shock everyone. It's been a long time since a new human has come here."

"This…this is amazing," breathed Effie as she began to bounce from one foot to the other, "A human—a human! Jasper! Does that mean that…?"

Jasper held up a hand to stop Effie, "Don't worry about that now. Come on. We'll be late for the Gathering."

Lydall frowned and narrowed her eyes at Jasper, trying to figure out why he had stopped Effie from asking her question. They both knew what she was trying to ask anyway. Fenelia had mentioned that Krekania only allowed lost humans to find it when it was in need of a new King or Queen. But they already had a Queen, and a young one at that. The nagging thought that kept entering her mind since she spoke to the Queen came back to her again: if she were to be the new ruler, then what would become of Fenelia?

Lydall didn't have more time to contemplate the matter as the trio emerged into a large clearing where many magical creatures were congregating. Some flew around the big open space while others chased each other, eliciting growls and snarls of displeasure from the larger creatures laying about. Floating above them were orbs of light in various undulating colors. The magical balls of light gave the clearing a warm, happy glow and instantly made Lydall feel a sense of ease.

"You have to meet the others!" exclaimed Effie as she danced around Lydall, "They're going to be so excited!"

Lydall smiled in amusement at the small elf, "Well I can't wait to meet them myself," she said, stifling a yawn. It had been a long day. It was hard to believe that early that morning, before the sun had even risen, she had arrived in Krekania. It had also been more than a day now since she had last slept.

"Don't worry," murmured Jasper as he touched her arm, leading her around the clearing, "After this you can sleep. I'll have Effie make a space for you in her home."

Lydall smiled gratefully just as three other elves approached them from across the gathering place.

"Look!" shouted Effie as she pranced over to the elves, "Jasper brought a human to the gathering! And she came through *An Chloch*!"

The three elves stopped, mid-stride, as they looked over at Lydall in shock. Mouths gaping, their eyes trailed slowly over from Lydall to Jasper, seeking further explanation.

Jasper shifted his weight from one foot to the other, "She's the one in the prophecy. For now though, she is our guest and she is the newest member of our Army. We'll figure the rest out in due time. Now," said Jasper as he walked over to the elves, "This is Syllus, Nyra, and Armus...the last of the surviving elves."

Lydall swallowed nervously. These three elves were considerably more imposing than Jasper and Effie. The one Jasper pointed to and called Syllus was large, muscular, and had long blonde hair that ran down his back. He stood a good three heads taller than Jasper. Despite his intimidating size, Syllus had a good-natured smile plastered across his broad face. The elf named Nyra looked as if she were ready to murder the entire world. Her long black hair swept over her eyes, giving her a guarded and aloof appearance. Armus, like Nyra, was scowling as if all of Krekania were out to get him. His white hair hid some of the scarring on the side of his face and his pale blue eyes seemed to cut right through Lydall.

Several creatures emerged from the edge of the woods and moved to stand beside the elves. A golden-colored griffon rubbed his head against Syllus' leg, while a massive grey winged-wolf eagerly whined at Nyra's feet. A white pegasus tossed his head and whinnied as he trotted over next to Armus, followed closely by the familiar black shape of Triton.

Lydall broke out into a wide grin as Triton knickered happily, moving away from the group of elves and other magical creatures. He hurried over to Lydall and bent down to breathe in her scent. Lydall hugged her pegasus around the neck lovingly.

The final creature to emerge from the gloom was a large cat-like animal with fangs that hung down from her upper jaw. The cat slunk around the other elves and their creatures and, with a purr that shook the ground, wound herself around Effie. The small elf giggled happily as she stroked the tawny-colored sabretooth cat.

"Alright, let's begin, shall we?" asked Jasper as he moved into the center of the clearing.

Effie tugged on the sleeve of Lydall's dirty white dress and indicated that she should sit next to her, "When this is over I'll have to find you some proper clothing," she giggled, "This little dress won't do well for battle training. We'll have to find you some leathers and armor and have you properly fitted."

Lydall smiled gratefully at the little elf, "Thank you. I was in a bit of a hurry when I left my world," she added with a slight smirk, remembering the mind-bending experience she'd had at An Chloch, "I haven't had a chance to find more suitable clothes."

Effie smiled kindly and turned her attention back to Jasper who had begun to address the crowd. The elves settled down and their creatures lay next to them, ready to hear what Jasper had to say.

"You are all aware by now that we have a new inhabitant of Krekania," he said, his voice echoing in the clearing.

Lydall felt the heat rise up into her neck and into her face as every eye in the glade turned toward her. The creatures cooed and growled in response to the news as they studied her. She reached out reflexively for Triton who had settled down on the other side of her. She nervously toyed with his black mane until the eyes of the Krekanians shifted back to Jasper.

"She has met Queen Fenelia and, between the Queen and myself, has been told the history of Krekania and the current threat we face. She is also aware of the prophecy and that she, more than likely, plays a vital role in its fulfillment. While we cannot say for certain what her role will be exactly, she is willing to join the Army and learn her purpose and her place here. "

Jasper's words were met with clapping and cries of approval from the creatures in the clearing. A young firefox scampered over to Lydall and leapt into her lap with a yip of excitement. Lydall gasped in surprise, worried for a moment that the little firefox's flames would singe her dress. She smiled sadly as she remembered the firefox in the infirmary. Her weak flames had not even felt warm to the touch. Lydall surmised that this must be part of the magic of these little creatures and reached out her hand to pet the brightly-glowing fox in her lap. The firefox cooed with pleasure as she ran her hands over his flame-like fur, amazed that it felt silky soft and without a touch of heat.

"As you can see," said Jasper, grinning crookedly, "Fire creatures seem rather fond of her. I suppose that is fitting given the prophecy of the Woman of Fire, no?"

Murmurs of amusement echoed throughout the clearing as Jasper continued with his speech.

"That being said, we need to ramp up our battle training starting tomorrow. The threat of the Dark Sorceress and her army grows stronger every day. We cannot let up. We cannot allow ourselves to become complacent. I understand that Caillic has not launched a raid in quite some time, but we are also aware that this means she is most likely preparing for a massive attack. The last time she went this long between her raids…we lost an entire village of elves before we could stop her."

Dismayed cries and whimpers followed Jasper's words. Lydall glanced at the other elves and saw that Effie had tears in her eyes while Nyra and Armus had pure rage reflecting in their violent, snarling faces. Syllus glanced nervously at Effie, concern drawing deep lines on his face as he noted her distress. These elves had been through so much already, and the war had not even begun.

"We know that she is lying in wait and that this next attack will most likely be one of her largest ones to date. I sent the griffons out on a scouting mission a few days ago and they returned to report that there has been no activity on the border. None of Caillic's beasts have crossed the line, to include Caillic herself. They are in their dark woods, feeding on the magic that they have stolen, and training. We must do the same. Now…"

Jasper's words were cut off abruptly as a deafeningroar ripped through the clearing. Lydall felt a thrill of fear as she gazed skyward and saw a monstorous black beast descending upon them, jagged wings and crooked teeth open wide as it unleashed another hellish scream.

"We're being attacked!" shouted Jasper desperately, his eyes glittering with fear and fury.

"It's her manticors!" shouted Nyra, baring her teeth like a wild animal, "Send them all to hell, Spellbinders! ATTACK!"

Lydall watched as the elves and magical creatures transformed from peaceful, welcoming beings into creatures of war. Even the little firefox, who had been lying peacefully in her lap, leapt to attention, his flames flaring with rage as he snarled in defiance at the deadly creatures cascading down around them.

Lydall felt a rush of panic shoot up her spine as the massive manticore landed, shaking the earth beneath it. Upon its back sat a slender woman with long, flowing white hair and cruel, black eyes. She turned her head and those dark eyes met Lydall's emerald gaze. In that instant Lydall knew true fear. She felt as if all the hope inside of her drowned within those dark pools of hate. Before her was the epitome of evil. The mistress of darkness.

The Dark Sorceress.

11

The clearing erupted in panicked and outraged cries as the Army of Spellbinders reacted to the surprise attack.

Lydall watched, frozen with shock, as unicorns, winged-wolves, sabretooth cats, firefoxes, phoenixes, and pegasi all launched themselves into the fray. Creatures that Lydall had never seen before fell from the skies, jaws wide open and teeth gleaming in the glow of the floating orbs. Dark winged-wolves with savage maws and glowing red eyes flung themselves mercilessly on the Spellbinders while ancient, monstrous manticores slashed with unsuppressed rage.

A loud crashing noise came from behind the wood line, catching many of the creatures' attention. A massive bull-like creature, whose entire body appeared to be on fire, stampeded over the trees, shaking its giant head as it charged into the clearing.

A brilliantly white unicorn cantered toward it, it's horn glittering, full of powerful Krekanian magic. The fiery bull skid to a halt as the unicorn whinnied and released its magic into the face of the beast. The white light that shot out of the unicorn's horn encased the massive bull, snuffing out its fiery aura. The bull cried out in pain and began to retreat slowly back to the woods as the unicorn was joined by more of her kind.

Almost immediately after the unicorns chased the fiery bull from the battle, a dark wolf leapt onto one of the unicorns' backs, tearing large gashes into the beautiful animal's pelt.

With shrieks of pain and terror, the other unicorns turned to face this new threat, desperate to save their injured friend.

Lydall's attention was pulled from the scene when another dark winged-wolf trapped Nyra's large grey wolf under its cruel paws. The dark beast's saliva dripped down onto the smaller wolf as its jaw descended.

"No!" screamed Lydall, leaping forward desperately. She dodged a screaming phoenix as it tried to tackle another dark wolf and side-stepped two sabretooth cats locked in a viscous battle with a manticore. She had no idea what she could possibly do to stop what was about to happen to Nyra's wolf, but she knew she could not just stand there and watch him be destroyed.

The dark wolf's teeth met the grey wolf's throat just as Lydall stumbled in front of them.

Crying out in desperation Lydall felt a sudden rush of rage, love, and a ferocity she had never felt before take over her body. The overpowering emotions shook her to the core and threatened to take her down to her knees. She felt something, a powerful force, pooling in her hands. A quiet voice in her head told her what she must do next. Without hesitation, Lydall flung her hands forward, palms out toward the dark wolf.

A loud squeal of pain and the sound of a body hitting the forest floor pulled Lydall from the overpowering sensation. She opened her eyes and stared in shock at the charred, smoking body of the dark winged-wolf. Gazing down at her hands Lydall saw small flickers of flame receding back into her palms.

Gaping in astonishment Lydall looked from her hands to the dark wolf's body and back again, trying to make sense of what just happened.

Nyra's wolf stood up and shook out his ruffled pelt and

gazed up at Lydall in admiration. He gave a quick bow of gratitude before he leapt back into the battle, locking teeth and claws with another dark wolf.

Lydall whirled around and looked across the clearing. Splatters of blood and bodies of creatures, Spellbinders and the dark army alike, littered the forest floor. Off to one side Nyra and Armus were fending off a large manticore with the help of a couple winged-wolves. Effie, her sabretooth cat, and Triton were unleashing physical and magical blows at a group of dark wolves, driving them away from a family of pegasi. Three griffons soared down on top of a couple smaller manticores, slashing them viciously with long claws as they tried to peck out their eyes.

The Dark Sorceress, Caillic, was still mounted upon her manticore monstrosity, gathering magic into her scepter from the fallen Spellbinders. One of the unicorns, who had survived the assault by the large dark wolf, cantered bravely toward Caillic, horn gleaming dangerously. With barely a glance in it's direction, Caillic lifted a hand and pointed her palm at the charging unicorn. Ice shot out of her hand and flew through the air at a blinding speed. To Lydall's horror, the ice pierced through the unicorn's chest, striking it dead almost instantly. The unicorn fell to the forest floor, body bloodied and crumpled as the magic poured out of it and into Caillic's scepter.

The calmness of Caillic's demeanor coupled with the little smile on her face made Lydall shudder. The ease with which she snuffed out an innocent life was utterly horrifying.

But what caught Lydall's attention next made her heart stop in her chest: Jasper.

On the far side of the clearing, the Captain of the Army of Spellbinders was facing down a tall, lean figure that looked like a mirror image of himself. Jasper's eyes were filled with hate and pain as the two figures exchanged words, circling one another slowly.

"Archer," breathed Lydall, realizing who the other elf must be.

Scrambling, Lydall began to make her way over to the circling brothers. A dark wolf slammed into her from the side, throwing Lydall several feet into the air. She landed painfully on her stomach, the air whooshing from her lungs at the sudden impact. Stunned, she struggled to get up, gasping desperately for air. A deadly snarling sound above her made Lydall scramble to right herself and face this new threat.

The black wolf lunged forward as Lydall twisted onto her back, hands raised to shield her face and throat from the inevitable attack. The overwhelming rush of magic overtook Lydall once again and she felt a surge of energy pour from her hands. For a second time that day, a dark wolf cried out in agony as its burning body fell to the ground.

Lydall's green eyes were wide with horror at the sight, but she had no time to think about what was going on inside her head. She struggled back to her feet, one arm wrapped around her sore ribs, and ran toward Jasper and his brother. The look on Jasper's face told her that her fears were correctly placed: he was utterly mortified to see his brother again, and full of undisciplined rage.

Diving around the various skirmishes in the clearing, Lydall drew closer and closer to the two brothers. Soon she was able to hear some of what they were saying to one another.

"You're a traitor and a murderer," snarled Jasper, his eyes hard with hate, "You helped *her*…she killed our family! We lost everything and it's because of *her*! And where were you when that happened? You were with her! You were there! I saw you in our village killing our friends, the elves who *raised* you! Why? Because of an elf who never loved you? Tiela loved me, Archer! She loved *me*. Your greed, selfishness and your hate killed her. *You* killed her. And now look at you: serving *Caillic*."

Archer sneered openly, "If only life were as simplistic as you make it seem, brother. If only things were so black and white. Then again, you were always the simple-minded of the two of us," he said, slinking around Jasper like a snake, fluid and cunning, "You let your heart guide you more than your own head. It is true that I loved Tiela. She foolishly loved you, but I knew her better than you did. I knew she wanted and needed someone more like me: someone bolder, stronger, and smarter to care for her. She just needed to be—pushed—in the right direction. Unfortunately, I guess I pushed her farther than she could handle. I guess she wasn't as strong as I thought she was. Perhaps she was actually the perfect fit for you, little brother."

Jasper tensed, prepared to leap at his brother in a fit of uncontrollable fury.

"You're only saying that because you're too prideful to admit that you made a horrible mistake. You killed her and instead of owning up to what you did, you ran away. You sought comfort from those who would understand you…and who better to understand a murderer than Caillic? You sold your soul to the dark magic just like she did. You're a coward. That's all you ever were and that's all you'll ever be."

With a howl of rage, Archer leapt at Jasper, sword drawn. Jasper leapt deftly to the side and reached into his own cloak to draw his twin blades, turning quickly to face his brother head-on.

"We'll see who the real coward is after this night," growled Archer as he lunged forward, striking his long sword against his brother's swords with a strength that nearly caused Jasper to fall to the ground.

Lydall braced herself to intervene. She knew deep down that this was a battle Jasper had to face on his own, but should he appear to be in mortal danger, Lydall would not be able to stand by and watch him die.

The two elves battled savagely, trading blow for blow, evenly matched. Lydall shuddered at how eerily similar they were to one another. Not only did the two elves look alike, they even moved alike. At times it became difficultto differentiate one from the other as they circled and struck relentlessly.

Lydall was distracted by a sudden cry of pain as an injured griffon slashed open the face of a dark wolf. The beast collapsed onto the earth, convulsed, and then finally lay still. The injured griffon collapsed beside the wolf, his breath coming in ragged gasps, until he too lay silent.

The scene made Lydall sick to her stomach, but before she had time to process it, a cry of surprise from Jasper jolted her back to the brothers' battle.

Jasper had fallen onto his back, his blades tossed to the side and out of reach, while Archer hovered over him. Archer was beaming with certain victory as he stood over his fallen brother, sword raised and ready to plunge into Jasper's heart.

"You should have picked the stronger side, brother," he said with a sneer, "Always following your heart and not your head. I told you that would get you killed one day."

Lydall heard herself scream, a sound ripping from her throat that startled the battling beasts around her. Without thinking, she raised her hands and, this time, the power that coursed through her made Lydall sink down to her knees. Hot, white, magical power blinded her completely as she struck out toward Archer, willing the elf to get away from Jasper.

When the moment passed, and her vision returned, Lydall watched in astonishment as a singed and furious Archer ran away from her. Her cry of panic had been just enough warning for the elf to leap clear of the full force of Lydall's magic and escape certain death. The dark elf ran toward the massive manticore in the center of the clearing and, with Caillic's help, climbed onto its back.

The Dark Sorceress let out a loud laugh that sounded like glass shattering on stone as the beast launched itself into the air.

"My warriors!" she cried, "To me!"

Immediately, the dark creatures separated from their battles with the Spellbinders and took flight, following their cruel mistress into the pitch-black sky.

"Let this be a warning to you all!" shouted Caillic, teeth bared as she gazed down at the remaining Spellbinders, "You'll never defeat us! I only brought a small selection of the creatures from my home to show you our strength and to deplete you of your own. We continue to grow stronger with every Krekanian death! Your Army, and all of Krekania is doomed. Save yourselves. Join us in the mountains and find your freedom or *die*!"

With a final battle cry, Caillic led her dark army into the night sky, leaving nothing but death and destruction in their wake.

12

Lydall stood up slowly, legs shaking as her eyes swept across Catha, taking in the scene around her. As the dark creatures fled into the night and the haze of battle lifted, the true horror of what had happened at Catha hit her with a crushing force.

The entire main clearing of Catha was littered with bodies and pools of blood. Cries and moans of pain echoed in her head as she turned around slowly, surveying the damage that Caillic had left behind. Her head and ribs throbbed with pain and she winced with every step.

Jasper looked shell-shocked as he scrambled to his feet. His eyes were glazed over and he looked lost. He gazed around and froze when he made eye-contact with Lydall. They exchanged despairing looks, grief and horror reflected in their eyes.

A loud whinny interrupted the somber moment. Lydall turned and saw Triton galloping toward her. Fresh claw marks decorated his haunches, but what was more startling than his injuries was the large horn protruding from his forehead.

"Triton?" whispered Lydall as she hugged her stallion, "What…what is this? What happened?"

"He was amazing," panted a disheveled-looking Effie as she emerged from behind Triton, "Cally and I were trapped by a bunch of those dark wolves and Triton came out of nowhere and saved us! He looked so fierce and angry and then this thing just came out of his head and fire came out of it and burned the wolves to ash!"

Lydall's mouth fell open in disbelief as she watched Effie's sabretooth, Cally, rub up against Triton's legs, purring with gratitude.

"How—how does that just happen?" stammered Lydall, running her hand over the new, shiny black horn that jutted out of Triton's forehead.

"I'm guessing the same way fire just shot out of your hands," answered Armus in his gruff voice as he, Nyra, Syllus, and their bonded animals gathered around them, "In times of great danger magic can reveal itself in astounding ways. It seems you two have found your magic."

Lydall's heart raced at Armus' words. She closed her eyes for a moment and remembered the rush of emotion that had flooded through her veins and the power that had erupted from her hands when she stood between her new friends and their enemies. Something about this newfound power was intoxicating and yet also very overwhelming.

Nyra winced and shifted her weight to her other leg. Armus moved quickly and wrapped an arm around her, supporting her weight. Nyra gazed up at the taller elf, her eyes suddenly full of love and adoration.

Lydall was surprised by her reaction. Nyra came across as cold, angry and fierce. The love in her eyes for the white-haired, muscular elf was a drastic change in her demeanor.

"I guess I twisted my ankle worse than I thought," muttered Nyra as she gave her foot a glare of annoyance.

"Syllus got cut up pretty good too," said Effie, frowning as she tried to wipe some of the dirt from one of the wounds on the larger elf.

Syllus' cheeks turned pink at Effie's touch and Lydall was

struck by the sudden realization that four of the five elves were rather close to one another. Her second epiphany was that this meant Jasper was even more alone than she realized.

Glancing over at the handsome elf, Lydall saw his eyes flicker briefly with envy as he watched the two couples tend to their wounds. He had lost his entire family and village, and his brother who was fighting on Caillic's side had just tried to murder him. Lydall could not imagine the level of loneliness Jasper must feel on a daily basis.

She felt an ache in her chest as she thought about her own family in Histair. At least she knew they were alive and out of harm's way. Jasper had no one, not even in some far-off distant land. He was truly alone.

A sharp cry of pain startled Lydall out of her own thoughts. Whirling around, Lydall saw a tiny firefox laying on its side and crying out in agony. With a pang of horror, Lydall realized it was the same firefox that had bonded with her at the gathering just before Caillic launched her hellish attack.

"Oh no!" cried Lydall as she hurried over to the bedraggled looking creature.

The firefox's flame had diminished to a grey, ashy hue, much like the firefox Lydall had seen in the Castle infirmary. The pitiful creature gazed up at Lydall, brown eyes large and filled with tears.

"Oh, please no," murmured Lydall as emotion threatened to choke her. She reached down for the firefox and cradled him in her arms, her tears spilling onto his dwindling pelt.

A rush of heat flooded down Lydall's arms and into her hands. Startled, she looked down at her hands as they cradled the young firefox. A soft glow emitted from her palms and began to transfer into the tiny animal. She watched in disbelief as, slowly, the firefox's flame began to glow bright again.

Blinking in surprise, the firefox gazed up at Lydall with round, grateful eyes, his flaming pelt vibrant and healthy.

"How—how did she do that?" stuttered Syllus as the elves' stared in bewilderment.

"I don't know what just happened," breathed Lydall as the firefox jumped out of her arms and began to run circles around them, yipping happily.

Lydall gazed down at her hands, her green eyes shining with amazement, "I—I healed him. But how? And why do I feel so tired now?"

Jasper walked up to Lydall and took her hands in his, running his thumbs in gentle circles over her palms, "I think you just transferred some of your power into the firefox. I don't know how you did that, but you did. Lydall you are the first magical being aside from the Seer that has ever been able to do that…and live."

Lydall gazed up into Jasper's eyes, her mouth open slightly as she tried to understand what he was saying to her. His light touch on her palms was making her warm in ways even her own fire magic could not and she swallowed nervously.

Despite the horrors around them, Effie could notsuppress an amused smile as she and the other elves exchanged knowing looks.

"Alright you two," interrupted Nyra, rolling her eyes, "There are dying creatures out here and most of Catha has been destroyed. There's a lot of work ahead of us. We need to find the creatures who stand the best chance of surviving and send them to the infirmary at the Castle. The others…we need to make as comfortable as possible."

Nyra's words made Lydall flinch, causing Jasper to drop her hands, his eyes glazing over with grief as he took in the scene around them. The little firefox was still running in happy circles around Lydall's feet, barking with joy and energy as he gazed up at her lovingly.

"You're right," said Jasper, clearing his throat and forcing down the emotions boiling inside of him, "And I think Lydall should lead them back to the Castle."

Lydall whirled around and gave Jasper a startled look, "Me? Why me? Don't you need help here rebuilding Catha?"

"You can *heal* them," whispered Jasper, fiercely, "They *need* you there. You may be able to save a few lives…the ones who aren't as injured and can be spared. I need you to lead them to the Castle. I'll have Nyra go with you for protection…and Triton and her wolf, Zephyr. Myself, Syllus, Effie and Armus will stay here and start the rebuilding process—and bury our dead."

Lydall flinched at that and looked away, "Okay," she said, quietly, "Let's start finding the creatures who can travel and get going. The sooner we get to the Castle the better."

Jasper gave Lydall a grateful smile as he and the other elves began to move through the devastated Catha field, assessing who could be saved and who would most likely not make it on the long journey to the Castle.

Lydall felt a rush of guilt at being unable to heal every single creature right here and now. She felt incredibly drained and could not even summon up a flicker of flame in her palms. She glanced down at her hands, frowning in frustration. Her magic was strong, but only for short periods of time. It would be awhile before she was able to use it again to help more of the magical creatures.

The firefox barked incessantly as he pawed her leg, startling Lydall out of her thoughts as he whined and pleaded with his large eyes. Lydall smiled and bent down to pick up the young creature.

"I suppose you'll be our stowaway," she murmured gently as the firefox curled himself up against her neck.

Lydall felt the firefox wrap himself around the back of her head and across her shoulders. The creature let out a coo of happiness as he settled down and watched Lydall as she began helping the other elves tend to the injured.

The night quickly slipped by as she and the elves worked feverishly to help those who could be saved.

Soon the sun began to rise slowly over the mountains in the distance, casting bright beams of light across the shattered ground and broken bodies.

Despite the horror around them and the unbelievable feeling of loss, the arrival of the morning seemed to rejuvenate the elves and Lydall. Caillic had won this battle, but she had not yet won the war.

Tomorrow was another day.

13

On the side of a cold mountain covered with snow and bitten by a cruel wind, stood a colossal black winged-wolf. The great beast snarled in defiance at the painfully-cold breeze as he scanned the steep slope below him. He settled back on his haunches, poised on the ledge in front of the entrance to the cave that was nestled deep into the side of the great mountain.

A sudden noise to his left made the wolf's ears swivel and he curled back his muzzle to reveal long, gleaming fangs. A deep snarl echoed in his barrel-like chest as he rose to meet his foe.

"Baalkor, easy," murmured a familiar voice as a figure emerged from the gloom, "It's just me."

The dark wolf relaxed his muscles and stretch his bat-like wings as he scented his master. The tall elf moved toward him and reached out, giving the wolf a grateful pat before he and the Sorceress entered the cave. A long line of dark and dangerous creatures followed him inside, all limping with injuries and extreme exhaustion. Baalkor greeted each creature as they returned from battle, pleased to see that a decent number of them had survived the ordeal. Once they had all entered the cave, Baalkor resumed his post as Guardian of the Mountain, his large black frame covered in a light layer of ice and snow as he glared balefully into the storm.

Archer tossed his cloak into a crevice of the cave and

walked over to light a fire in the center of the large open space. He glanced at the back of the cave where he could see Caillic, her back to him as she preened in front of her ice-mirror.

Archer frowned as he turned back to the fire pit and fought with the flint, his thoughts moving once again back to the battle they had just survived. He glared at the burns that crossed his arms and hands. The fire-wielding human had singed him with her unexpected and ferocious attack. He was grateful that he'd moved swiftly, acting on instinct, and managed to avoid the full power of her magic. Had he not moved he would surely have ended up as charred as the dark wolf he had watched her slaughter.

It had been a long time since he had seen his brother, Jasper. The very thought of his brother sent a rush of fury through Archer's very core. The brother who had taken the one woman he had ever loved and then became the captain of the Army of Spellbinders. He had never hated anyone more than he hated his older brother.

Jasper claimed that Teila loved him, but Archer knew how false that statement was. He knew the looks that little minx had given him and what they had conveyed. Jasper may have thought she was an innocent little elf who was longing for love and affection, but Archer knew she was just looking for attention—and she had sought it from him more than once. She had fooled Jasper and most of the village as well. But Archer had put an end to her lies and trickery. A permanent end.

His brother was too stupid and too stubborn to see the truth. The self-righteous, bleeding-heart leader of the Army of Spellbinders blindly followed the rule of the Queen, a woman with her own secrets. Fenelia had wronged her sister Caillic many times over the years. Caillic simply just had enough of her. The Queen was just as proud and self-important as Jasper. The two were a perfect match. It was no mystery to him why they'd become allies in the war for Krekania.

Archer sneered as he contemplated what his brother was naively fighting for: Krekanian magic. The magic that had destroyed everything they both had ever cared about. Caillic had found a way to manipulate the Krekanians' magic. He knew that she would make a great ruler one day. She had suffered just as he had and, in the end, they would both prevail and overcome the Krekanians and their ignorant beliefs.

"Don't worry," spoke Caillic, her voice as smooth and cold as the ice surrounding them, as she brushed out her long, white hair, "Their time is coming. Today was a warning. Today was just the beginning of the end. More of them will die in the days to come. They will all pay. I promised you that long ago," she added as she sat her brush down on her ice-vanity.

Archer glanced over at the Sorceress as she approached him, his eyes glittering with suppressed fury, "I know. I'm just impatient for it all to be over with."

The Sorceress watched as Archer struck the flint again and smiled down at her loyal captain. She knelt next to him just as the fire roared to life, "I know you are, my love. And that is why you are my captain, and my partner, and my everything," she added, her voice low and husky as she leaned in and gave him a passionate kiss, "But for now, think not of them and their magic. Think only of this."

Caillic stood slowly and began to remove her cloak. It slid gently down to the floor of the cave like snow falling from the mountain. She began to take off her black leather armor, piece by piece. As the final garment fell to the ground, Caillic knelt down again next to Archer and began to remove his clothing, stopping occasionally to kiss him and run her hands through his long, black hair.

Archer felt something stirring inside of him at the

Sorceress' touch. Caillic smiled wickedly at his reaction and bit her lower lip. In that moment, Archer banished every thought of his brother and the Krekanians from his mind and turned his full attention to the beautiful ice queen as she gently guided him down to the cave floor.

. . .

"We're nearly there," said Nyra as she glanced back over her shoulder at Lydall.

Lydall nodded as she tried to catch her breath. She wasn't accustomed to such long journeys through the woods without riding on Triton. At the moment her stallion was pulling the large carriage, filled with whimpering creatures, as they trudged toward the Castle.

Lydall smiled slightly in spite of her exhaustion. She was clothed in layers of leather with steel enhancements, meant both to adorn and to protect her. It was quite the improvement from the small, dirty dress she had been wearing since she had arrived in Krekania.

Just before she and Nyra left for their mission, Effie had insisted that she provide Lydall with proper gear for the journey. Lydall's dirty dress had been little more than a torn up rag after the battle in Catha, much to little Effie's horror. Despite the time that it had taken for Effie to select the proper-fitting pieces, Lydall was deeply grateful. She felt less like a princess and a lot more like a warrior, ready to battle the foes that threatened Krekania's very existence. The layers of supple leather enhanced with sturdy and dangerous metal bits made Lydall feel powerful, a feeling that was still rather new to her.

Lydall walked alongside Triton, patting him encouragingly as he pulled the carriage along the winding path. Nyra and Zephyr led the small caravan, scouting ahead for any danger on the trail. They had traveled straight through the day, exhausted but determined to make it to the Castle.

As the sun set in the distance, Lydall was painfully reminded that it had been nearly two days since she had slept. She shook her head, willing herself to keep moving. The animals on the wooden carriage were depending on them, and Lydall could not bear to lose any more than they already had. Sleep would come soon enough. Getting these magical animals to the infirmary was all that mattered now.

"We'll spend a night or two at the Castle," said Nyra, giving Lydall a knowing look as she slowed down to walk next to her, "We'll need to regain our strength for the journey home. At least it will be a lot easier, and faster, since we'll be able to just ride on Triton and Zephyr. We can leave the carriage at the Castle. There are others in Catha if we need them later."

Lydall nodded, "I just want to get the injured to the infirmary as soon as possible," she said she turned to look at the carriage, frowning in concern, "I'm afraid we'll be too late. So many have died already."

Nyra gave Lydall a sympathetic look, "Perhaps, but those we cannot save may be useful still. We can use their magic to restore some other creatures in the infirmary. Their deaths won't be in vain, we'll make sure of that."

Lydall bit her lip, fighting back her emotions as she forced her feet to keep moving forward. The firefox, still perched on her shoulder, nuzzled her and whined softly. Lydall had just reached up to stroke the soft, glowing creature when a loud sound startled them both.

Zephyr unleashed a booming howl from up ahead on the trail, causing Nyra to unsheathe her twin swords, eyes flashing with the light of battle. She paused as she listened to her wolf's howl, a smile slowly forming on her face as she deciphered its meaning.

"We're here! Zephyr just gave us the signal—the way ahead is clear!"

Lydall felt her spirit fill with hope as Triton picked up the pace. She felt a sudden burst of energy as they crested the hill and saw the gleaming white Castle in front of them. Her heart soared as the power of the magic emanating from the Castle touched her very soul.

The haggard group moved as fast as they could across the long bridge. The two large white wolves, Akira and Logan, stood to attention with their ears and tails erect as they sniffed the air. The wolves caught the scent of the injured creatures and whined sadly, moving quickly to open the gates.

"Thank you," said Lydall as she gave them each a brief pat on their gigantic heads and then stepped quickly inside the Castle.

"Fenelia!" shouted Lydall as she helped Triton haul the carriage into the Castle, "Queen Fenelia!"

Almost immediately, Fenelia moved out of the gloom, eyes wide with surprise as she took in the number of creatures piled onto the carriage. She eyed the bedraggled-looking elf and human, concern and fear etching deep lines in her face.

"I was just tending to the wood nymphs," she muttered in shock, "What…what happened?"

"We were ambushed," explained Nyra as she began leading Triton down the passageway that led to the infirmary, "Caillic," she added, tossing the name over her shoulder with an air of fury and disgust as she moved down the hall.

Fenelia flinched as if she had been hit and closed her eyes briefly, "How…how bad was it?"

Lydall forced herself to not show frustration with the Queen. She knew that Fenelia deeply regretted her decision to banish her sister years ago instead of having her killed, but Lydall had a difficult time accepting it. Had Fenelia taken care of Caillic five years ago, the horrible deaths and injuries Lydall had witnessed today would have never happened.

"It was bad," she managed to get out, gritting her teeth as she followed Nyra and the carriage, "We didn't stay long enough to see exactly how many died, but it was bad. Jasper and the other elves are burying the dead aswe speak."

Fenelia followed them down the passageway, her hand over her stomach as if she were going to be sick. Nyra and Zephyr went on ahead to clear the hallway, making room for the carriage while Lydall helped the weary Triton pull it through the Castle's corridors.

Lydall felt as if they were never going to make it to the infirmary. Every step she took made her aching muscles scream in protest. Triton was huffing, head low as he tried to gather his strength for the final stretch of the corridor.

As they finally rounded the bend, Lydall could see the light from the infirmary entrance.

"Come on boy," she said as she tugged on the reigns, "We're here...just a few more steps."

Triton snorted, pawing the ground with one hoof as he strained to pull the carriage through the narrow entryway. The instant they were inside the large room, Lydall moved to unhook her bone-weary destrier.

"Quickly," ushered Nyra as she moved to start unloading creatures, "We have to move faster than this, let's go!" she added as she glanced over at Fenelia.

The Queen had entered the room behind the carriage and was leaning against the far wall, eyes shut against the unseen demons that danced in her mind.

"Do something about her," snarled Nyra through her teeth, "We don't have time for this."

Lydall frowned over in Fenelia's direction. Her frustration with the Queen was beginning to reach fever-pitch. Lydall had not slept in days and had just fought in her first magic battle against the Queen's evil sister, Jasper's twisted brother, and an army of demonic creatures that should only exist in nightmares. Her ability to tolerate Fenelia's guilt and emotional issues was at an end.

"*Queen*," said Lydall as she stalked over to Fenelia, "We need you *now*. You can't do this. I need you to show me how to transfer the magic from the dying so we can save some of the others before it's too late."

Fenelia was taking deep, panicked breaths as her eyes flickered open, full of fear and guilt, "This is because of me...all my fault...again...they're dead because...because of me..."

"Fenelia!" snapped Lydall, green eyes flashing with fury as she reached out and grasped the Queen's shoulders, "Stop it! We don't have time for any of this. They need you now. You can be there for them *now*. The longer we stand here the more animals die today. They're depending on you. This isn't the time to stand around and dwell on the past...we need you in the present."

Fenelia clenched her teeth and shut her eyes, fighting her inner turmoil before she looked back up at Lydall. Steadying her breathing, the Queen pushed herself off the wall and straightened her back. Her brown eyes were bright with pain as she stilled herself.

"You're right," she said, steadying her voice, "I'm fine. They need me."

Lydall gave Fenelia a doubtful glance. The Queen still looked pale as a ghost and weak with grief as she walked slowly passed Lydall to the carriage.

A sharp bark startled them as Lydall's firefox leapt from her shoulder and bounded across the room. He raced down the aisles filled with beds of the sick and injured creatures and came to a stop at a tiny one near the back of the room. Yapping desperately, he tried to jump into it, insistent on getting to whatever was in laying in the bed.

"What is he doing?" asked Nyra as she began to help Fenelia lift an injured unicorn out of the carriage, "Lydall, make him stop that racket before he gets the other creatures riled up."

Lydall sighed in annoyance as she jogged down the aisle in pursuit of the firefox, but as she reached the bed he was so desperately trying to jump into, she froze.

"Oh!" she said, as she gazed down at a verybedraggled looking firefox. Her flame was nearly extinguished completely. She looked up at Lydall with sad brown eyes. The poor creature looked more like a fox-shaped pile of ash than she did an actual firefox.

Lydall's jaw hung open in disbelief as she realizedthat this firefox was the same pitiful creature she had met the last time she had been in this room. Lydall wasastounded that the creature was still alive, but even more surprised that she seemed to recognize her.

"You know her?" asked Lydall, glancing over at the other firefox as she reached down to pick up the sickly creature in the tiny bed.

Immediately, the male firefox began to bark and claw at Lydall's legs. Wincing Lydall quickly laid the female on the ground and watched in amazement as the healthy firefox began to groom the sickly one. His cries of despair echoed in the cavernous room, causing Lydall's heart to clench with sadness.

After a moment, Lydall got down on her knees beside the two firefoxes and began to gently pet the injured female. She felt the heat of her magic begin to curl up inside of her and extend to her arms. Closing her eyes, Lydall gave herself over to the magic, willing it to emerge from her palms and heal the pitiful creature under her hands.

The male firefox jumped back in surprise as a bright light emitted from Lydall's hands, encasing the ashy female firefox. After a few moments, Lydall opened her eyes and gazed down. What had once been a nearly-translucent, pitiful creature was now a bright, vibrant firefox. Her fur glowed with magical power as the flames flared with life once more.

Lydall heard Fenelia gasp behind her and turned around. The Queen and Nyra had stopped to watch what she had been doing with the foxes, their eyes round with amazement and disbelief.

"You…you healed her?" stammered the Queen, "But—you're still alive? Transferring magic from one being to another ends in death. How is—how is this possible?"

Lydall rose to her feet as she watched the two firefoxes leaping and wrestling with joy. She smiled at the sight and turned to face Fenelia, face flushing slightly under all the attention.

"I'm not sure," she said hesitantly, "I've only done it one other time—when I healed the other firefox after the battle with Caillic. It…it makes me tired, so I'm not sure how many I can heal at once. It's a limited part of my magic I think."

Fenelia was staring at Lydall in amazement, "'The fate of magic rests on The Woman of Fire. She alone holds the power to save and to destroy, for power is not held by the darkness, but by those who control the light.'"

Lydall felt her heart beat out of cadence as she listened to Fenelia recite part of the prophecy. As if on cue, a strange-looking, and yet very familiar creature emerged from the gloom. His eyes were large glowing orbs moving through the shadows as he slowly entered the infirmary.

"Seer," whispered Lydall in awe as the unique creature strode gracefully into the room on his long, thin legs.

"Woman of Fire," replied the Seer in his deep, gravelly voice as he bowed his dog-like head, "I told you we would meet more than once along your journey. And here we are."

Nyra looked utterly perplexed by the strange creature in front of them and cast an anxious glance between Lydall and Fenelia. She placed a hand on one of her swords, preparing to draw the blade should this bizarre creature attack them.

"It's alright," murmured Fenelia to Nyra, "The Seer is an old friend. He can see the future and is closer to magic than any living creature in Krekania. He is the one who brought us the prophecy of the Woman of Fire."

The Seer gazed kindly at Fenelia, "I have reason to believe that I will not be the only one with this relationship to magic. Lydall will soon find she is closer to the ancient magic than any living creature has ever been. It appears she has learned she can not only destroy…but also restore. This is an important lesson, young Lydall. Your power does not merely destroy your enemies, but it also heals your friends. I think you will find such power will serve you well in the dark days to come."

Lydall gave the Seer a small bow of respect, "I hope I can serve the Army of Spellbinders to the best of my ability. We…we've suffered a lot of loss. Caillic came—and she came prepared."

The Seer nodded and cast his large, sad eyes on the carriage, now only half-filled with injured creatures. Several wood nymphs and winged-wolves had arrived and were gently placing the wounded onto beds, sorting them by those who were close to death and the ones who could still be spared.

"Yes, you have," he said as he returned his wide-eyed stare on Lydall, "However, this loss will one day feel rather small compared to what is coming."

Lydall felt a thrill of fear course through her veins,

"What have you seen? What's coming?"

The Seer bowed his dog-like head as his long antlers began to glow. He summoned the ancient magic, his very soul conversing with it as the magic began to fill the many dangling baubles on the end of his antlers.

"The great battle that I prophesied when you were last here, Lydall? That very battle is coming sooner than you and the Army realize. You must be prepared. You must be ready, or all will be lost. Lydall, you will find yourself faced with temptation…and what you choose to do will determine the fate of Krekania itself."

Lydall felt icy tendrils of fear sink deep into her bones and her hands began to tremble as she stared at the Seer.

"What choice? What choice do I have to make?" she asked, voice shaking, "I need to know more…I…"

The Seer shook his head as the magic began to fade from the baubles. The light inside the strange orbs dimmed as he began to speak, "I am afraid this is up to you, Lydall. There is nothing more I can reveal. Follow your heart, follow your magic, for both will guide you in the way you should go, in the end."

Without another word, the Seer turned around and walked away from them. As quickly as he had arrived, the Seer vanished, disappearing back into the far wall of the infirmary.

Nyra stood stock-still, eyes wide with disbelief as she watched the strange creature walk straight through a wall as if it were not even there.

Lydall looked over at Fenelia. The Queen was forcing herself to look in control, but her entire body was quivering and her gaze was glassy as she looked around the room. Nyra was staring at Lydall as if she were a stranger, eyes wide with alarm.

In that moment, Lydall realized she could no longer be the

scared little girl she had once been. She had just been through a battle and seen death firsthand, unleashed death itself upon her enemies, and healed wounded creatures. She was in a strange land that was ruled by magic and being threatened by a Sorceress and her dark army. In a very short amount of time, the sheltered life that Lydall had known was gone. Now, she just needed to let go of the girl she had once been and become the Woman of Fire that Krekania needed her to be.

"There's nothing we can do about what the prophecy says, or what the Seer revealed," she said, forcing her voice to be strong and lifting her head high, "When the time comes for me to make this choice, whatever it is, I know I will make the right one. For now, we need to focus on the task at hand, and that is saving as many of these creatures as possible. After that, Nyra and I need to go back to Catha and help the Army with repairs. I'm sure Jasper will want us to start some battle-training too. We have a lot to do to get ready for the war the Seer spoke of. We can't stand around here worrying and wallowing in our own fear. We don't have time for that. Not now."

Nyra gave Lydall a small nod of respect. She smiled slightly as she looked at the young human, "Well said Woman of Fire. Let's get to work then, shall we?"

Fenelia nodded in agreement and reached out to Lydall, grasping her arm briefly and giving her an encouraging smile.

"You will make a great leader one day, Lydall," she said, her voice soft and kind.

But as Lydall gazed back at the Queen, she thought she saw a glimmer of sadness deep in the woman's deep brown eyes. Fenelia turned away quickly under Lydall's inquisitive stare and moved to continue helping Nyra with the injured creatures.

Lydall frowned as she watched Fenelia walk away. The Queen knew something that she wasn't telling them. The realization made her uneasy, but she didn't have time to dwell on this new revelation. There was a lot of work to be done in the short amount of time they had left. The sooner they got their assignment at the Castle complete, the sooner they could return home and start prepping for the war to come.

And if Lydall was being honest with herself, there was a certain elf back in Catha that she was beginning to miss.

14

After hours of transferring magic into the creatures who could be saved and burying the ones who were lost, Lydall collapsed on the plush Castle bed with a sigh of relief. The process of healing and transferring magic had sapped what little remained of her strength. It was mid-morning the next day and Lydall could not remember the last time she had actually slept.

The little firefoxes whined on the ground as they tried to jump into the large bed with Lydall. She smirked slightly in amusement as she reached down to lift them both up. They had insisted on following her wherever she went since the moment she healed and reunited them. Lydall had a feeling she was more or less stuck with the little fiery creatures from here on out.

"You two need names," Lydall muttered sleepily as she watched them curl up together on her bed, "Maybe something that has to do with fire? Hmm…I think I'll call you Aidan," she said as she stroked the male firefox, "It means 'little and fiery,' and you," she said as she reached out to the female firefox,"I'll call you Shula, the old word for 'flame.'"

Satisfied, Lydall closed her eyes and let herself drift into a deep sleep. Almost instantly images from the fight at Catha and the dying creatures in the infirmary flashed through her mind.

Lydall bolted out of bed, gasping for air as cold sweat

poured down her back. She looked over at the large window in the guest room and saw that the sun had set long ago. She could have sworn she had only closed her eyes for a brief moment, but apparently several hours had passed.

Lydall rubbed her bloodshot eyes with her hands and then threw her disheveled hair up into a loose bun, tying it with a bit of ribbon she found in one of the dresser drawers. After taking several deep breaths to steady her racing heart, Lydall slowly climbed out of bed and made her way to the wash room. A cold bath would help erase the horrific images that had been racing through her mind the past several hours.

After a quick soak and a good scrub, Lydall put on her leather and metal garb Effie had given her. She smiled as she thought of the little elf back in Catha and allowed herself another moment of quiet gratitude that Effie had found pieces that fit her.

Moving slowly, her muscles aching with exhaustion from the past few days, Lydall made her way down the long winding hall toward the room the Queen had lent Nyra for the night. Aidan and Shula followed her, nipping playfully at her ankles as Lydall walked. She reached Nyra's tall, wooden door and slowly opened it, peering inside. Nyra was curled up into a tight ball in the center of her large bed, her winged-wolf Zephyr snuggled up against her.

Lydall smiled at the sight of the elf and her bonded creature. She was eager to go out to the Castle's pastures and see Triton again. Although they had only been apart for a few hours she'd begun to feel his absence.

"Nyra," said Lydall as she walked over to the bed, "Nyra! Come on we have to…"

Nyra flew out of bed faster than Lydall's eyes could follow. She was a whirlwind of black and silver as she spun in the air. The next thing Lydall knew, she was against the far wall with the breath knocked from her lungs, gasping desperately.

The firefoxes squealed with terror while Zephyr, who had launched himself to the other side of the room, hovered in mid-air, wings flapping rapidly and eyes wide with fear.

Nyra stood, panting as she stared at Lydall, wild eyes sparking with rage. Lydall lay crumpled against the wall, groaning in pain.

"What the hell do you think you're doing?" snarled Nyra with rage, "Sneaking up on someone like that? Sneaking up on *me* like that? Are you crazy?"

Lydall coughed as she tried to force air back into her lungs and slowly stood back up, "I wasn't sneaking," she said between her teeth, glaring at Nyra, "I was coming to wake you up so we can go home. If we leave now we can reach Catha by tomorrow morning. *You* don't have to be such a paranoid spaz."

Nyra narrowed her eyes at Lydall, "If you'd lived the life I've lived you would understand. You're still new to Krekania and all of the horrors that go along with it. Give it time, Woman of Fire. You'll soon have night terrors and plenty of paranoia to share."

Lydall sighed, "As encouraging as that is, we need to go. I'm going to get Triton ready. I'll meet you outside the gates."

Nyra muttered something under her breath as she stormed off to her washroom. Lydall rolled her eyes as she walked out of Nyra's quarters, massaging her shoulder and wincing in pain. Nyra had shoved her into the wall harder than she realized. That was going to leave a mark.

Aidan and Shula followed Lydall, more subdued than they were before, as the trio made their way to the main gates of the Castle.

Lydall paused briefly in front of the throne room. She saw Fenelia sitting on her throne as she spoke with several wood nymphs gathered around her. The Queen glanced up when she heard footsteps and her eyes met Lydall's stare. Fenelia offered her a hesitant smile and a quick nod. Lydall lifted her hand and waved in return as she walked toward the main doors of the Castle. Under different circumstances, Lydall may have stayed to talk with the Queen, but plenty had been said the day before and all she wanted to do was get back to Catha.

Thinking about Catha gave Lydall an ache in the center of her chest. She wanted to return to the devastated camp and help Jasper, Syllus and Armus repair the damage. More than that, she also wanted to start her battle training. As the most inexperienced of all the members in Jasper's Army, Lydall knew it was imperative that she get up to speed on battle tactics and learn more about the enemies they faced.

A small part of her heart told her she also wanted to see Jasper again. She swallowed nervously at that thought and tried to push the sudden rush of emotion away. There was no time for those feelings. Not right now anyway.

She turned and made her way down into the fields outside the Castle where a large barn stood. The heads of several pegasi and unicorns emerged to gaze at her from their barn, but as Lydall looked around, she realized Triton was not among them.

A loud whinny off to her left made Lydall burst into a wide grin. She recognized that sound instantaneously.

"There you are!" she exclaimed as the inky-black stallion landed gracefully in the clearing, "Off exploring, were you?"

Triton tossed his head up and down with joy and gently brushed up against Lydall.

"Whenever you two are done, we're ready to leave," said Nyra as she and Zephyr emerged from the Castle. Her long black hair was half-braided, and it looked as if she had applied dark makeup across her eyes, giving her an even more unapproachable look than normal.

"We were waiting for you," retorted Lydall with a small, sarcastic smile as she climbed onto Triton's back, "Whenever *you* two are ready."

Nyra rolled her eyes as she climbed onto the back of her large winged-wolf,w "Let's go Woman of Fire. I'm ready to go home."

...

The stars glowed bright as Nyra and Lydall flew through day and into the night back to Catha. Aidan and Shula clung tight to one another, tangled in Triton's mane as the powerful pegasus soared through the sky. Lydall smiled at the small firefoxes and gave them reassuring strokes as they gazed up at her nervously.

"It's okay little ones," murmured Lydall, "We'll be home soon enough."

The firefoxes could not bear to be apart from one another, so Lydall had decided to return them both to Catha. The rest of the injured magical creatures would stay to heal in the infirmary. They would then be allowed to choose to return to Catha and continue fighting, or staying in the sanctuary of the Castle with the Queen.

Nyra rolled her eyes at the sight, "You get too attached, you know."

Lydall frowned in annoyance, "Perhaps you should try it sometime. It's actually kind of nice having friends."

Nyra's eyes hardened at that, "I did once. Didn't do me much good. I've found it's easier to stay away. Put a wall up. It keeps you from getting hurt again."

Lydall flinched and glanced away for a moment. Nyra was a lot colder and more direct than her other elf companions. On occasion, her brazenness made Lydall uncomfortable. She could not understand why Nyra was so viscous and unwelcoming. She never let anyone get close—at least no one other than the white-haired elf, Armus.

"What happened to you?" asked Lydall after a long, awkward moment of silence, "What made you...like this?"

Nyra narrowed her eyes as she looked at Lydall, "What is *that* supposed to mean?"

Lydall cleared her throat and shifted on Triton's back, feeling the weight of Nyra's glare, "I meant...what happened to you and your family? Jasper told me his story, but I don't know yours, or the other elves for that matter. I have a feeling that none of your stories are very—easy to talk about."

Nyra's eyes shifted slightly as a wave of unpleasant emotions coursed through her. She took a deep breath before turning to look back at Lydall.

"My story is about as pleasant as Jasper's," she said quietly, "I'm not sure it's something you want to hear."

"Try me," challenged Lydall, looking fully into Nyra's tense face.

Nyra attempted to sneer but it turned into more of a smirk, "You're unusual, Lydall," she said quietly, "Krekania gave you powerful magic even though you're a sheltered princess from a land without magic. And despite my doubts, you've quickly found your warrior spirit. You just might make a great leader one day."

Lydall frowned slightly, weighing Nyra's words. They were not so different than the ones the Queen spoke to her, and they unnerved her just as much, "I'm not brave enough or prepared enough for that. I think most of my courage is...an act."

Nyra laughed, "Oh, so you didn't step into battle and stop attacks from Caillic's horde then? That was fake? And when you've had the courage to speak the words inside of you...that was fake as well? You're odd, yes. Annoying? Well I find most living things annoying, but you are far more than what you appear to be. You will need to accept that sooner than later, Woman of Fire."

Lydall smiled slightly, "Will you tell me your story or not?" she said, eager to change the subject.

Nyra's lip curled up in amusement as she noted Lydall's discomfort, "Very well. Much like Jasper, my village was raided in one of the attacks by Caillic. My family was one of the first to die in this raid. They came for our end of the village first. I remember very little about the initial attack, aside from my father throwing me out of the way as our roof caved in. He managed to toss me out the back dooras our house collapsed. A manticore landed on the roof and crushed everything inside. The great oaf destroyed everything within seconds. I fled down our street and dove into an alleyway, trying to avoid Caillic's winged-wolves. They fell from the sky like rain. It was disorienting and chaotic.

"I hid in the alley for as long as I could, but two of the dark wolves found me. They trapped me against the wall of a fallen building. I had nowhere to run, no weapons on me, nothing. In that moment I knew I was done for. I remember feeling relieved, though. At least now I would join my dead family. I wouldn't have to continue on in this life without them for very long.

"That was when Armus arrived. He came out of nowhere, cut, bleeding, but fierce and powerful. He brandished two long daggers and sliced with a fierce rage at the two wolves. In seconds the fight was over and the wolves lay dying in their own blood. He reached for my hand, gave me one of his long daggers, and together we took off into the night.

"Armus and I had been seeing one another before that day. He was the most handsome and the deadliest warrior in our tribe. He was also the only one who could tolerate my love of weaponry and fighting. Not once did he make me feel as if I should be daintier or less aggressive. He embraced my fighting warrior spirit and for that, I love him. But the day he fearlessly came to my aid, armed me, and saved me, I knew I would be with him forever.

"He is one of only two things in this life I still cling to: him and Zephyr," Nyra said as she lovingly rubbed Zephyr's head, "Zephyr found us in the woods shortly after the attack. He led us back to the winged-wolf pack he was alpha of and took care of us. It wasn't long after that when we heard word of Jasper's Army of Spellbinders. There was no hesitation on mine and Armus' part, nor Zephyr and some of his pack. We journeyed to Catha and found Jasper and his small Army and joined them. Since the day I joined, the Army of Spellbinders has tripled in size."

"And Armus' family?" pressed Lydall, "Did he lose them too?"

Nyra nodded, "Yes. We both lost everything that day. We were the only two elves who survived in our village. We both feel guilty for running when we did—but to stay meant certain death. We were outnumbered and unprepared. But we vowed to serve Jasper, the Queen, and the Army with everything we have left. We will avenge our families' deaths and we will stop Caillic from destroying magic."

Lydall smiled encouragingly at Nyra, "You're both very brave. To have lost so much and yet to be so strong. You've overcome a lot. It makes my problems look so much smaller in comparison."

Nyra shook her head, "You may not have lost your family in the way that we did, but that does not make your losses any less, Lydall," she said, her deep-brown eyes boring into Lydall's emerald gaze, "Your family would have forced you to be with someone you did not love. That is a fate worse than death…I believe so anyway. I could not imagine not being allowed to choose my path. I had a lot taken from me, but I could still choose who I loved. That, that is the true power. That is what keeps me going. You had a difficult decision to make, and it's one you must always live with…just like us."

Lydall nodded sadly. She felt the familiar ache of lossas she thought about her parents and her brother. She had wondered more than once if she had made the right decision, but a big part of her knew that if she had not left Histair, she would have lived a life of misery, void of real love and freedom. She knew her brother would be a good heir to Histair, and he would have more freedoms than she would have had as a woman in her land. Her brother would reign with intellect and empathy and Histair would continue to prosper under his rule.

More than that, her brother wouldn't have to leave their home. The Westland's young daughter would be betrothed to him and she would be expected to move to Histair and rule alongside him when the time came. Lydall felt a momentary flash of sympathy for the Westland's daughter. She would be forced into a fate much like the one Lydall had once faced.

"And what about Effie and Syllus?" asked Lydall after a moment, "Do you know their stories?"

Nyra nodded, "Yes. They're about like mine and Jasper's, although their villages were raided last. They were more prepared because they had heard what happened to the rest of us, but they still were no match for Caillic. They are both the only survivors of their respective villages. Jasper and I suspect that Syllus has quite the crush on little Effie," she added with a smirk, "But he's so quiet and nervous around her that I don't think she's noticed just yet. That and Effie is quite the excitable little thing. She doesn't stand still long enough to even notice the signs."

Lydall smiled happily at that, "They'd make a great couple," she agreed. A warm feeling of hope coursed through her as she thought of the love that had survived even the most horrific of tragedies. Despite the threat they all faced, love was still able to grow and survive. Lydall could think of nothing more rebellious than that.

"So do you and Jasper," said Nyra boldly, her eyes dancing with mischief.

Lydall felt the blood rush to her face and her mouth opened in surprise, "What? Me and Jasper? I mean…we just met. We aren't…. that is to say, we don't…"

Nyra laughed loudly, cutting Lydall off, "Time is nothing, Woman of Fire. Sometimes you just know the moment you meet the right one. And trust me, we've all noticed how you two are around one another. Don't even bother denying it."

Lydall felt her face flush even more as she shook her head, trying to contradict Nyra's words.

"There's Catha now," said Nyra, still giving Lydall a bemused look, "We better hurry. I'm sure Jasper's been worried."

Lydall glared at Nyra as the black-haired elf laughed with mirth. Nyra and Zephyr soared quickly down toward Catha, leaving Triton, the firefoxes, and Lydall behind in a sudden gust of wind from the wolf's wings.

As Triton began his much-slower descent, Lydall felt her heart skip a beat. As much as she tried to deny Nyra's words, part of her was overjoyed at the thought of seeing Jasper again. Maybe the dark-haired elf was right after all. Maybe what she was feeling was real. What if it was? Would Jasper even want to be with a *human* like her? She shook her head in frustration as Triton broke through the last layer of clouds. That was a problem for another day. For now, she wanted to focus on returning to Catha, and preparing for the coming war.

15

The joyous uproar took Lydall by surprise as she and Triton landed next to Nyra and Zephyr. The winged-wolves let out a chorus of howls the moment they saw Zephyr emerge from the cloud cover, causing the rest of the Army of Spellbinders to emerge from their homes.

"You're back!" shouted Effie as the tiny elf danced around Nyra and Lydall, "You made it! Not that I doubted you, of course."

Lydall laughed as Effie clung to her, brown eyes bright with happiness. The little elf was a couple years younger than Lydall, but her youthful spirit and small stature made her appear to be very child-like. Lydall always felt as if her heart was going to burst with joy when Effie was near.

"Did the leathers hold?" asked Effie, her eyes taking on a more serious gleam as she began to inspect Lydall's clothing.

"They were perfect," assured Lydall, "You picked out just the right ones for me to wear."

Effie clapped her hands with happiness, "Then wait until you see the battle armor I've been making for you while you were away. Syllus was helping me with bending and shaping the metal, but it was all my design."

Nyra and Lydall exchanged a knowing look as Syllus approached them, smiling with pride, and something else entirely, as he looked at Effie.

"Did you have any trouble while we were away?" asked Nyra as Armus emerged from the crowd of magical creatures.

"No, my love," said Armus in his quiet, gravely voice, "And you?"

"All is well," purred Nyra as she settled into Armus' embrace.

"Catha looks almost as it did before the battle," said Lydall quietly, gazing around, "You all got a lot done."

Effie nodded, "Yes, Jasper and the others were working on repairs while I was designing your armor. I'm too small to be much use with the cleaning up and all. And...I don't think they wanted me to deal with, um, burying the...you know..."

Lydall nodded kindly as she gave Effie another hug, "I understand. I think Jasper was wise to let you design my armor instead. You have quite an important role here."

As if on cue, the handsome elf captain emerged from the crowd, eyes dancing with happiness as they met Lydall's green gaze.

Lydall broke out into a wide grin, her heart hammering an unsteady cadence in her chest as Jasper approached.

"It's good to see you again," said Jasper quietly as he reached out and gently touched Lydall's arm.

"You as well," she breathed. The place on her arm where Jasper had rested his hand felt as if it were alive with electricity.

Nyra and Armus exchanged amused looks as they watched their captain and Lydall greet each other.

"Well, I suppose I can't speak for Lydall, but I am exhausted after that trip," said Nyra as she gave a long, cat-like stretch, "I'm heading home to rest," she added, giving Armus a long, knowing look.

The tall, muscular elf grinned wickedly as he followed Nyra

up to her home situated in the tree across from Jasper's.

"You must be exhausted as well," said Jasper, eyeing Lydall.

Lydall nodded in agreement. In that moment, however, she did not feel even the slightest bit tired. Her skin still tingled where Jasper had placed his hand on her arm and her heart was beating erratically as she stared into his deep brown eyes.

Jasper glanced over his shoulder for a brief moment to call for Effie. He smirked as he realized that Effie and Syllus were talking, their eyes bright with happiness, as they planned their next session at the forge. Syllus' love of metal work and Effie's passion for design and clothing seemed to be helping form a rather close bond between the two elves. Jasper decided in that moment to leave them both alone. Besides, it provided an excuse to spend more time with Lydall. He could not explain the feeling in his chest every time he saw her. All he knew was that he wanted to be around her as much as possible, and that when she was away it felt as if a part of his very soul was absent.

"Effie seems to be preoccupied at the moment," said Jasper with a smirk, "But, if it's okay with you, you can come back to my house to rest?"

Lydall felt her heart leap at the thought. A rush of excitement and nervousness overwhelmed her as she fought to control her emotions.

"Oh, yes, that would be fine," she stammered, attempting to sound normal and calm, "I would like that, actually."

Jasper's face lit up, "Really?" he pressed, his gaze hopeful.

Lydall bit her lip, eyes glowing, "Yes…really."

Jasper gazed at Lydall a moment more before he made

his move. Lydall gasped, startled by his sudden closeness as Jasper put his hands on either side of her face and stared into her eyes. Her breath caught in her throat and she was convinced that her heart had ceased to beat as he pulled her in and kissed her with a fevered passion.

The moment their lips touched Lydall felt a rush of energy surge through her veins. It felt like experiencing all of her fire magic, both destructive and healing, all at once. In that moment, all Lydall's fears and doubts vanished. She knew she was meant to be here, in this moment…and with Jasper.

A chorus of cheers and whistles interrupted their moment as the Army lent voice to their opinion on the matter.

Lydall blushed furiously as she and Jasper pulled away. Jasper was smiling shamelessly, and even laughed a little at the Army and their antics.

Triton and Dionysus side-eyed one another, clearly not approving of this new dynamic.

"Come on," said Jasper quietly to Lydall, "Perhaps we should go somewhere a little less…out in the open?"

"That would probably be best," said Lydall, her entire face red with embarrassment from all the attention they were garnering.

A sharp bark distracted Lydall. She laughed when she saw the two firefoxes gazing up at her questioningly, pawing at her legs and whining pitifully.

"I have a couple of stowaways," she said as she bent down to pet the gently glowing creatures, "It turns out that these two are mates. They recognized each other in the infirmary, and they wanted to return together to Catha with me."

Triton snorted as he eyed the creatures with annoyance. He stomped a single hoof and turned his rear to the firefoxes, Lydall, and Jasper. Dionysus gave a loud caw of agreement as he too turned away from the group.

"Triton was not a fan," explained Lydall, rolling her eyes, "The little guys clung to his mane rather tightly the whole journey, I'm afraid."

Triton let out another snort of frustration, looking rather exasperated as he stomped his hoof into the ground again. The firefoxes gave cries of alarm at the reaction of the large destrier and darted quickly under a nearby bush, out of the reach of Triton's hooves.

"I guess they won't be friends anytime soon then," said Jasper as he watched the little firefoxes glare at Triton from between the branches of the large bush.

"I suppose not," agreed Lydall with a nervous laugh as she tucked a stray strand of bright red hair behind her ear, "But it looks like Triton and Dionysus finally found common ground."

Jasper looked over at the irritated pegasus and griffon who were giving each other conspiratorial glances.

"Let's leave them be then," he said as he reached out to Lydall and gently took her arm, leading her away from the throng of creatures and deeper into Catha, "They can work all that out themselves."

Jasper and Lydall slid out of the mass of celebrating magical creatures and quietly made their way back to Jasper's tree house. They climbed up the wooden ladder and entered the small home, unnoticed by the others below.

Lydall made herself comfortable on the wolf pelt that lay across the main portion of the house. She glanced shyly up at Jasper, biting her lower lip as she waited to see what he would do.

Jasper hesitated for just a moment before he joined her, happiness dancing in his eyes as he settled himself down in front of her. His hands shook slightly as his nerves got the best of him.

Lydall felt another jolt course through her body as Jasper stared at her for a long moment before speaking.

"I'm glad you made it back safely," he said, his voice low, "I was worried something may have happened to you."

Lydall nodded, "We stayed to rest before we returned. I tried to heal as many of the wounded as I could, but my magic tires me quickly. We helped as many as possible and then left the rest to Fenelia's care. Magic-willing some will return to us," Lydall hesitated a moment before she continued, "I was worried Caillic had returned while we were away. I didn't say anything to Nyra because I didn't want her to worry as well, but I could not stop thinking of what we may come home to."

Jasper smiled and glanced away for a moment, "Home?"

Lydall gave him a quizzical look and inclined her head, "Yes? Here, Catha. I was afraid she had come back to finish what she had started."

"You called Catha your home," murmured Jasper, eyes soft.

Lydall blinked in surprise, "I—I suppose I did. I guess it feels that way now, after fighting for it and all. And choosing to join the Army of Spellbinders. And…because you're here. And that just feels—right. It feels like I belong here."

Jasper turned away for a moment and swallowed back the emotion that was slowly choking him.

"It does feel right that you should be here," he said, his voice trembling slightly, "It's been a long time, Lydall. A long time since anyone has made me feel as if I belonged. When I lost Tiela…and then my village, my family, my friends—I thought I had lost everything forever. I made a family the best I could with Syllus, Effie, Armus and Nyra, but it never felt the same. I thought, all this time, that those feelings were lost to me forever—until you arrived."

Lydall realized she had forgotten to keep breathing and

gasped for air, coughing slightly. She leaned in closer to Jasper, silently encouraging him to continue.

"You changed everything the moment you stepped through that stone in Histair," breathed Jasper, "The moment I saw you, I knew things would be different. I felt that jolt in my chest. Before you even spoke to me, I just knew. And then when I saw you in the Castle—your fierce warrior spirit and your kind, caring heart—that feeling grew even more. Then in the battle when I watched you stand and fight despite your fears, despite never having wielded magic or faced such creatures before in your life, I knew that there would never be another like you in all the worlds—in all the lifetimes. There is only one Lydall. One 'Woman of Fire.'

"All I know now, Lydall, is that I want to be around you as much as I can. Life is short in this world. Time is fleeting. Whatever time we have left, even if it isn't that long, I want to spend it getting to know the Woman of Fire…if she'll have me?"

Lydall felt tears running down her cheeks, but she did not bother to wipe them away. She was too enthralled by Jasper's speech to care about anything else.

"Yes, she will," she said, voice cracking as she tried to speak, "Your bravery, the way you love and lead your Army, the way you did not give in when everything was taken from you…all of who you are makes me want to be with you. I know this world is still new to me and I have much to learn, but I hope you will be the one to continue to teach me. Train me. I want to be a true warrior in the Army of Spellbinders. I want to fight to save Krekania and all of magic. This is my home now. This is where my heart truly belongs."

Jasper leaned in and grasped Lydall's face for a second time that day, pulling her into a kiss. His hand snaked around to the back of her head, deepening the kiss, while his other hand found her lower back and pulled her body into his.

Lydall moaned into Jasper's mouth as she felt his muscular body pressing into her. Every touch set her on fire—body, mind and soul. Nothing had ever felt so right, or so good. For the first time in Lydall's young life, she knew where she belonged.

Jasper gently laid Lydall down on the wolf-rug, moving with her so that he would not break their passionate kiss. He let his hands explore, stopping every so often to look at Lydall, studying her reactions and requesting permission before he continued.

Lydall nodded each time without hesitation. The last thing in the world she wanted was for him to stop touching her. He slowly removed each article of clothing with delicate care, studying her face as he did so.

What normally would have mortified Lydall to do with a man suddenly felt like all she wanted to do. Soon, they were both stripped down to nothing, their bodies pressed together, both breathing hard from nervous excitement.

Jasper could not pinpoint the exact moment when he started to feel this way for Lydall. In a way, it snuck up on him. The moment he saw her, she had taken his breath away with her beauty. But as the days continued, he began to notice the way her mind worked, how she so quickly picked up on things, her empathy and her fierce spirit—all of it combined to form this perfect woman before him. Every look from her crystal-clear green eyes, every slight touch they had exchanged, every moment had led to this. The distance between them on her journey to the Castle had only strengthened these feelings. He had missed her terribly in ways he had never missed another being before—not even Tiela.

With a final nod of permission from Lydall, Jasper gently took her, their bodies becoming one in an embrace that somehow felt even more powerful than magic itself.

16

Lydall blinked against the harsh morning light and gazed around the unfamiliar room. She froze when she realized she was stark naked under a warm fur blanket. Her eyes widened with alarm as she tried to recall what happened last night.

The sound of metal clanging against metal and the cry of an animal in distress snapped Lydall out of her sleep-induced fog. Scrambling, she threw on her pants, shirt, and the leather pieces Effie had picked out for her. She threw open the door of the small tree house and gazed down below, heart pounding with adrenalin.

"Wow, it's about time sleeping beauty!" called Nyra with a smirk on her face as she deftly avoided a blow from Armus, "Hurry up! Battle training started an hour ago!"

Lydall blinked in surprise as she watched Armus and two winged-wolves gang up against Nyra, "What?" she muttered to herself, still in a daze as she slowly climbed down the wooden ladder.

Lydall jumped down, skipping the last few steps on the ladder and turned, nearly running right into Jasper.

"Good morning," he said with a bemused smile, "I'm sorry I didn't wake you earlier. You were sleeping so soundly I didn't want to disturb you."

Lydall's heart was beating irregularly again as her mind quickly flashed through the events of last night, making her blush furiously.

"Oh, it's okay," she said as she nervously tucked a stray strand of hair behind her ear, "I'm sorry, I wasn't aware that we were going to start training today I would have woken up sooner."

Jasper gave her a devilish grin, "Well I forgot to tell you last night because I was a little distracted by other matters I was attending to."

Lydall felt her face go as red as a tomato as she bit her lip, "Yeah...I suppose we both were a little distracted."

Effie giggled as she, the firefoxes, Triton, Dionysus, and her sabretooth, Cally, sat on the side of the training ring watching them intently.

"Well, we have quite the audience apparently," said Lydall as she tried to smooth out her frizzy red hair.

"I think everyone is eager to get to work," said Jasper, his face taking on a more serious tone, "The attack Caillic led on Catha has everyone on edge now."

"That's understandable. Do I get to train today?" she asked, her green eyes bright and hopeful.

"Of course," replied Jasper, smiling with approval, "Effie and Syllus will be done with the rest of your armor in a few days, but for now, you and Triton can practice harnessing that fire magic you wielded during the battle. It's important you understand how to summon it and control it when necessary. I'll have Armus and Syllus bring over some wooden targets and you can begin practicing on those."

Lydall's eyes glowed with excitement as she shifted from one foot to the other, "Sounds great to me. The sooner we start the better. I have a feeling Caillic won't wait much longer to come after us again."

Jasper leaned forward suddenly and grabbed Lydall's chin in one hand, pulling her in for a quick kiss. Lydall stared back at the elf as he pulled away, her eyes wide with surprise.

"I needed to give you a proper good morning greeting," he said, his voice low and husky, sending shivers straight down Lydall's spine.

"*'It's not like that, Jasper and I aren't like that,*'" mocked Nyra as she dodged another practice attack from the winged-wolves, her eyes glittering with amusement.

"Oh shut up," said Lydall, eyes narrowed as she shot the dark-haired elf an annoyed look.

Jasper raised an eyebrow, "I see you two have—bonded—on your journey."

"That's one way to put it," said Lydall, her voice laced with feigned frustration as she tried to hide her smile. It was clear to Jasper that the two had grown rather close on their journey, despite their vastly different personalities.

"Whenever you're ready Woman of Fire," said Nyra, still taunting Lydall as she finished her mock battle with the wolves and Armus, "The ring is all yours, princess."

Lydall gave Nyra a mock bow, making the dark elf laugh as she playfully shoved Lydall on her way out of the training ring. Lydall stuck out her tongue in reply and stepped out of the way of another feigned attack from the dark-haired elf.

"You're all set, Lydall," announced Syllus as he finished setting up the wooden targets in the center of the ring. The large elf stretched out his bulging muscles as he moved out of the way, joining Effie and the other creatures along the sidelines.

The wooden targets were nothing more than large sections of trees that had fallen in the forest and had been harvested by the Army of Spellbinders for use in battle practice and for repairing their homes. Syllus and Armus had set up three rather large wooden pieces side by side in the center of the training ring, equally spaced from one another.

"Thank you," replied Lydall as she stepped forward.

The creatures and elves who had gathered to watch and participate in the battle training all moved out of the way. There was no telling what might happen when a human was exercising a new magical ability. It had been years since a human had been granted magic by Krekania, and there was no precedent for Lydall's particular abilities.

Lydall glanced over her shoulder and saw Effie giving her an encouraging nod as she walked toward the targets.

Taking a deep breath, Lydall forced her mind to vacate the training ring. She had only used her power in the battle with Caillic when tensions were high and she had felt desperate to save her new friends. Part of her, some deep internal instinct, told her that this was how she was able to use her magic: when she needed it to save those she loved. In order to get her magic to ignite, she knew she had to mentally put herself back in that battle and imagine that there were horrendous creatures surrounding her, threatening to destroy Catha.

With her eyes closed, Lydall steadied her breathing and began to picture the battle. She saw Caillic, laughing wickedly on her monstrous manticore; Archer as he lashed out at Jasper, knocking him to the forest floor; a wounded pegasus being tortured by a black winged-wolf; a brave firefox leaping fearlessly onto the back of another dark wolf as he tried desperately to save his friends.

The more she saw in her mind's eye, the angrier Lydall became. She felt the overwhelming sensation of battle combined with the desperate love she felt for the creatures and elves she saw being attacked. Soon, the burning, passionate feeling radiated from her heart down to her arms and through her hands. As her eyes snapped open, she no longer saw three wooden targets. She only saw

Caillic, Archer, and a dark winged-wolf, teeth bared and dripping with the blood of the innocent.

Flames danced in her eyes as Lydall unleashed her wrath upon her imagined enemies. The flames shot from her palms and devoured the wooden targets in a matter of seconds, turning them into nothing but piles of ash, scattered by the wind.

After a few seconds, Lydall found herself on her knees, gasping for air as if she had just run several miles through the woods. The magic took every ounce of her energy, yet she had never felt more alive. She had been able to channel her magic on command…and controlled it.

The Army erupted into joyous cheers as the creatures and elves stood to their feet, utter amazement on their faces as they gazed upon the Woman of Fire.

Lydall could not hide her satisfied smile as she gazed around the clearing at the Army of Spellbinders. The look on Jasper's face set the butterflies in her stomach to flight and the awed stares from the other elves made her heart soar with pride.

Once the cheering began to die down, Lydall stood slowly and exited the ring, making room for a couple of pegasi and more winged-wolves who wished to practice their skills next.

"You were perfect, Lydall," said Jasper, excitement dancing across his features, "Your power marks a significant change in the war for Krekania. This is a power that can possibly counter Caillic's ice magic. In fact, it may be the only magic that can."

Lydall frowned and glanced away, "Except for the fact that every time I use the fire magic, or even my healing magic, it drains my energy completely. What if that happens in a battle where I have to use my magic more than a couple of times? What use would I be after that? I could get myself killed—or worse, I could get one of *you* killed."

Jasper gave Lydall a reassuring look, "Don't worry.

Practice should make it easier. We will keep training. We'll push your limits every day. Perhaps this magic is like your muscles: the more you train the stronger it becomes. The Queen has said that when Caillic was young her magic was limited, but as she grew older and used it more often, she began to find that the ice formed easier, quicker, and caused her less strain. The same will happen with you, Lydall. Have faith."

Lydall smiled, reassured by Jasper's words, "Maybe you're right," she said quietly.

Lydall turned to watch the pegasi face off against the pair of winged-wolves. The mock-battle was evenly matched, and it was evident that it would be a good while before there would be a decisive winner.

"We should join the others," suggested Jasper as he nodded to where the other elves were sitting, their bonded animals curled up around them.

Lydall nodded and followed Jasper over to her new friends—her new family. As the five elves, human, winged-wolf, two pegasi, sabretooth, and griffon settled in around one another, Lydall felt warmth spread through every part of her body. This was true love. This was what it felt like to care this deeply about other creatures and to *belong*. This was everything that her soul had been craving for solong.

Lydall glanced down at her hands as the warm feeling coursed through her. Suddenly curious, she narrowed her eyes in concentration, staring at her palms.

As if on cue, two tiny twin flames emerged from the palms of her hands, flickering gently in the wind.

Effie gasped in surprise as she looked over to see what Lydall was doing. Nudging the other elves, Effie pointed at Lydall.

"She's learning to control it already," observed Armus, nodding in approval.

Lydall stared, fascinated by the tiny flames. She extinguished the one in her right hand and held up her left. Focusing, she increased the flame until it filled the entirety of her palm. It glowed and flickered, but did not shoot from her hand, nor did it lose its spark. Lydall kept the flame carefully at the level she wished it to burn. With a confident smirk she glanced over at the elves, the flames dancing in her emerald eyes as she raised her hand up near her face.

"I think I'm beginning to get the hang of this..."

The Army of Spellbinders trained long into the day, taking turns facing a variety of opponents in the ring. As evening drew close, Jasper held up his hand to stop the final skirmish.

"That's enough for today," he said, voice echoing across the large open area, "Let's call it a night and continue in the morning."

Lydall grumbled a bit under her breath as she sat on the dirt in the center of the training area, brushing the debris off her clothing while Nyra gave her a victorious smirk before turning away. Lydall gave Nyra an annoyed look in return as the slender elf sauntered out of the training circle, sashaying her hips and winking at Armus as she walked by.

As the various creatures split off from one another to return to their homes scattered around Catha, Jasper reached down and grasped Lydall's hand, lifting her to her feet.

"Walk with me before dinner?" he asked quietly, his eyes shining with an emotion that turned Lydall's insides to jelly.

She nodded, biting her lower lip as she glanced away. She felt a sudden rush of shyness overtake her as she thought back to the events of last night. Making herself vulnerable for the first time left her feeling rather uneasy, and yet it also made her feel incredibly free. She had never wanted marriage. Such a thing bored her to tears, yet Jasper set her soul ablaze. She wanted nothing more than to return to his home and continue what they had started last night.

Jasper took her arm in his and gently led her to the path that wound around the edge of Catha.

"I thought perhaps I could show you the lake," he said as they made their way to the main village gates, "It's beautiful, especially as the sun is setting."

"I would love to see it," replied Lydall as she leaned slightly against Jasper's well-muscled arm, warmth spreading through her body at his touch.

They made their way out of the village gates and into the woods, following the well-worn path made by the Army of Spellbinders over the years. The lengthening shadows in the forest made Lydall shudder. She did not fear the darkness, but she was now very aware of what it could conceal. Images of Caillic's dark army flashed through her mind and she shook her head slightly, eager to rid herself of the memories that would be with her forever now. This was not a time for dwelling on such things. For now, Lydall wanted to focus on the handsome elf who was leading her on a romantic walk through the woods.

"I'm glad you came to us, Lydall," said Jasper after they left Catha behind them, "I know it must still be overwhelming for you in many ways, but I believe we are all beginning to see why Krekania, and magic itself, chose you to come to us."

Lydall smiled slightly, "I'm still not sure what it wants from me exactly," she said, her eyes taking on an anxious gleam, "But I do know now that I have the ability to play my part in saving it. I'm willing to fight in your Army—and next to you."

Jasper smiled at Lydall's words, "You've gone from a scared runaway to a fierce warrior in a matter of days," he remarked, "I think you always had the fighter's spirit inside you. All you needed was the opportunity to let that part of you shine through."

Lydall bowed her head under Jasper's praise, her cheeks burning once again, making her even more grateful for the quickly-fading light as the sun continued its descent.

"If Caillic destroys Krekania," continued Jasper, his voice grim as they walked through the lightly glowing flora, "All of magic will be lost. It will not only be lost to Krekania, but also to Histair and all the lands beyond. Our world and your world will never be the same. Your ability to travel back home, should you ever wish to do so, will be taken away from you. There is so much more at stake than most of the Army realizes...and I have chosen to keep it from them. I'm sure they are aware of it to an extent, but to explain it to them in detail, as I do with you, would only cause them to panic. There's no need to belabor the point with the others."

Lydall nodded wisely, "And what we need from them now is courage in the face of the worst threat your world has ever known. Hesitation or lack of confidence could cost them their lives…maybe even the war itself."

Jasper sighed, relieved that she understood his predicament. For so long he had to hide his inner turmoil from the Army to spare them the same anxiety that he was forced to face every single day the past few years. It was exhausting, but more than that it was lonely. With Lydall next to him, Jasper began to feel as if perhaps he wouldn't need to feel so alone anymore.

"Exactly," he said as he flashed her a quick smile, "Despite what we know, we have to keep up a brave front for the rest of them. Some do not have the warrior mindset that you and I possess."

Lydall could not help but smile a little, "Effie," she said quietly, thinking about the small, good-natured elf.

"Yes, her and a few of the creatures as well," agreed

Jasper, "Their personalities may not be capable of handling the darker truths. There's no need to frighten them unnecessarily. There will be plenty of time to face fears and battle inner demons in the days to come."

"So…when do we launch the attack?" asked Lydall, brows furrowed as she contemplated her own question, "How will we know the time is right to go after Caillic?"

Jasper took a long, slow breath before he answered, "That—that is the hardest question to answer. It is one that the Queen and I have discussed at length. For now, her orders to me are to grow our numbers and train you all. Once she and I reach an agreement that we are at the fighting strength we need to eliminate Caillic and her horde, then we attack. We have also agreed that should Caillic's attacks escalate, then we will launch our attack early and—do the best we can with what we have. It isn't the most thorough plan, or the safest, but it's all we have."

The unspoken message concealed behind Jasper's words made Lydall swallow nervously. It would be a war they knew they could not win if they had to attack before the Army was fully prepared. Caillic's forces were already overwhelmingly strong. If the Army of Spellbinders was unable to quickly gain members and grow, then the probability of saving Krekania was very low at best.

"We're here," said Jasper, pulling Lydall out of her bleak thoughts, "Look!"

Lydall's eyes followed Jasper's finger as the elf stared out at the scene before them. Sure enough, through an opening in the trees was a glittering lake. A myriad of colors danced across its surface as the sun seemed to disappear right into the water. The sight took Lydall's breath away. She had never seen anything quite so stunning. The sunsets in Histair were nothing compared to the beauty that stretched out across the immense body of water in front of her. Yellows, oranges, reds, and purples, all in shades she had never seen, intermingled and covered the rippling lake.

A sudden splash grabbed Lydall's attention as a mermaid leapt from the depths, twirled in the air, and then landed with a graceful dive back into the multi-colored lake. Three more mermaids and two mermen followed her lead as they leapt and dove for the sheer pleasure of being alive.

Bright starlight began to twinkle on the surface of the water like a mirror image of the night sky. The flowers and trees around them began to glow brighter as the sun finally set, casting an ethereal light around them.

Lydall found herself wiping away a tear that had escaped from her eye and gently rolled down her cheek. She had never seen anything like this before in her life.

"Just when I thought I had seen all the beauty of Krekania," she breathed, looking up at Jasper in awe, "This—this is the most amazing thing I have ever seen."

Jasper smiled as he stepped up behind Lydall, wrapping his arms around her, "This is what I fight for," he murmured quietly in her ear, his eyes taking on a fierce glint as he stared out at the lake, "This is why I will die long before I let Caillic and Archer destroy this place. I cannot live—I refuse to live in a world without magic."

Lydall pulled away, her green eyes shining with equal passion, "Then I'll die with you if necessary," she said, her jaw set with determination, "Because without magic...we are all already lost."

Just then, a panicked howl erupted from the woods behind them, causing Lydall to push away from Jasper and extend her palms to the forest, ready to attack whatever emerged from its depths.

Likewise, Jasper unsheathed his two longswords and glared into the gloom, eyes alight with the prospect of battle.

Lydall took a moment to admire his strong frame and snarling face, the scars on the side of his face crinkling as he silently threatened whatever was coming for them.

A winged-wolf crashed through the brush and skidded to a halt in front of them. One of his wings was crooked and a large gash on his side steadily dripped blood onto the glowing grass. He gazed up at Lydall and Jasper and gave a low whine, his eyes wide and pleading.

"The wolves," breathed Jasper, his heart hammering in his chest, "It's Caillic. She's attacking the wolves—the ones that didn't join us at Catha—the rest of Zephyr's old pack."

"How'd he find us?" asked Lydall, eyes flashing with rage as she imagined what was being done to Zephyr's pack. She placed a hand gently on the injured wolf's head, her heart cracking in two at the pain she saw reflected in his silver eyes.

"He probably sensed your magic and tracked us," replied Jasper, his voice tense.

The wolf whinnied piteously and licked Lydall's hand to get her attention, his eyes wide with alarm anddesperation.

"We have to go now," said Lydall as she stared into the wolf's eyes, "I don't know if you can understand me—but can you howl? Call for Zephyr. Tell him the news. Tell him to meet us at his old pack?"

The winged-wolf cocked his head to one side, ears forward as if he were listening to Lydall's words. After a few moments, he threw back his head and let out a booming howl that shook the trees around them.

"He understood!" said Lydall in astonishment.

Jasper nodded, "Some of the wolves understand enough to get by," he turned to the wolf and looked in its eyes, "Go to Catha and seek help there. They'll tend to your wounds."

The wolf gave a quick bark before it plunged into the woods, it's gait unsteady but determined as it took off toward

Catha.

"Let's go," said Lydall, clenching her jaw tight as she prepared herself for the battle they were about to face, "Zephyr will bring the others, but we can't afford to just sit here and wait for them."

Jasper nodded once, eyes burning with fury, as he turned and took off into the woods, Lydall following close behind.

18

Lydall felt her lungs burn with exertion as she ran behind Jasper, dodging branches and large glowing plants as they raced through the forest. Her legs began to tire, but the thought of the winged-wolves suffering at the hands of another Caillic raid forced her to keep moving.

Jasper stopped suddenly and ducked behind a tree, gesturing for Lydall to do the same. She could hear snarling up ahead and the cries of injured wolves. Peering over Jasper's shoulder, Lydall could see large black shapes circling several smaller grey ones. The smaller wolves were huddled together, shaking and whimpering with fear.

Lydall felt the adrenalin pump through her veins as she watched the scene unfold. As she tensed her muscles, preparing to leap into action, Lydall felt the familiar burning sensation coursing down her arms and pooling into the palm of her hands.

Jasper quickly put an arm in front of Lydall and pushed her back, hissing between his teeth, "*No!* We don't know who else is here. This may be a trap. Wait, observe, then we'll move."

"Look at them, Jasper," whispered Lydall fervently, eyes flashing with desperation and fury, "What if we're out of time?"

"And what if they kill us?" countered Jasper, his eyes hardening as he contemplated their options, "It won't be long before Zephyr arrives with reinforcements. The longer we can stall this out, the better."

"Then let's stall," growled Lydall through clenched teeth as she turned to look at the circling dark wolves, "Standing here and doing nothing will guarantee their deaths. Fighting the dark wolves would distract them—*that* is us stalling."

Jasper's eyes flashed with fear as he thought over the consequences of Lydall's suggestion. Action or in-action, living beings would be harmed today. There was no easy answer. After a moment he sighed and looked back at Lydall.

"Whatever you do, do not get yourself killed," he said, staring at her intently.

Lydall smirked, "Who saved who last time?"

Jasper narrowed his eyes, a smile playing briefly on his lips as Lydall straightened herself and ran into the glade.

Instantly, loud snarls erupted as the dark winged-wolves shifted, sensing Lydall's presence a moment before she made herself known.

Lydall moved quickly to stand in front of the huddle of grey wolves, balls of fire burning brightly in the palm of her hands as she stared down Caillic's beasts.

The largest of the dark wolves moved forward on stiff legs, jagged maw hanging low as his yellow eyes fixated on Lydall, glittering with hate.

With a small shudder of horror, Lydall realized that his teeth were stained by the blood of the Krekanians he had slaughtered for Caillic. Disgust made Lydall snarl back as she felt Jasper's reassuring presence next to her. Swords drawn, the elf captain assumed his battle stance and shifted his weight in anticipation of the impending attack.

Lydall took a moment to glance around her as the dark wolf slowly approached them. There were five of the monstrous dark winged-wolves, one dead on the edge of the clearing, with four grey winged-wolves dead and scattered about. The three remaining grey wolves with two small pups huddled together in the center of the clearing, eyes wide with terror.

"Caillic sent you," stated Lydall, eyes bright with rage as she challenged the gigantic brute.

The great beast halted his approach, lips pulled back in a hideous snarl, a low growl rumbled in his barrel-like chest as he studied Lydall.

Lydall smiled as she realized that just saying Caillic's name had an effect on the monster, "Caillic. Your master. You're nothing more than her slave, her puppets, her little pets. That's why you're here isn't it? You do her bidding. And for what? What promises has your great Dark Sorceress made you? And were you so stupid that you actually believed what she said?"

The wolf roared with fury and lowered its head, teeth flashing dangerously as it bunched its muscles under its thick pelt, preparing to leap.

"Lydall!" hissed Jasper, beginning to panic at the creature's reaction.

The remaining dark wolves began to fan out behind their alpha, circling Lydall, Jasper, and the grey wolves. They lowered their heads, snarling quietly as they waited for the command to attack, their eyes gleaming with hunger and excitement, confident their victory was assured.

But Lydall's anger had flared—and so had her magic. She felt the hot, burning sensation of the fire flowing through her body. The thrill of battle began to overtake her fears and doubts. In that moment, the only thing Lydall could see was the monster roaring in front of her, and all she could feel was righteous fury at the injustice that had been dealt by his slavering jaws. The fire burned bright in Lydall's hands as she felt her lips pulling back, snarling in fury at the black wolf before her.

In a horrifying instant, the great wolf moved. Lydallfelt a momentary thrill of terror at the unexpected speed of the powerful creature. She saw its wings spread open wide and watched its jaw descend as it leapt. Out of the corner of her eye, Lydall saw the other dark wolves move in unison as they followed their alpha into the fray.

The burning sensation took over and Lydall felt herself losing her vision as she raised her palms toward the alpha. A blinding orange light exploded from her hands, confusing and horrifying the dark wolves. They whined and skid to a halt, tails between their legs as they watched the fiery assault on their alpha.

The moment was over in a matter of seconds. Lydall smelled the results of her handiwork before she saw them. The scent of burning flesh scorched her nostrils as she looked up and saw the charred body of the massive wolf. She realized she was on her knees and out of breath, the energy wiped from her very core, just as it had been the last time she unleashed the full force of her fire.

After a brief moment, the remaining dark wolves moved forward, eyes glittering with indignation at the sudden and unexpected death of their leader.

Lydall shot Jasper a desperate look as she fought to regain some of her energy. Gritting her teeth, she forced herself to stand and face the black wolves, grimacing as she realized she may no longer be capable of protecting the grey wolves trembling behind her.

Jasper swung his twin swords through the air in a threatening display and gave out a deafening battle cry as the dark wolves charged.

Suddenly, a roar shattered the glade as a large grey winged-wolf landed heavily in front of Jasper. The wolf was drooling, its eyes rolling with psychotic rage as its rider leapt off its back, daggers in hand.

"Nyra!" shouted Lydall, feeling a wave of relief.

Nyra gave Lydall a quick wink before she walked over to Jasper. Several other grey winged-wolves began to fall from the night-sky. They quickly surrounded Lydall and the wounded wolves, growling fiercely. Effie and her sabretooth landed next, followed by a screeching Dionysus and several pegasi, including her own. Triton whinnied and reared up on his hindegs, hooves slashing the air threateningly as he faced the startled dark wolves.

"We couldn't let you have all the fun!" said Effie as she bravely leapt off Cally's back, "Armus and Syllus are guarding Catha—I made them let me go this time," she added, smiling with satisfaction at her own bravery.

Lydall smiled back, her heart lifting as she felt the powerful surge of love coming from her friends as it refilled her exhausted soul. A sudden rush of energy coursed through her and, grinning with pure joy, Lydall realized there were two small flames flickering from her palms.

Lydall gave a wicked grin when she looked up and saw the panic and defeat reflected in the glowing yellow eyes of the dark wolves. The beasts continued to snarl, feigning bravery as they slowly began to retreat back toward the woods.

Stepping forward, Lydall glared coldly at the beasts, "Army of Spellbinders don't let them escape today," she hissed, her words dripping with venom, "Today Caillic's servants will pay dearly for what they have done."

Zephyr let out a deafening howl, urging the remaining members of his former pack to join in on the final attack.

With a chorus of snarls and growls, the Army of Spellbinders surged forward, Lydall and Jasper leading the charge. Fear turned to blind panic as the dark winged-wolves whirled around, seeking an escape route and whimpering with terror as the fury of the Army reigned down upon them.

The attack was swift and brutal. Zephyr's old pack, alongside their reinforcements, were enraged by the deaths of their former packmates. They fought next to one another with a ferocity that shook the dark beasts to their core. Soon the remaining black winged-wolves lay bleeding upon the forest floor, their blood draining into the soil.

There remained only one dark wolf as the battle came to an end. He staggered to his feet, whimpering and cowering under the violent snarls of the grey wolves. Lydall held out her hands, flames surging from her palms as she ordered the Army to stop their attack.

"We'll let this one return to his master," she said, eyes glittering as she knelt down next to the wolf, "Return to Caillic. Tell her what happened here today. And make sure you tell her…the Woman of Fire has risen."

Lydall unleashed her fire magic, igniting a spot just in front of the dark wolf, causing it to squeal in terror as it scrambled to its feet and fled into the woods.

As the wolf disappeared into the forest, the sound of bushes rustling behind the Army caused them to whirl around, anticipating a secondary attack.

Lydall's breath came out in ragged gasps as she braced for whatever was about to emerge from the depths of the woods. She silently prayed that her fire magic would hold strong. She could feel the exhaustion from unleashing it earlier and her heart plummeted. Whatever was coming, she felt in her very bones that she had nothing left to give. The second wave of energy she had acquired from the arrival of her friends had passed and now she felt even more drained than before.

Lydall's mouth dropped open in astonishment when she realized it was the Seer. The odd creature stalked calmly out of the darkness, his tall frame moving with effortless grace as he approached the Army. Even more surprising than the Seer's arrival was the woman walking behind him: Fenelia. She carried her scepter, blue totem glowing vividly on one end. Her long black hair cascaded in beautiful ripples down her shoulders as she pushed back the hood of her cloak.

"Good evening, Army of Spellbinders," said the Seer, his voice both gravely and ethereal.

"What are you two doing here?" asked Jasper, moving to stand next to Lydall, "You journeyed all the way from the Castle? How'd you know where we were?"

Nyra sneered, "More importantly, why'd you arrive after the party was over?"

Effie cringed at Nyra's condescending tone as the darker female elf glared defiantly at the Queen.

The Seer's eyes twinkled with amusement, "I have magical abilities beyond your understanding, brave elf. It only took us a moment to arrive. As for arriving late, I saw the battle in my mind's eye. The magic of Krekania revealed your location to me and we left immediately. I'm afraid that by the time I was aware of your predicament, it was too late for us to aide in the fight. No matter though, as we came for other purposes."

Jasper lifted an eyebrow as he glanced at Lydall. The Seer was an odd creature, physically and socially, and often difficult to understand.

"We came to see how you were getting on," said Fenelia, giving Lydall a kind smile, "I had all the faith in the world that you could handle the battle against the dark wolves," she added, glancing out the corner of her eye at the scowling Nyra.

Lydall felt her insides curl up slightly as she looked at the Queen. Fenelia's past was known to all Krekania and while most had been forgiving, Lydall still had a difficult time reconciling the decisions the Queen had made regarding her sister.

"I see you have saved a few of Zephyr's pack today," said the Seer as he approached the wounded wolves.

Jasper nodded, "Those who chose to stay here at least. The rest of the pack is part of my Army."

Zephyr was busy nuzzling and grooming his bedraggled former packmates, whining with sadness as he stopped occasionally to glance at the others who had fallen and would never rise again.

The Seer knelt next to the surviving wolves and stared at them intently. The Army watched, eyes wide with surprise as the grey wolves began to bark and whine. The Seer responded accordingly, pausing every so often to listen to the wolves' replies.

After a moment he straightened back up and gazed at Lydall, "The survivors wish to join the Army of Spellbinders. They are all that remains of the wild members of Zephyr's pack. They wish to avenge the deaths of their packmates and help fight against Caillic and her dark army in the war to come."

Lydall glanced over at Jasper who was looking rather excited by the news.

"All are welcome," he said as he approached the wolves, "We would be honored to have you as members of the Army of Spellbinders."

Lydall smiled happily as Effie bounced up and down next to her sabretooth.

"Let's go home then," said the little elf as she threw an arm around Cally's broad, golden shoulders, "We should throw a celebration party!"

"We should bury the dead before we all go," said Fenelia as she stepped closer to Lydall.

Effie immediately stopped her happy dance and blushed furiously, embarrassed that she had temporarily forgotten some of the grey wolves had died today.

Lydall gave the Queen a sidelong glance before she nodded, "The Queen is right. We need to honor the wolves of Zephyr's pack who died today defending their home."

Jasper gave a quick nod as he turned around and began giving orders to the rest of the Army. The uninjured wolves began to circle, sniffing the ground. Soon, one of the smaller wolves stopped and gave a quick yip as she began to dig in the softer soil. The other creatures gathered around her and began to help dig several holes into the earth beneath a copse of gently glowing trees.

"I know you don't particularly care for me, Lydall," murmured Fenelia as she moved closer, "And I don't blame you for that."

Lydall clenched her jaw and kept her eyes carefully neutral, gazing around the clearing while the Queen spoke.

"But I will promise you, Woman of Fire, that I will not repeat my past mistakes," she said, her eyes full of regret, "I intend to protect Krekania with my own life—by taking my sister's—as I should have done years ago. When the time for the final battle is here, I promise you, and all of Krekania, that I will make sure Caillic is gone forever."

Lydall took a deep breath, measuring her words before she spoke, "You did what you thought was best at the time," she conceded, "Was it a mistake? Yes. But I don't think anyone knew how terrible Caillic was going to become—or the things she would be willing to do once she had the power to do them. How could anyone, even you, have known she would wage a war against all of Krekania and all magic?"

Fenelia lowered her head, nodding sadly, "I knew my sister had a darkness in her. I knew the day she killed our parents that my relationship with her was severed forever. There was no repairing what she had done to us that cursed day—what she had done to Krekania. But I never thought she would raise an army herself and slaughter Krekanians the way she has. I thought that—perhaps exacting her revenge on our parents for favoring me over her all those years—I thought that would have sated her bloodlust. Clearly it was only the beginning."

Lydall frowned slightly. In her mind it was rather obvious that the moment Caillic was willing to murder her own family, she would do anything to achieve the power, control, and honor she believed she deserved. But perhaps the Queen's relationship to Caillic caused her to turn a blind eye to her sister's true nature.

"Now you know," said Lydall in a low, firm voice, "And now there won't be any room for excuses—or forgiveness—not this time," she added, green eyes glaring into Fenelia's brown gaze.

Fenelia's eyes flickered for a moment as she stared at Lydall. Had anyone else spoken to her in such a manner she would not have tolerated the insolence. But Lydall was the future of Krekania—and she wasn't wrong.

The two women bowed stiffly to each other before they turned to watch the rest of the Army finish digging the fallen wolves' graves.

Nyra and Jasper were beginning to gently lift the bodies and place them into the ground. The surrounding creatures bowed their heads out of grief and respect for the lives that were lost. The grim task caused a hush to fall over the glade. Soon, the fallen wolves were in the earth and the Army began to fill their graves with dirt.

"They will run free forever now," said the Seer, standing near the edge of the woods, "They roam theSpirit Realm, where the creatures of magic who have earned their rightful place in the next life, reside. They are free of pain and free of sadness—and free of the darkness."

The Seer stood and padded over to the gathered

Krekanians. He bowed his head to Fenelia and Lydall and gave them both a long, hard stare.

"I have come for more than just this battle and checking on your well-being, Lydall," he said as he fixed his yellow eyes on her face, "Krekania's greatest threat is closer than ever before. In the days leading to the Final War, there will be many battles. Those battles will end with much death, but also much life. For those who survive will journey to you, Jasper. They seek the Woman of Fire who fights next to the Elf Captain, for they have heard the prophecy and they will know this is their only hope. When your numbers grow and your strength increases, you will find the time is right. Do not fear the final day—embrace its inevitability. Prepare. Wait. All will be revealed."

The Seer turned his yellow orbs to Fenelia who gave a nod of consent as she moved toward him, "Take care, Lydall—Jasper," she said quietly, "I am glad I was able to speak to you both again. Should you need anything, send word to the Castle. The Seer will help bring me back to you."

Jasper nodded, "Thank you for coming to us, Queen," he said with a bow.

"I hope one day we will be able to meet and talk under better circumstances," said Lydall as she gave the Queen a final nod.

Fenelia smiled as she touched the Seer's head. He closed his eyes and the baubles on his long antlers began to glow bright enough to blind them all. After a few seconds, a loud popping sound startled them, and the Queen and the Seer disappeared before their very eyes.

"What a useful magical ability," murmured Jasper, a smirk playing on his face, "Would come in handy if the strange creature actually managed to show up for a battle."

Lydall rolled her eyes and smiled, "He's just a Seer who harbors the last of the ancient magic. I suppose such arole comes with a few additional eccentric assets…and maybe limitations as well."

"Fair enough," said Jasper as he gazed at Lydall for a moment, "Well-fought by the way. I don't think your fire magic has worked quite so well before. And you recovered quickly."

Lydall's eyes twinkled with excitement, "I think it was the Army," she said as she turned to face all the creatures who were looking eagerly up at them, "When you all came here and stood in front of me, ready to defend us, I felt something. It was almost as if your presence recharged my magic. Perhaps all I need to recover—is all of you."

"We need each other—all of us," agreed Jasper as he kept his eyes on Lydall, "Without one another, we are lost. Alone we fall, together we stand. And together we will stop Caillic. We have a lot of training ahead and a lot of preparation. We all heard the Seer…the Final War draws close. Let's go home."

The Army howled, roared, and neighed with excitement as they began to walk back into the woods in the direction of Catha.

Jasper and Lydall brought up the rear of the group, making sure the injured wolves did not fall too far behind. As they walked, Jasper reached over and felt for Lydall's hand, intertwining his fingers with hers.

Lydall felt herself smile at Jasper's touch. Whatever this was with him, it felt completely different than anything she had ever experienced. Before, the thought of belonging to someone else was the opposite of romantic. To Lydall it felt almost like a prison. But here in Krekania, she was free to choose her own life, and free to choose who she loved. Jasper made Lydall feel as if she were more than just a girl on his arm. The elf captain made her feel as if she were a powerful woman, capable of her own decisions. He valued her thoughts and took what she said seriously. Her new life in Krekania, with Jasper by her side, made Lydall feel something she had never once felt in Histair: whole.

19

The sun began to rise over the distant hills as theArmy of Spellbinders arrived home from their journey to save the winged-wolf pack. The bright rays of the sun blinded Lydall as she and Jasper crested the last hill and began to walk down toward the main gates of Catha.

"They're home!" shouted Armus as the two large, grey wolves moved quickly to pull open the gates.

Syllus ran over from where he was working in his forge, his eyes roaming over the Army, searching.

Lydall smirked as she realized who Syllus must be looking for. Little Effie was currently riding on the back of her sabretooth, laughing at the antics of the wolf pups who were chasing Cally's tail as they walked. The sabretooth growled softly in protest as she whisked her tail out of the reach of the restless pups and their sharp milk-teeth.

When Effie looked up and saw Syllus, however, she slid off Cally's back without hesitation and took off running, arms flailing as she nearly tripped in her rush to get to the larger elf.

"Syllus! Look! We saved some of the wolves and even brought back their pups. Aren't they adorable?" she asked as she reached down to pick up one of the small grey balls of fur that had chased after her.

Syllus was grinning from ear to ear as he stared down at Effie's beaming smile, "I'm just glad you're okay. I was so worried about you."

Effie rolled her eyes in exasperation, "How many times do I have to tell you? Just because I'm little doesn't mean I'm constantly in danger, or any more likely to die than any of *you*. Size isn't everything you know, you great brute."

"Says you," protested Syllus, smiling good-naturedly as Effie attempted to punch him in the arm.

Armus raised an eyebrow at Syllus and Effie as he walked over to Nyra. He grabbed her in a powerful hug, his long white hair a stark contrast to her pitch-black locks.

"Come on," he said after a moment, "You must all be hungry. We'll start a fire and heat up some stew. Syllus and I caught a few of the wild rabbits down in the valley before the sun rose."

Lydall felt her stomach growl appreciatively at the offer, "That and some sleep would be wonderful," she added with a yawn as they all began to gather around the main fire pit, "I had no idea there were rabbits here," she said as she settled down on a tree stump near the edge of the fire pit, "Are they normal rabbits? Or magic?"

Jasper laughed as he sat down next to her on a nearby log, "There are some creatures in Krekania who do not have magic. Deer and rabbits are the most common and a few species of birds."

"As magic started disappearing, more non-magic creatures began to show up," added Nyra as she and Zephyr settled down next to them, "But it feels as if there are even more of them these days."

"Or perhaps it's just because there are less of us," muttered Armus as he brought over a large cast-iron pot.

Jasper frowned slightly, "I'm afraid that's most likely the case."

"Enough of that talk," fussed Effie as she helped Syllus

haul over some baskets of vegetables, "We need to eat and rest. Today was a good day. We fought off those dark wolves and managed to save some of Zephyr's old pack. We should be celebrating."

The three adult winged-wolves they had rescued intermingled with their former packmates and were laying near one another, grooming each other and watching the two pups wrestling in a patch of long grass. The sight warmed Lydall's heart as she watched the young wolves play without a care in the world, unaware of the fate they had narrowly escaped today.

As Lydall looked around the clearing, she felt her heart lift with hope. Syllus and Effie were laughing and flirting as they prepared the vegetables from the little Catha garden and tossed them into the pot. Armus was cutting strips of meat to add to the soup, keeping one eye on Nyra who was stroking Zephyr contentedly next to the fire. Jasper was sitting next to her, his eyes a mixture of happiness with a flicker of battle-light, always ready for the next fight. Triton nickered softly as he settled down onto the ground next to her, his new black horn gleaming in the early morning light.

The elves' other bonded creatures gathered around the fire, cooing, cawing, and whining with pleasure. Dionysus gave Triton a side-long glare out of the corner of his eye, their temporary truce clearly at an end, as he settled down on the opposite side of the fire. Cally curled around Effie, her golden fur smooth as silk against the young elf's skin. Mallen snorted happily as he joined Armus, Nyra and Zephyr, while Augustine sought out Syllus' great form, the griffon's feathers shimmering beautifully in the light from the fire.

As Lydall gazed at the scene in front of her, she realized she finally had all she could ever want right herein Catha. That thought both thrilled and terrified her as she thought about what might be lost when the final battle came to pass. There was so much to gain, but also so much more to lose.

Lydall shook away the gloomy thoughts and focused her attention on the elves and magical creatures who had quickly become her entire world. This was all that mattered…at least for tonight.

…

The days flew by in a whirlwind of training, reinforcing Catha, and gathering supplies. Lydall felt her body, and her magic, becoming stronger and stronger with each passing day. The mornings started with her and Jasper going for a long run through the woods, testing their endurance and building their stamina. The afternoons were filled with battle and strength training exercises as the Army advanced into more intense drills, challenging them and pushing them past their limits.

One morning, after her run with Jasper, Lydall watched as Effie joyfully skipped over to her. The small elf gave Lydall a wooden box wrapped in large leaves, her face beaming with pride.

Lydall was bent over as she tried to catch her breath, but she smiled wide when she saw the excited look on her friend's face.

"What is this?" she asked as she slowly regained her breath. She reached out and took the box from Effie's hands.

"Your armor," said Effie, smirking confidently, "I know you've been using the hand-me-down leathers we found for you when you first arrived a few weeks ago, but these are the ones Syllus and I have been working on especially for you."

Lydall felt a thrill of joy at the thought of having her very own, custom armor. She smiled at Effie, her eyes sparkling as she began to open the box.

Dark brown leather, reinforced with bits of metal, stone,

and other materials, made up her sleeves and the bodice. A pair of leather gloves that went up to her elbows with knuckles made out of obsidian caught Lydall's attention.

"They're magically reinforced as well," said Effie, bouncing from one foot to the other, "So your fire won't burn them. It's a special kind of leather coating. Syllus and the wolves bought the material and the magical coating from the Castle stores when they went to get supplies last week."

Lydall's jaw dropped open in astonishment as she handled the gloves. They were supple, beautiful, ornate, and somehow both delicate and strong at the same time. She had never seen anything quite so lovely before.

Jasper smiled as he hung back a couple of paces, letting the two friends enjoy their moment. The look of awe on Lydall's face and the pride that shined in Effie's excited gaze filled Jasper with a rush of joy. This was how things were meant to be.

"Effie they're perfect," breathed Lydall as she slipped on one of the gloves.

"Wait til you see your boots!" said Effie as she reached into the box and pulled out a matching pair of dark leather boots, "We made the leather parts ourselves and formed the metal reinforcements. The soles we bought from the Castle supply stores, but the rest was all me and Syllus."

Lydall was at a loss for words, "How long did it take you to create these?" she managed to ask after a moment.

"We started working on your armor right after you got here," replied Effie as she continued to bounce from one foot to the other, "Some of the enhancements we added as we got to know you—and learn about your fire magic."

Lydall beamed down at the little elf as a sudden wave of emotion overwhelmed her.

Just then, a cry of pain startled them. Effie and Lydall whirled around in time to see a group of bedraggled looking creatures stumbling in through the front gates of Catha. The two winged-wolves guarding the entrance moved aside to let them in, their ears and tails tucked down in distress as they watched the injured horde painfully take the final steps into the safety of Catha.

"What happened?" demanded Jasper, transforming from the care-free elf he had been on the morning run with Lydall, to the stern Captain of the Army of Spellbinders. His brown eyes widened in astonishment as he took in the variety of animals and their horrible wounds.

Lydall and Effie moved quickly through the various wounded creatures, seeking those who were suffering the most, and began to tend to their damaged bodies.

The noise attracted the attention of the other members of the Army as they emerged from their homes, eyes round with shock as they took in the scene before them.

"Those are wounds from dark wolves and manticores," said Nyra as she and Zephyr approached, "I'd know those injuries anywhere," she added, her mouth set in a thin, grim line.

"There are so many," said Armus in his monotone, calm voice, "So many different species…traveling together?"

"Let's get them to the grassy clearing," said Lydall as she tried to help support an injured unicorn, "We can make beds for them and see who needs help the most."

"We came here to fight."

Lydall nearly fell over as the unicorn she was helping began to speak. The elves and other creatures who had come to lend a hand froze in disbelief, mouths gaping at the abnormally-large white unicorn.

"I learned your language a long time ago," said the

unicorn, shaking his head impatiently, "My magic is stronger than most. Not quite as strong as the great Seer, but it is strong enough. Unfortunately, it was not sufficient to fend off the brunt of the Sorceress' horde today."

Lydall shook her head, trying to clear her now-scattered thoughts, "Um, alright, let's get you all settled then you can explain to us what happened."

Jasper nodded in agreement as Armus and Syllusjoined them, eyes wide with disbelief as they listened to the talking unicorn.

Armus shook his head as he and Syllus began to help carry some of the injured animals to the grassy knoll next to the training field.

"A talking unicorn? Now I've seen everything."

…

Lydall was amazed by the variety of creatures that had found their way to Catha: unicorns, pegasi, wolves, firefoxes, a couple sabretooth tigers, a phoenix, wood nymphs, and griffons.

They had just finished tending to the animals' wounds and were settling down around the firepit. The elves had prepared quite the feast for their new guests in an effort to help the injured heal faster.

Lydall remained near the strange unicorn, her curiosity peaked after the large beast had spoken.

"What is your name?" she asked, her eyes bright with wonder as she stared, "And how did you all find one another? Your group looks a lot like our Army of Spellbinders—so many different species living together."

The unicorn settled himself down on the ground next to the fire. Triton seemed rather intrigued by the unique creature as well. He laid down nearby and stared, snorting occasionally as if he were trying to get its attention. The unicorn flicked his ears kindly at Triton before he turned his piercing blue gaze on Lydall.

"My name is Corvus and I have been gathering the victims of the Sorceress' attacks. These are the stragglers and the survivors who would have been left behind to die on their own. We are misfits, separated from those we loved because of *her*. There is protection in numbers, as I am sure you have found with your Army here in Catha. My ragtag group was attacked last night by the Sorceress and her mate, that darker elf that is always with her now. She brought the dark wolves with her and those horrible manticores as well."

Jasper visibly cringed. They had not heard a word about Archer in quite some time now. The mention of him now sent a fresh wave of guilt, anger, and horror through the elf captain's mind.

Lydall put her hand over Jasper's as she looked away from Corvus and stared into at the fire.

Corvus flicked his ears and snorted quietly, "You know of this elf then?" he asked as he studied their reactions.

Lydall nodded, carefully avoiding Jasper's tormented gaze, "Yes. We know who he is. He's…"

"My brother," finished Jasper, his voice full of bitterness and pain, "His name is Archer. He left our family before Caillic began her reign. He's caused nothing but pain and suffering since the day he left us—and killed the girl I was with at the time."

Corvus tossed his head, his long white horn glowing with a rush of magic, "He killed my mate as well…in the raid that destroyed my herd."

Jasper looked away quickly, his face flushing with shame.

"Do not bow your head because of what your brother has done," said Corvus, flicking his forelock out of his eyes, "His actions are not a reflection of yours. It is he who should be ashamed."

Jasper looked up at the unicorn and nodded slowly, "I know. It's just hard to hear what he's done, and the torment he's inflicted on so many. Being related to someone so evil…it's difficult to accept at times."

"I understand," said Corvus, sagely, "But you will stop him, I am sure of it. You lead the greatest Army in all of Krekania. Your warriors will fight and defeat the darkness. I have faith. This is also why we have come to you."

The creatures who had followed Corvus gazed up at him in admiration, their eyes glittering at the mention of going to battle with Caillic's horde.

Lydall was grateful that their injuries had not been life-threatening, and they would all make a full recovery. Just looking at the energy and battle-light in their eyes, Lydall knew they would prove to be invaluable to the Army in the days to come.

"You wish to join the Army then?" asked Syllus as he shifted on the log he shared with Effie.

Corvus nodded, "Yes. I have been traveling all over Krekania, gathering the survivors of the Sorceress' evil work for the sole purpose of finding your army and joining the fight. You see, all of Krekania knows of the Army of Spellbinders and the elf-captain Jasper who leads them. We have also heard tale of you, Woman of Fire. I would say it is safe to assume all of Krekania now knows of the prophecy spoken by the Seer. We know it is you who will save us. What better group to join than the Army who is fighting to save Krekania, and the Woman of Fire who is prophesied to be our savior?"

Lydall glanced away sheepishly as she felt all the eyes of the newcomers turn toward her.

"I just hope the Seer is right," said Lydall, quietly, "I hope I can live up to what has been promised to you. I'm still not sure what it is I'm supposed to do. Part of the prophecy makes it sound as if…if I make the wrong decision, then all is lost. All of Krekania is depending on me to make this right decision and I don't even know what it is," she said, her voice barely above a whisper as she self-consciously tucked her hair behind her ears.

Corvus snorted as he began to recite: "*Upon the day that darkness rises once more, the Woman of Fire shall appear. A decision will alter the future. A war will ravage the land. A powerful love will unite or divide. The fate of magic rests on The Woman of Fire. She alone holds the power to save and to destroy, for power is not held by the darkness, but by those who control the light. In the end the Woman of Fire shall rise, or darkness shall reign for all eternity.*'"

A hush had fallen over the grassy knoll as the Army and Corvus' creatures listened with rapt attention to the reciting of the prophecy.

"I believe, dear Lydall, that the prophecy is referring in general to the decisions you make and the path you choose to take," said Corvus, his blue gaze intense as he stared into Lydall's eyes, "You have already chosen to join the Army. Before arriving in Krekania, you were a princess in a far-off land. You knew nothing of magic or battle, death, or any such thing. And despite that, you chose to enter into a pact with the Army and you have since then chosen to fight, risking your own life in the process. You have saved creatures; you have destroyed darkness. Lydall, you have chosen well."

Lydall felt her heart lift at the unicorn's words, her eyes glowing bright with realization. Perhaps her decision had already been made!

"However," said Corvus, "If that were the decision the prophecy was referring to, I believe the Seer would have stopped visiting you. He only visits those who have an active role in prophecies and the fate of Krekania. This is why he is always with the Queen. He rarely visits anyone else, and as I understand it, you have seen him several times now?"

Lydall nodded as fear began to creep back into her mind. Her role in the battle for Krekania and all of magic sounded as if it were far from over.

"It is for that reason I believe you have yet another decision to make that will alter the future for Krekania," continued Corvus, "But I would not fear this decision, Woman of Fire. You have already chosen wisely thus far. I believe your final decision will be your greatest challenge, and I believe it will come before the final battle begins. In fact, it may be the thing that determines when the battle will be waged. I am not the great Seer, but I have been around long enough, I have seen enough, and I'm more in touch with magic than most creatures here, to know that there is more to come before the final battle can be fought and the victor determined."

Jasper put a reassuring arm around Lydall, his eyes kind as he gazed down at her, smiling warmly, "We have faith in you," he said quietly, "Don't fear the future. We are all here and we are all fighting this together. And now," he added as he looked up at Corvus and the creatures gathered around him, "We have even more creatures on our side than ever before."

Corvus tossed his head happily as he realized what Jasper was saying: they had just been officially accepted into the Army of Spellbinders. The new wolves, griffons, pegasi, and sabretooths howled, growled, and cried out with joy as they began to dance around the fire, intermingling with the Army of Spellbinders in a joyous celebration.

The wood nymphs had crept from the shadows and joined in on the festivities. The pull of magic was too strong for even the shyest of creatures and it drew them from the woods in droves.

Syllus quickly finished his stew and upended his large bowl, tapping out a beat as Effie began to sing. The haunting melody filled Catha as Nyra and Armus began to seek out other pots and pans to use as instruments.

Jasper laughed as he stood, reaching down for Lydall's hand, inviting her to join in the chaotic, joyful dancing. Lydall smiled as she took his hand and allowed him to lead her into the throng of excited creatures.

The sounds of laughter and music soon filled the entirety of Catha and of Lydall's very soul. She threw back her head and laughed as she and Jasper twirled around and around, colors and light blurring as they both gave themselves over to a moment of pure joy.

The abundance of magic made the surrounding trees and flowers glow brighter than ever. The orbs of light that hung over the glade began to bounce in the air to the beat of the music as the elves steadily increased the tempo. And in that moment, Lydall thought magic had never felt more real.

20

Archer paced restlessly in front of the cave entrance, muttering to himself under his breath. The past few raids had been extremely successful with numerous Krekanian deaths. Theoretically, he should feel elated, but deep-down Archer knew that if they had any chance of eradicating his brother's Army of Spellbinders, they had to find a way to destroy the Woman of Fire.

Archer gritted his teeth as he thought about the young woman. Curse Krekania and its magic for choosing to gift her with such powerful magic! She had killed Baalkor, the alpha of the dark winged-wolves, in their most recent attack against the Krekanian wolf pack in the southern region.

Archer closed his eyes against the wave of grief that threatened to overtake him. He had grown close to Baalkor, the massive brute. He had fiercely guarded their home and led many a battle against the most powerful of Krekanians. He was the one who was supposed to lead their horde into the final battle, and now his body was nothing more than ash—because of *her*.

Caillic watched her captain pacing and growling under his breath as she sat upon her ice throne at the back of their cave. He was so much more attractive when he was raging.

"Archer," she said, her voice as sharp and cold as the ice she sat upon, "What is it?"

Archer stopped pacing and looked over at the Sorceress. Her undeniable beauty, lithe body, and the fierce look in her eyes always made his heart race. The last woman to do this to him had been Tiela and she had betrayed him—the little slut. But Caillic—Caillic was his and only his. That fact never ceased to excite him.

"The Woman of Fire," said Archer through clenched teeth as he walked toward Caillic, his gait smooth and purposeful.

Caillic smirked, "She is quite the powerful enemy," she conceded as Archer drew near.

"She needs to be slaughtered," he snarled as he knelt down before the Sorceress.

"So—kill her," said Caillic simply, sneering as she looked down at Archer, her cold eyes flashing with the thought of the Woman of Fire giving her last breath.

"If only it were that easy," replied Archer, his brow furrowed in frustration, "I would torment her…make her pay for what she has done. What she did to Baalkor is unforgiveable. She must be held accountable for her actions."

Caillic smiled slowly, "I do love it when you're angry," she purred as she reached down to stroke his long, black hair, "She is smart, for a human new to this land, and she will not be easily defeated, but your magical ability just might work on her. Perhaps it is you who must be her undoing. Manipulate her mind. She could be rather useful to our cause. However, if she fails to choose the correct side, she must be dealt with— permanently."

Archer raised an eyebrow as he looked up at Caillic. The Sorceress was a mere two inches from his face as she continued to run her fingers through his hair and flashed him a seductive look that made his heart hammer in his chest.

"Catch her alone," crooned Caillic, pausing briefly to kiss him, "My wolf spies tell me she takes walks around that lake near Catha. Catch her out there on one of her strolls. You know what to do after that."

Archer felt his breath catch in his throne as the Sorceress slipped gracefully off her ice throne and slid down into his arms. All thoughts of the human fled from his mind as he ran his hands over Caillic's slender frame and lost himself to her enchanting spell.

. . .

Lydall laughed as Triton galloped wildly through the clearing. She threw back her head and cried out in pure joy as the gently glowing plants flashed by in a blur of color.

The weeks had passed faster than Lydall had realized. The warm days and cool nights had quickly been replaced with chilly days and considerably colder nights.

Effie and Syllus had been hard at work creating warmer garments and additional layers of clothing for her, the elves, and the more cold-sensitive creatures.

Corvus, and his group of survivors, had fully healed and began to train with the Army of Spellbinders. Jasper had begun to rely heavily on Corvus' commanding presence and wisdom. The elf captain and powerful unicorn worked together as one to train and prepare the Army for the war that was steadily approaching.

Nearly every day another wounded creature appeared in Catha, seeking refuge after surviving one of Caillic and Archer's raids. The Sorceress had grown wise to Jasper's winged-wolf spies he had been sending out to thwart her plans. The Army had been successfully putting an end to Caillic's raids before they even began, up until recently. Since then it was becoming increasingly more difficult to determine when and where Caillic and her army would strike next.

Lydall tried to shake her worries off and urged Triton to gallop faster as they flew through the trees, deep in the heart of the Krekanian wilderness. It had been a long day of training and Jasper had not been in the best mood for the majority of the day. The stress of preparing the Army for the inevitable war had been weighing on him more than usual, and Lydall needed to escape it all, even just for a few moments.

Shortly after their rounds of training had ended, Lydall and Triton had slipped away. Lydall felt a twinge of guilt for leaving and not telling Jasper, but the elf captain had been preoccupied with his battle plans and training schedule. Chances were he wouldn't even notice they'd gone off for a little while.

Lydall saw a stream ahead and slowed Triton down to a trot. It had been a couple of days since she had bathed last. The frigid temperatures made bathing on a regular basis a rather difficult and uncomfortable chore.

Lydall slid off Triton's back and knelt next to the frozen stream. Triton whinnied irritably at her, realizing what she intended to do next. Lydall glanced over her shoulder at her stallion and gave him an amused look.

"We can't go any longer without cleaning ourselves, Triton," she said as he whickered in disagreement, "Jasper may kick us out—well he will at least kick me out from his bed that is for sure."

Triton flicked his ears as if to say he harbored absolutely no concern for Lydall's predicament and took a step back from the stream.

Lydall rolled her eyes at him as she grabbed a rock and slammed it down into the frozen streambed. The ice cracked and splintered, revealing running water underneath. Lydall stood and walked back over to Triton. She opened the pack she had strapped to the side of his saddle and removed two clean cloths. Lydall placed them along the edge of the stream with a bar of soap Effie had acquired on a supply run with Syllus.

"It's best to do this quickly," she muttered, more to herself than to Triton, as she prepared to wash.

Lydall stripped down as quickly as she could and grabbed one of the long cloths, dunking it in the frozen water. She snatched up the soap and rubbed it rigorously on the cloth, then began to wipe off her body. She grimaced as the icy-cold water touched her bare skin. Once she was certain that the dirt and sweat from the day's training had been successfully removed, she rinsed the soap off her body, gritting her teeth against the chill.

Lydall wrapped herself up in the other cloth, trying to rid herself of the cold water trickling down her skin as quickly as possible. Triton stubbornly stomped his hoof on the cold ground, casting a baleful look in Lydall's direction.

"Fine," she said, relenting, "You sleep outside with the other unicorns and pegasi anyway."

Triton snorted at her and pointedly looked away as Lydall began to put her clothes back on. She frowned slightly as she tied up the leather laces on the front of her shirt.

Unexpected memories raced through Lydall's mind, causing her to fumble with the laces: her and Angus running around the green grassy hills of Histair all day, then winding up in the stream near home; bathing in the stream and splashing one another without a care in the world; returning home to their parents; being scolded for getting so muddy and being sent off to bathe, then returning for a hot supper and reading Angus' fairytales by the fire before they retired to their separate chambers; her brother escaping from his room and sneaking into hers so they could tell one another more stories and plot out the next day's adventures.

A pang of sorrow washed over Lydall. It had been quite some time since she had thought of her life back in Histair, or of her family. Training, Jasper, Krekania, and

Caillic had dominated her thoughts these days, leaving little room for much else.

Shaking her head as if emerging from the depths of the ocean, Lydall turned back to Triton.

"Let's get out of here," she murmured, her green eyes still glazed over with memories, "Jasper will be wondering where we've gone."

Triton tossed his head, pleased to be leaving the frozen stream. He waited impatiently for Lydall to climb onto his back before he tensed, preparing to run again through the woods and the large clearing.

"Let's fly this time," said Lydall, patting Triton's neck, "It'll be faster—and I want to feel the sky."

Triton whinnied excitedly as he spread his massive wings and began to run. He flapped them hard as he ran and they quickly took off into the evening sky. The setting sun created a dramatic backdrop of oranges, reds, and yellows as the pegasus and his rider flew back to Catha.

...

Lydall returned from her trip to the stream with Triton just in time to see the Army of Spellbinders gathering in the main clearing of Catha. The sight took her mind off her brother and Histair. She found herself smiling as she and Triton landed in the middle of the gathering creatures. Returning to Catha, even after only being gone for a short time, always made her feel warm inside.

"Lydall!" shouted Effie excitedly as she ran up to her friend, "I made you a gift today," she said as she handed her a bundle of material.

Lydall smiled back at the joyous little elf and began to unwrap the gift, "You spoil me, Effie," she said with a wink as she opened up the garment.

As Lydall opened the gift she realized it was a jacket made

of fine leather and lined with the fur of rabbits they had hunted for their stews. The workmanship made it rather evident that Effie had toiled on this project for many days. The leather was dark and supple and matched the other leather garments Effie had created for her over the past few months.

"Effie," breathed Lydall in awe as she slipped the jacket on, "This is beautiful! How can I ever thank you?"

Effie beamed under Lydall's praise, "Since you're new here I realized you probably didn't have any other warm clothes—so I thought that might help."

Lydall scooped Effie up into a hug, her heart soaring with happiness, "It helps so much."

Suddenly, they were interrupted by the cacophony of what sounded like several musical instruments playing off key all at the same time.

"What in all of magic is that?" exclaimed Lydall as she looked around for the source of the racket.

Effie laughed as she started bouncing up and down with excitement, "It's the new stuff Jasper said Nyra and Armus could get when they went to the Castle for supplies earlier this week! The Queen has plenty and she gave them to us…instruments!"

Lydall raised an eyebrow at this revelation, "Jasper said we could have instruments?"

"I figured they could use the morale building," said Jasper as he walked up behind Lydall, sliding an arm around her waist, "The closer we get to the final battle with Caillic, the more anxious everyone is becoming. I thought perhaps this would allow them to enjoy themselves a bit and take their minds off the war—plus banging on pots and pans is a poor excuse for dance music," he added with a wink.

Lydall smiled up at Jasper as she leaned forward to kiss him, "I think that's brilliant."

A screeching sound erupted through the clearing, causing some of the creatures to scatter and others to laugh uproariously at the elves as they attempted to familiarize themselves with their new toys.

"Clearly it is going to take some practice," said Jasper, wincing painfully as he moved away from Lydall and walked over to Nyra, Syllus, and Armus.

Armus was struggling to turn the crank on a peculiar looking instrument that was unleashing the hellish racket. Jasper stopped Armus before he could give it another crank and reached down to take it from him. Armus frowned at the contraption in frustration as he released it to his captain.

"Don't feel bad," assured Jasper as he settled down on an overturned log, "It took me years to learn the art of the Hurdy Gurdy."

Lydall and Effie exchanged bewildered looks, "Hurdy Gurdy?" asked Lydall, "What in all of Krekania is that?"

Jasper laughed, "It's a string-based instrument. The sound is created when the musician turns this handle here," he said as he grabbed the wooden handle at the end of the violin-shaped instrument, "There's a wheel inside that rubs against the strings, and the keyboard here," he added as he pointed to several keys that lined the side of the wooden contraption, "These create the different notes that then create a melody— when played properly."

Armus' frown deepened and he rolled his eyes, "I think it's just broken," he said as he crossed his arms irritably.

Jasper just smiled as he adjusted the Hurdy Gurdy and began to turn the crank. Almost immediately, a beautiful sound reverberated throughout Catha, causing the Army to quiet down as they listened to Jasper play.

Lydall watched in amazement as his hand flew over the little keys while his other hand cranked the lever at various speeds. The melody that poured out of the unique instrument astounded her. It sounded as if there was an entire band playing a variety of instruments all at once. It was a sound she had never heard before and she was as mesmerized as the rest of the creatures in Catha.

Effie walked over and picked up a small violin and placed it on her shoulder. She gently moved a little bow across the strings and her instrument sang in tune with the Hurdy Gurdy. Nyra lifted a small harp and began to strum the strings, while Syllus began to play an organ-like instrument.

Armus stood off to the side with Lydall, clearly giving up any hope on his musical ability, or lack thereof.

The lulling melody began to pick up the pace as Jasper led the elves into a more rambunctious song, the kind that made one unable to stand still for long.

Corvus was bobbing his large head to the music and shuffling his hooves, whinnying to Triton. The dark stallion trotted over and began to mimick the white unicorn's movements. Corvus shook out his mane in excitement as reared up on his hide legs, pawing the air with his hooves as he and Triton continued their equestrian dance.

Cally swayed with the music, her silky golden fur rippling in the low light as Mallen, Zephyr and Augustine began to join in on the dance. Zephyr lifted his head and howled long and low, adding an ethereal element to the melody.

Strigs hooted and hollered, their little owl-like bodies zipping around in the air as their feathers changed to nearly every color in the rainbow. The firefoxes yipped excitedly and flicked little spurts of flame into the air from their tails, while the wood nymphs emerged from the forest, hesitant but intrigued by the beautiful sounds from the Hurdy Gurdy.

Soon, nearly every creature in Catha was swaying, sashaying, dancing, or stomping to the beat.

Lydall glanced at Armus. The solemn elf had sat down on a nearby log and was glowering irritably as he watched the scene unfold. Lydall hesitated only a moment before she reached out and grabbed his arm, pulling him into the center of the clearing, close to the fire.

"What do you think you're doing?" demanded Armus, his cold eyes flashing in annoyance.

"Forcing you to have fun," said Lydall as she began to twirl and dance to the beat.

The other creatures followed Lydall's lead and began to leap and dance around the fire, howling, neighing, and growling with the music. Magic itself seemed to come alive and many of the creatures began to glow while they danced.

Armus frowned at the spectacle as he slowly began to move along with the music, "Only this one time," he growled at Lydall as he began to dance with her.

Lydall gave Armus an encouraging nod as she moved her hips to the haunting melody that Jasper was creating. The elf captain looked up from the Hurdy Gurdy and stared at Lydall. She swayed with the music as if it were part of her, controlling her in fluid, beautiful movements of her slender frame.

Lydall gasped as she felt the magic inside of her awaken, feeding off the energy of the Army of Spellbinders as they danced around the flames. The fire inside her sang, desperate to be released. Lydall closed her eyes and let herself go. She felt the fire gently emerge from her palms and dance up her arms. The fire skated across her skin, forming a thin layer of flame as it completely encased her.

Jasper watched, utterly mesmerized by the scene in front of

him. Lydall was covered in gently flickering orange flames as she danced, the fire and the human becoming one in a magical embrace. And in that moment, Jasper had never seen anything more beautiful.

21

As the Army continued their celebrations, Lydall slipped out of the throng. Despite how much fun this night had been, thoughts of her brother and Histair kept creeping back into her mind. After a few hours of giving in to her magic, dancing, feasting, and celebrating, Lydall was in need of some spaceand quiet to think. Her head felt heavy with memories as she quietly removed herself from the dancing horde of magical creatures and elves.

She found her way to the path that led to the lake Jasper had shown her. Jasper had never questioned her reasons for needing to escape to the lake once in awhile. In fact, it was almost as if he knew why she needed to get away from everyone, including himself. She smiled slightly. Jasper understood her better than most and it showed time and time again. He had been through so many horrific things in his young life that he seemed to understand the need to exist within one's own thoughts for periods of time.

Lydall felt her heart lift as she neared the lake. Ever since Jasper had taken her to this special place, she had found that it brought her peace in ways nothing else really did. The calming waves, beautiful colors, and leaping mermaids restored her restless spirit.

Lydall frowned slightly as she turned her thoughts back to her brother and the adventures they used to have. Even as they had grown older, she and Angus had remained close. She smiled briefly as she remembered how he had tried to cheer her up when she faced the arranged marriage and that awful, scrawny little lord of Westland. If only her parents and Angus could see her now—in a relationship with an elf captain who led a magical army against the darkest forces the world had ever known, while she herself wielded powerful and destructive fire magic with healing properties. Her family only knew her as a young and rebellious little girl. They wouldn't know what to do with "The Woman of Fire."

Despite the rift that had formed between her and her family, Lydall missed them dearly. Their memory was still so fresh in her mind that sometimes she felt as if she had only just left Histair. She doubted that returning to her land would ever be a real option. Nothing would ever be the same ever again.

Lydall wondered if her brother had been betrothed to the Westland's daughter. That match would suffice to maintain the peace and the stupid age-old treaty. She just hoped that Angus would be content with the girl he would be forced to marry. Perhaps the O'Connor's daughter was at least attractive, unlike their scrawny son.

A sudden movement in the woods caught Lydall's eye. She turned swiftly, acting on instinct and her training, as she slid into her fighting stance. With her heart hammering in her chest, Lydall searched the darkening woods with her piercing gaze. She stood frozen for a long moment, listening and watching for any signs of life.

Although she saw nothing, a deeper instinct told Lydall that she was not alone on her walk tonight. She moved forward slowly and carefully, treading lightly in the leather boots Effie had made. The supple leather made her footsteps nearly silent on the forest floor as she edged further along the path, keeping to the shadows.

"I thought the Woman of Fire would have seen me by now," said a deep, sardonic voice from the woods behind her.

Lydall whirled around, red hair flying out behind her as she spun. She felt her heart go into overdrive as she realized that somehow this person had managed to get behind her. The thought sent a thrill of fear through her as she glared into the gloom.

Her blood turned to ice as she recognized the figure that seemed to materialize out of the woods. With pale skin and hair as black as the night sky, Archer stepped into a shaft of moonlight, his eyes dancing with mirth as he noted Lydall's fear.

"Good evening, Lydall," purred Archer as he slowly stalked forward, like a large cat approaching his prey.

Lydall forced her body to react, pushing away her fear and feigning bravery as she fought to steady her emotions.

"Archer," she replied coolly, "What brings you to my neck of the woods tonight?"

Archer's lip curled up in amusement, "It won't be yours for long, don't worry," he said, his laugh deep and rumbling as he continued moving toward her, "Not very wise of you to be out here alone at night. You never know what could be lurking in these magical woods."

"I could say the same to you," she retorted, taking a step back, desperate to maintain an even distance, "Where's your mistress? Did she grow tired of her little pet?"

Archer's smile widened, "Oh, Lydall if you knew the things I could do, *you* would want me as your pet."

Lydall pulled back her lips in a disgusted sneer, "No thank you. Your brother is more my type."

Archer's eyes flashed dangerously for a moment before he controlled himself. The short slip-up was enough for Lydall to realize she had struck a nerve with the elf.

"That sounds like a challenge," he crooned as he bit his

lower lip, eyeing Lydall up and down with a hungry stare.

A sudden powerful rush of emotion slammed into Lydall. She felt as if a magnetic force was suddenly pulling her toward Archer. Lydall shook her head in frustration and took another hesitant step back, suddenly feeling very confused and unsure of herself. The sudden and overwhelming feeling of desperate longing for Archer made her feel sick. It felt so strong and so tempting in the moment that it alarmed Lydall with its intensity.

"Something the matter, Lydall?" asked Archer in a deep, sultry tone. He quirked an eyebrow and flashed her a cocky smile as he moved steadily closer.

Lydall noticed that Archer's hands were up, the palms facing toward her as he slowly moved forward. She couldn't see anything pouring from his hands, but something deep down told her he was using some power against her. She could taste the magic, but it felt wrong. It wasn't the pure Krekanian magic, like her fire. This…this was dark magic.

"What are you doing?" she demanded, feeling her mind go fuzzy as Archer drew closer and closer to her.

Lydall had to physically force herself to keep taking steps back. Each step away from the elf was becoming increasingly more difficult.

"I'm awakening your deepest desires," he said soothingly, pressing forward, "I'm setting you free, Woman of Fire. Give in to the feeling, the emotion, the rush. You want this. I can tell that you do. Think of how much easier life would be with us—with me. You would be on the winning side. Caillic would treat you like a princess and I would—well—I would do things to you my brother could only dream of. There are things he cannever accomplish without my power."

Lydall felt a wave of revulsion pull her out of Archer's

hypnotic spell. She lifted her hands to release her fire and was shocked to realize that only small flames flickered weakly from her hands. She tried to force herself to increase the flames, but something inside was telling her to stop resisting Archer's power as it washed over her again and again.

Archer smiled in satisfaction as he realized that his magic was taking hold, "Oh Lydall, let's not be hostile," he remarked as he saw her desperately trying to engage her magic, "You know you don't truly want to hurt me. I think I know what you want," he said, edging closer, "You want to be free. That is your deepest desire, is it not? That is why you are in Krekania after all."

Lydall felt the last tendril of her will bending at Archer's words. She stopped trying to move away from him and stood completely still, staring into Archer's eyes. She felt almost care-free, as if what was happening did not concern her in the very least. This elf was one of Krekania's most hated enemies, and Jasper's traitorous brother, and yet Lydall felt completely at ease with her proximity to him. She began to feel compelled to be near the dangerous elf—to close that small gap that existed between them.

"I—I am," she found herself answering, "I just—wanted to make my own choices."

Archer nodded sagely as he reached out and ran a gloved-hand through Lydall's bright red hair, "Yes, love. As you deserve to. No one should force you to do anything you don't want to do. All I want is for you to choose. You did not get the option to choose when you arrived here. You just met my brother first. Had you met me first, I would have shown you a world—a freedom—like nothing you have ever known. You would have been immediately elevated to a status that would have made every single one of your wildest fantasies come to life."

Archer traced Lydall's face with one finger, gently grazing her jawline and then moving down to her neck, his lips dangerously close to her own.

"But that doesn't matter now," growled Archer, his eyes becoming wild with hunger and desire as he spoke, "You have the opportunity here and now to join us. Join me and Caillic. Join our forces. Become one of us and learn what real freedom is. You'll never have that serving in my brother's Army. That is no life—no true freedom. That is servitude—servitude to a Queen who is weak and unworthy of her position. To serve Caillic is to serve a real, true Queen: one who has the power and the knowledge to take this pathetic Krekania and turn it into the most powerful kingdom in all the worlds. Give in to me, Lydall. We shall become one, and in doing so you will becomeone with the darkness. You will become mine and I will grant you your freedom."

Lydall felt a small jolt and frowned at Archer's words. *Grant* her freedom? Jasper had never granted her anything—he never even alluded to *allowing* her what she had already acquired for herself by fleeing Histair. Who did this elf think he was? He spoke as if she would be his slave and he would give her the freedoms she was permitted to have, but under his guidance and control. That sounded like anything *but* freedom.

Archer's fingers moved down Lydall's neck to the bare skin along her collarbone where he began to trace gentle lines across the soft skin. The single touch pulled her back under his trance and Lydall felt her inner voice go silent once again. She heard herself sigh with pleasure and felt a moment of mild shock as she realized that she was enjoying this.

Archer's hands roamed gently over Lydall. He moaned quietly, his lips grazing hers briefly, sending a shock through her body. Leaning forward those last few centimeters, Archer kissed Lydall, his lips aggressive and insistent as his hands began to slide up under her shirt.

The sudden movement startled Lydall—just enough to break Archer's powerful magic for a brief moment. With a cry of shock, she shoved Archer away from her, nearly causing herself to fall as well. Lydall felt a rush of rage course through her veins and felt her fire come to life in a sudden burst of energy. Flames flew from her hands with a vengeance as Archer cried out, diving out of the way of Lydall's furious assault.

He quickly moved behind a glowing tree, his eyes glittering with fear and frustration. The cool, collected, confident demeanor evaporated as he cowered behind the foliage.

"Lydall," he said, attempting to use his soothing voice, "My love, don't…"

"Do *not* call me that," seethed Lydall through clenched teeth, "I am not yours and I am most certainly not your *love*."

Lydall felt the fire pooling in her hands again as she stalked forward, green eyes bright with unrestrained fury, "Get out of my woods. And tell your precious Sorceress that the Woman of Fire has made her choice—she fights for Krekania and for Queen Fenelia, the rightful ruler of this land. Your dark magic has no place here and it certainly has no power over *me*."

Lydall lifted her hands again and shot jets of fire toward the tree where Archer was hiding. The force of the blast made Lydall close her eyes and grit her teeth as she felt her energy draining through her hands.

As the fire died down, Lydall took several shuddering breaths, trying to regain some of the energy that had been sapped out of her body from both Archer and her fire magic. Brushing her hair out of her eyes, Lydall looked around, trying to see what had become of the sadistic elf.

But Archer had disappeared.

Jasper threw a kettle across the open space in the center of Catha. The nearby Spellbinders ducked as it smashed into a tree, leaving a rather large dent in the heavy pot. The tree shuddered with the impact and its glow dimmed briefly as it recovered from the unexpected assault.

"Is he going to keep doing this until we have no dishes left?" demanded Effie, arms crossed irritably as the elves stood next to one another, watching Jasper lose his temper.

Lydall had run back to Catha as fast as her feet could carry her. She found Jasper and told him what had happened on her way to the lake. Since then, Jasper had been throwing everything within sight, unleashing his rage on whatever he could pick up and toss.

"So, I guess now we know Archer wields some sort of dark magic," said Armus grimly, "I am willing to bet Caillic gave it to him somehow, or she enhanced an ability he already possessed?"

"Or the Dark Pool did it," said Nyra, her lip curled up as she glanced back at Jasper, "I wonder what Archer meant by his whole 'if you sleep with me you will be one with the darkness' bit?"

"Maybe there are other ways of giving in to the dark magic other than going to the Pool itself," suggested Syllus as he kept a watchful eye on Jasper as the enraged elf tossed a plate across the clearing, "Perhaps sleeping with one who possesses dark magic serves as some kind of ritual? It could be a way of giving in or giving yourself up to the darkness I suppose. Maybe like to giving yourself over to the Dark Pool?"

Nyra nodded, "That would make sense. It's sick, but then again so is everything else about Caillic and Archer."

"I'm pretty sure anything having to do with dark magic is just plain disgusting," said Effie with a sigh as she watched another plate soar through the air, "It's unnatural as it is. So in joining it you would have to do something horribly wrong to become fully part of it. It makes sense—in a twisted sort of way."

"Jasper would you knock it off?" shouted Nyra as a log from the fire pit sailed over the heads of Lydall's little firefoxes, Aidan and Shula.

The two tiny fire creatures hissed in annoyance and shot sparks in Jasper's direction before they scuttled off under a bush. They huddled together and glared balefully up at the tall elf.

"Jasper, come on," urged Lydall as she gave the furious captain a desperate look, "This isn't helping anything."

"I'm going to kill him," snarled Jasper as he put down the next log he was preparing to throw, "I'm going to destroy him!" he shouted, beginning to pace.

"Yes, we know," said Nyra, rolling her eyes, "You're the big bad brother who's going to destroy his evil dark-magic-wielding little brother for messing with your woman, we know. Now would you come over here and talk like a civilized Krekanian for a moment?"

Jasper shot Nyra an irritated look as he stalked over to the rest of the elves.

"I wanted to say, now that Jasper isn't trying to murder us

with flying objects," said Nyra as she cut him a look, "That I think Lydall has fulfilled another part of the prophecy."

The other elves froze as they gazed at Nyra with keen interest. Lydall swallowed nervously.

"Remember the part when the Seer said *A decision will alter the future. A war will ravage the land. A powerful love will unite or divide?*" asked Nyra as she began to walk in a circle around the group, "Well—what if that decision was to choose the Army and Krekania? She was faced with powerful dark magic—but she fought it off. She choose us over the darkness. And the powerful love part? She just chose Jasper over Archer. Both are powerful loves, but one is a choice and one was forced. One had the power to unite, and one the power to divide us all. I think—I think Lydall has fulfilled all of the prophecy other than the whole 'war ravaging the land' thing."

"And she has the power to save or to destroy," added Effie in her tiny, excited voice, "Lydall has saved those of us who are injured and destroyed the darkness whenever she can. All that is left is to—to fight the final war."

Jasper stopped pacing and stood still, staring off into the woods. His eyes glowed with a mixture of excitement and battle-fever as he turned back to face the elves and Lydall.

"Then that means it's time," he said, his voice low with intensity as he clenched and unclenched his hands.

The elves and Lydall exchanged wide-eyed looks as they read the meaning behind Jasper's words.

"It's time to go to war," stated Lydall after a long moment.

Jasper met her bright green gaze and nodded slowly, "The prophecy is fulfilled. Caillic continues to launch her raids and now she has sent my brother to try and take away our greatest asset. We have no choice now. The time has come. It's time to defend Krekania—for once and for all."

...

Early the next morning, Lydall woke up to the sounds of the Army shuffling around Catha. She blinked against the harsh morning light and rolled over to see that Jasper was stirring as well.

"What are they doing?" she muttered as she rubbed the sleepiness from her eyes.

Jasper yawned as he sat up and stretched, his pale skin glowing in the bright rays of the sun, "I'm not sure," he said, frowning as he slid out of bed and made his way to the door.

Lydall caught herself staring at Jasper's half-dressed form as he moved across the small treehouse. The muscles in his back rippled under a patchwork of scars that sent chills through Lydall. He was both formidable and handsome, a combination that made her heart flutter.

As he opened the door, Jasper saw that the Army was hard at work: reinforcing the walls, setting up extra watch posts high in the trees, gathering firewood, and repairing broken weapons and armor. Effie was standing in the center of Catha, organizing the patrols for the day, her high-pitched voice cutting through the rest of the racket.

Groaning in protest, Lydall forced herself to get out ofbed and join Jasper by the doorway. She looked out over Catha and a slow smile spread across her face.

"Look at them," she breathed, "Working together. Just a few weeks ago many of them were no more than strangers— and here they are, working as if they'd known each other their entire lives. That's your Army," she said as she gazed at Jasper, her eyes glowing in admiration, "You did this."

Jasper smiled and looked away, "So did you," he murmured, "Without your leadership and the woman you've become—the Woman of Fire—they would have lost hopea long time ago."

"I guess we make a pretty decent team then," said Lydall as she playfully nudged the elf captain.

He laughed as he grabbed Lydall and pulled her into his arms, "I guess we do," he said, his voice low and seductive as he bent down to kiss her.

"I'm sorry about yesterday," said Lydall quietly as they pulled apart. She gave Jasper a sad, regretful look as she bit her lip nervously.

"What do you have to apologize for?" asked Jasper in bewilderment, "My brother used his magic on you—he is to blame for what happened yesterday. And besides, you fought him off and won. What could *you* possibly have to apologize to *me* about?"

Lydall pulled away from Jasper and turned from him, hugging herself as guilt threatened to overwhelm her.

"Because I kissed him back," she blurted out, refusing to turn back around to face him, "He kissed me and—and touched me. And I didn't stop it. For a moment I thought that—that I liked it. I feel horrible," she said as her throat began to tighten and tears spilled from her eyes.

Jasper flinched slightly at Lydall's words and closed his eyes for a moment. The wave of fury washed over him again as he imagined his brother with his hands on Lydall—just like he had done to Teila so long ago.Nothing had changed. His brother was still the same deceitful, manipulative, misogynistic elf he always had been. If Archer wanted something he took it, regardless of the consequences to those around him.

"Lydall," said Jasper after a long, tense moment.

Lydall turned slowly back around to face him, arms still wrapped around herself protectively as she slowly lifted her eyes to his face, tears staining her pale cheeks.

Jasper walked forward until he could reach out and touch her, placing his hands on her arms as he looked down into her eyes.

"My brother did this very same thing to Tiela, the elf I told you about," he said, his voice rough with emotion, "Tiela was not a magical elf. She held no special ability or magical power. She was a normal elf like the rest of us. Tiela wasn't able to defend herself. She gave in to Archer—and it killed her. I'll never know the truth of what happened that night, but now that we know more about Archer's magic, I believe he used it to seduce her too. She probably had a moment like you did and tried to escape."

Jasper turned away from Lydall for a moment, his eyes distant and brooding with the painful memories of his past.

"Archer has always been violent and always had a quick temper," he said quietly, "I imagine Tiela tried to fight, but his magic was too strong. He took her, made her his, then destroyed her. It wasn't Tiela's fault. Archer alone is responsible for her death. But you—you were too strong for him. You escaped and you ran back here to Catha—to me. You chose me and you chose Krekania and overcame the power of dark magic. If nothing else, the Army of Spellbinders all love you now more than ever—and so do I."

Lydall choked on her tears as she looked up at Jasper, "I love you too, Jasper," she whispered, "And I will always choose you—and Krekania for as long as I live."

Jasper smiled as he wiped away Lydall's tears with his thumb, "And I you. Now put Archer and his wickedness out of your mind. Let's go down and see what 'orders' our Effie is doling out, shall we?"

Jasper leaned down to give Lydall a quick kiss. He reached for her hand and led the way out of the tree house and down into the heart of Catha, his heart filling with hope under the piercing stare of those emerald eye.

23

Effie happily walked through the woods next to Cally and a few of Zephyr's winged-wolf pack. She was feeling rather pleased with herself today. Effie had taken it upon herself to rouse the Army early to begin preparations for the coming war. After Jasper's declaration, she had begun feeling anxious about making sure that everything, and everyone, was ready.

So Effie had spent the morning assigning teams to work on the wall reinforcements, supply runs, and patrols for the forest boundary. Part of her secretly hoped her patrol would run into some of Caillic's horde. She was in a fighting mood after the story Lydall had told them. She shuddered slightly as she thought about Archer trying to seduce and trick Lydall into giving herself over to the darkness. The thought of losing Lydall to Caillic's army was horrifying. She said a silent prayer of thanks to the magic of Krekania for lending Lydall the strength to fight off the darkness and return to Catha unharmed.

As the patrol moved through the woods, they saw a group of pegasi clustered together in a small clearing.

Effie smiled at the sight, her heart lifting as she watched the pegasi grazing and frolicking peacefully. This was the Krekania she remembered: full of magical creatures, at ease and enjoying their world without fear. But, as they drew closer to the herd, the pegasi lifted their heads, ears erect in alarm and muscles bunching as they prepared to flee at a moment's notice…and the spell was broken.

Effie sighed in resignation as she watched the startled creatures. Perhaps Krekania would never be the same after Caillic's existence. What if, even after Caillic and her army were defeated, the creatures who remained lived forever in fear? Perhaps there would never be a way to return to the way things were before.

"It's alright!" said Effie as they approached the startled pegasi, "We're with the Army of Spellbinders. We're just patrolling the woods to make sure everything is safe."

The pegasi snorted and tossed their heads, trying to throw off their fears as they studied the approaching group.

Cally sniffed curiously at a small pegasus and leapt back in surprise when it gave a shrill whinny of alarm, much to Effie's amusement. The winged-wolves circled the clearing, sniffing around the trees and underbrush with their ears upright, alert for signs of trouble.

As Effie turned to glance at the patrolling wolves, she saw one of them freeze, the fur along her shoulder blades beginning to lift. Effie felt a cold chill course through her body moments before the wolf lifted her head and unleashed a howl of warning.

The other wolves immediately circled the pegasi, creating a protective barrier between them and whatever startled the winged she-wolf. Effie removed the small twin blades from their sheaths on her back and took up a fighting stance. She tried to think back to her training in the glade and the battle moves that Jasper and Nyra had taught her. Cally stood next to her, snarling as they faced the shadowed forest.

Shapes began to slowly slink into the clearing. Silent, lethal forms with slavering jaws and wicked eyes surrounded the patrol and the herd of pegasi. The dark wolves grinned malevolently as the massive creatures noted how greatly they outnumbered the Krekanians. They lowered their heads, growling softly as they stalked forward.

In that moment, Effie had never been more afraid. In her heart she knew they were doomed. Nearly a dozen monstrous brutes were closing in on her, Cally, and five grey winged-wolves. The pegasi herd was nearly helpless to defend themselves against these creatures. Closing her eyes briefly, Effie sent a prayer to the magic of Krekania, and braced herself for the battle.

Then, with jaws open wide and teeth stained with the blood of the innocent—the dark wolves attacked.

…

Meanwhile, back in Catha, Lydall was playing with Aidan and Shula. The firefoxes leapt around on her lap as they play-fought, tiny teeth bared and fiery pelts blazing.

Lydall laughed at their antics, her heart feeling full as she watched them frolic around one another. She remembered the moment they had been reunited and she had realized they were mates, separated after being attacked by Caillic's beasts. It was a moment that had made Lydall realize what they were all fighting for: freedom, love, and peace. Moments like this revealed what Krekania could be like one day—once Caillic and her army were removed from their world.

Lydall was laughing as Shula tripped over her leg and rolled over in the dirt, when the cry of a panicked and injured creature shattered the peaceful morning.

A grey winged-wolf landed painfully near the center of Catha by the fire pit, her wings ruffled, and long gashes raked down her sides. She collapsed on the ground, breathing hard as her eyes rolled around, searching desperately.

"Jasper!" shouted Lydall as she raced over to the injured wolf, her heart plummeting with dread.

Jasper was in the middle of sparring with Nyra and Syllus when he heard Lydall scream his name. He dropped the wooden training swords immediately and sprinted across the glade, Nyra and Syllus on his heels. Armus emerged from his home, one of his jagged daggers drawn as he prepared to fight whatever it was that had caused Lydall to cry out.

Lydall was desperately trying to stop the flow of blood from the struggling wolf's wounds as she gazed down at her, "What in all of Krekania happened?" she breathed as she tried to soothe the suffering creature.

The grey wolf whined loudly as she gazed beseechingly into Lydall's eyes, trying desperately to convey a message.

"Where are the wolves that went out this morning?" asked Armus, his voice trembling slightly as he and the other elves approached. His muscles were tense as he stood next to Lydall and the wolf, his feet planted in a fighter's stance.

Lydall looked up slowly as a horrific realization settled in the pit of her stomach. She looked into Syllus' eyes and saw the same panic reflected in his stare as the color quickly drained from the elf's face. Feeling a sudden pang of nausea, Lydall clutched her stomach.

"Effie."

...

As Triton soared through the night sky, Lydall felt her heart hammering in her chest at an unsteady pace. She felt the wind whip her hair around her face as Triton surged forward and could faintly hear the sound of the Army below and behind her, following close as they charged forward.

Effie.

The name rang through her mind over and over again as Triton's great wings pumped harder. She could hear Zephyr unleash a battle cry as he flew behind them, Nyra on his back and the rest of his pack fanning out behind him.

Dionysus flew just behind the wolves, Jasper clinging to his feathers as the griffon cawed angrily, eyes bright with battle light. Mallen and Augustine brought up the rear of the rescue party, Armus and Syllus upon their backs. A small group of unicorns tossed their heads and whinnied, their horns glowing with magic as they led the charge down on the ground below.

Jasper had ordered Corvus and his band of creatures to stay behind and guard Catha. The massive unicorn had bowed his head sagely and taken up watch outside the main gates next to the two grey-wolf guardians of Catha. The chances of Caillic launching an attack while half of Catha was out of the compound was too high of a risk to take lightly.

The sounds of dying animals startled Lydall out of her thoughts and made the blood in her veins freeze.

Triton dove out of the sky and landed in a small clearing where they could hear the horrible sounds. He whinnied in fear as he smelled the blood. Lydall felt time slow down as she gazed around the clearing. It was littered with broken bodies and blood that coated the gently glowing grass. Several wolves and pegasi lay on the ground, some writhing in pain while others lay ominously still.

But it was what lay on the far side of the clearing that made Lydall double over in horror. She slid off Triton's back and half-collapsed onto the ground, a guttural scream coming from somewhere deep inside her. A wave of agony unlike anything Lydall had ever felt cascaded over her like a black wave.

Jasper, Syllus, Armus, Nyra and the rest of the Army thundered into the clearing, gazing around in utter shock at the sight in front of them. Zephyr whined piteously as he moved from one injured wolf to the other, desperately seeking for signs of life from his packmates. The other creatures fanned out and began to check the devastated bodies of the pegasi herd, their heads and tails hanging low in despair.

Jasper felt his heart clench with the terrible realization that none of the pegasi were moving and only two of the wolves showed any sign of life. The others lay dead, their blood spilled across the forest floor.

Another gut-wrenching scream pulled the elves' attention away from the bodies of the dead animals. Jasper felt the blood rush from his head as he realized that the awful noise had come from Lydall. Racing over to where Lydall was hunched over on the ground, Jasper felt bile rise into his throat. He saw Lydall cradling something in her arms and he felt his body go numb. Jasper realized what she had to be holding—what had to have happened to cause her to scream in such a terrible way.

Lydall was slowly rocking back and forth, tears streaming freely down her grief-stricken face. Her eyes found Jasper's and she gave him a look that Jasper knew he would never forget as long as he lived.

A broken and mangled Effie lay limp in Lydall's arms. Jasper did not need to look any closer to realize that there was no possible way she was still alive. Effie was gone. Effie was dead. Sweet, gentle, tiny Effie—was dead.

Another cry of grief echoed through the clearing, this one deep and full of angst. Syllus stumbled over to where Lydall was crouched, clutching Effie, and sank to his knees. Lydall glanced up at Syllus, her eyes bright with sadness and utter disbelief as she allowed him to take Effie from her arms. Syllus bent over the small figure and began to wail. The heart-wrenching sound cut right through Lydall as she felt the sharp pain of loss stabbing into her very soul.

Suddenly, Zephyr gave a loud howl of anguish, startling the rest of the Army. He was standing over the large body of a creature nearly covered completely in crimson blood. Lydall recognized the remains as Cally, Effie's sabretooth, and felt the breath rush from her lungs.

Dionysus cawed in alarm as he hopped over to Zephyr. The two creatures leaned on one another for support as they mourned the loss of one of their dear friends. Triton, Mallen, and Augustine moved to join them. They brushed against one another, trying to provide comfort as they stared down in shock at Cally's body. The sight was enough to shatter Jasper and Lydall's hearts.

Nyra sank down to the ground, overwhelmed by grief as she tried to absorb what had happened. Armus crouched next to her and held her in his arms as tears began to fall down his normally-stoic face.

"How could they do this?" asked Nyra, choking on her own tears, "How could even *she* do this? It was Effie— EFFIE!"

"Dark wolves," said a deep, guttural voice from the edge of the woods.

Lydall looked up for a moment, briefly startled out of her grief as she recognized the voice of the Seer. The odd-looking creature slid into the clearing with his smooth stride, his yellow eyes bright with shared mourning as he looked upon the bloody scene before him.

"The dark wolves did this," repeated the Seer, his head bowed and his tail hanging low, "I was on my way to visit you, Lydall," he said, lifting his head to face her, "I arrived in Catha only to discover you had just left—and quickly by the scent of it. I spoke with Corvus and he told me where you'd gone. I am sorry, although I am afraid there is not much my magic could have done to stop *this*."

The Seer stepped through the maze of bodies, pausing at each one and bowing his head in a sign of respect and remorse as he honored each fallen creature.

"I came to Catha to tell you that the time has come,"

he said, his voice barely more than a whisper as he walked among the dead, "But I believe after this—this horror before us—you have reached this conclusion already."

Lydall gazed blindly in the Seer's direction, his form just a black watery shape in her grief-filled eyes.

"I saw what happened in the woods with the dark elf," continued the Seer as he gazed fully into Lydall's face, "I watched as you were tested beyond your abilities—beyond all reason. I have watched Archer use his powers before and destroy those he manipulates with his magic. I have never seen anyone survive it, much less defy it and fight back. You made the choice Lydall—the one the prophecy spoke of. Had you given in to his twisted version of love and power, you would have destroyed Krekania forever. Your power would have turned dark and all of Krekania would have burned until it was nothing but ash."

Lydall heard the words the Seer was saying and fought to make sense of them. She felt lost in her despair. It felt as if nothing else mattered now that Effie was gone. What was Krekania without Effie's gentle and pure soul? What was the purpose behind anything now that the most innocent of them all lay broken and dead?

She had died alone. She'd had Cally, the wolves, and a few wild pegasi—but she had died without the elves. Effie had fought without her closest friends—without *her*. That thought alone sent waves of unimaginable grief and rage through Lydall. She felt as if the emotion might break her into a million tiny pieces and scatter her to the wind.

The Seer bowed his head to Lydall, "I know you are suffering and that your pain is great," he said gently, "Look upon my words at another time, but do not wait for long, Woman of Fire. The time has come. I have had visions of the final battle and the images are becoming more and more clear with each passing day. Caillic readies her dark army—they are plotting even as we speak. The Sorceress grows impatient and

I have seen that she will send out her beasts in the coming days. Time is a luxury that is now lost to us."

The Seer stepped closer to Lydall until he was only a couple inches from her face, "You must channel this grief, Woman of Fire. You must use your pain now to save us all. Your final part in this prophecy is about to begin. I have faith in you, Lydall. You have fought the worst that dark magic has to offer. This will be your final test. All will be lost, or all will be gained. Krekania's fate hangs in the balance, and in those final days, the Woman of Fire alone can save us. The Woman of Fire must rise—so rise young Lydall, rise!"

As silent and graceful as a shadow, the Seer slipped away from the grieving Army and back into the woods, leaving Lydall with her anguish and the promise of war on the horizon.

24

The Army trudged back home with heavy footsteps and even heavier hearts. The bodies of the fallen lay upon their backs as they returned to Catha to bury their dead. Effie was wrapped in Syllus' cloak. He carried her body as if it were a baby, clutching her to his chest as he choked out sobs and declared his eternal love for her.

Lydall felt as if she were breaking. She had never felt pain this strong before. Of all her physical injuries from training and the battles she had fought, this one cut the deepest. She wasn't sure if there was a salve or a bandage suited for healing this particular wound. Her heart felt as if it had shattered, the remaining shards poking into her body, piercing her chest.

Jasper lead the Army through the front gates of Catha. He had wanted to walk with Lydall, but one look into her tormented eyes told him that she needed to be alone. There was little he could do to heal this particular hurt. The thought sent a thrill of fury through him as he realized that Caillic's horde had dealt a blow to his Army that they would feel forever—and there was nothing that he, the Captain of the Army, could do about it.

The Army laid the bodies in the center of their home and gathered around in a circle to grieve. Jasper had given them permission to leave the bodies out until the morning so that they could mourn properly. Once the sun rose, they were to take them to the burial ground on the outskirts of the Catha camp and lay them to rest.

Lydall settled down next to Syllus and reached out to stroke Effie's short brown hair. The wispy layers felt painfully familiar in Lydall's fingers. She thought back to all the moments where she had sat with Effie and lovingly took a hand through the little elf's hair or had ruffled it playfully after she had said something cute or witty.

The realization that these moments were lost to Lydall forever made her heart ache with a pain that she could not put into words. She would never again hear Effie's voice; see her smiling face as she presented Lydall with new armor or clothing; long nights by the fire sharing stories and learning more about each other's worlds—it was all gone. All taken by Caillic's demonic beasts.

Lydall felt the rage surge through her body, but she forced it back down. She swallowed her hate, knowing that now was the time to remember Effie and to mourn. The moment to seek revenge and unleash her fury would come—and it would come soon.

The night moved quickly as Lydall sat next to Syllus and grieved their loss. Jasper, Nyra, and Armus sat across from them, eyes bloodshot with lack of sleep and shock after the day's events. They sat together in a silent vigil. The only sounds were the occasional sob or sniff as they all let their sadness take hold.

The early rays of the sun made Lydall squint, her stomach clenching with dread as she realized what the rising sun meant. Although burying Effie would not change the fact she was gone, the idea of never physically seeing her again made something in Lydall break.

"It's time," murmured Jasper as he stood, gazing sadly at Syllus and Lydall, "Let's let her rest—she wouldn't want us sitting here forever. She'd want us to keep going—keep fighting."

Lydall nodded, closing her eyes against the waves of

pain as she forced herself to stand. She watched as Syllus slowly rose to his feet, his legs shaking with exhaustion as he clutched Effie's tiny broken body in his arms. Armus wrapped an arm around Nyra as the elves and Lydall slowly trudged out of the camp. Formidable Nyra suddenly looked like a young girl as she leaned into Armus' embrace, her fierce demeanor evaporated.

Jasper turned to the Army and ordered some of them to help carry the bodies of the other fallen creatures. It was a somber order as the wolves, firefoxes, pegasi, unicorns and griffons who answered Jasper's command, bowed their heads low and tucked their tails between their legs as they lifted up their fallen friends.

Dionysus hurried to Jasper's side, his eyes glassy with sadness and worry as he gently nuzzled against the elf.

Jasper smiled and gave the white griffon a friendly pat on the head, "It's alright, Dionysus," he whispered quietly, "We will survive this. We have to. We have to make sure that Effie did not die in vain."

Dionysus cawed softly in reply as Triton trotted over. The two creatures eyed each other warily. Dionysus chirped a quiet greeting at Triton. The black destrier bowed his black head in reply, snorting softly as he walked alongside them, a temporary true established in the wake of their mutual loss.

Zephyr moved forward to stand next to Nyra, rubbing against her for support. Armus' white pegasus, Mallen, trotted forward with Syllus' golden griffon, Augustine. Together the elves, Lydall, and their bonded creatures led the solemn march out to the cemetery near the edge of Catha.

...

The burial was a simple, quiet affair. The graves had been dug overnight by some of Zephyr's wolves. All that was left was to gently place the fallen into the earth. Even the surrounding woods seemed unusually quiet as they gently laid the fallen creatures, and their dear friend Effie, to rest.

Lydall watched as Jasper stepped forward to put a handful of dirt over Effie's grave. Nyra, Armus, and Syllus followed suite. She moved to do the same, her heart collapsing once more as, slowly but surely, the dirt began to cover her friend. She realized in that moment that Effie was truly gone from this world.

Lydall felt her breath quicken as her chest tightened against the sudden onslaught of pain and rage. The conflicting emotions became too much as everything rushed in on her, wave after wave.

Gasping for air, Lydall turned and ran back toward Catha. She had to get away from this—this place. She had to get away from the elves, from their grief-stricken faces, from the death that seemed to surround them all. She needed to just—get away.

Lydall ran toward the main gates of Catha at full tilt. The two guardian winged-wolves moved out of her way, their ears flattening against their heads as they recognized the sorrow that had overtaken her.

The rage boiling inside of Lydall was choking her. She had to let it out before she lost control completely. Shehad never felt anything so powerful, so intense, and so terrifying in all of her life. The pain was being channeled into pure hatred and fury, giving her a rush of energy as she raced toward the clearing they used for battletraining.

The fire was flowing through Lydall's veins,threatening to explode. She thought of Caillic, the Sorceress' malevolent black eyes and her stark white hair as she rode atop her manticore, destroying all the innocent lives around her. A vision of Archer's attempt to seduce her with his manipulative magic, and of the pack of dark wolves tearing the Spellbinders to shreds, pushed Lydall to her breaking point. Finally, the image of Effie's broken body, permanently etched in her mind's eye, sent her straight over the edge.

In that instant Lydall felt the fire within her surge forward. It poured from her body like an endless fountain and she let it take control. Within seconds she felt herself losing 'Lydall' and becoming the fire. All she could feel was righteous fury and endless pain as she unleashed the full power of her fire magic, destroying every training target in sight.

Jasper had followed Lydall, worried about what she might do after seeing her reaction to Effie's funeral. He felt the death of the little elf deeply in his soul, but the look in Lydall's eyes concerned him. As he walked through the gates of Catha, he realized that all he could hear was the roar of fire and the sound of crackling wood as it succumbed to the flames.

Jasper raced toward the training field where he could see the flames leaping through the foliage. The other Spellbinders peaked out of their doorways, hesitant to disrupt the raging Woman of Fire, their eyes round with anxiety.

When Jasper reached the clearing, his eyes grew wide with shock. Lydall was a pillar of fire, her human form barely recognizable as flames danced over every square inch of her skin. They poured out from every part of her body and her eyes were glowing embers. She had given herself over to the fire and was reigning hell upon anything and everything within her sight.

But as Lydall turned around and saw Jasper, the flames in her eyes dimmed slightly. She watched as he held up hishands, in a gesture meant to calm her, his eyes wide as he gazed upon what she had become. Lydall tried to steady herself, closing her eyes and focusing on her breathing as she fought to control the magic inside her.

Slowly, the flames flickered and died, leaving Lydall untouched in the center of the clearing, surrounded by charred grass and ashy remains of the logs that had been set up for target practice.

"Sorry," she managed to gasp as she fought to catch her breath, "I—I needed a moment."

Lydall felt a pang of regret as she realized what she had done—and what she had become—in those few moments. She had completely lost control. What if she had hurt someone?

Jasper moved toward Lydall, wrapping his arms around her from behind. Lydall gasped at his touch, startled for a moment before she relaxed under his steady grasp. She felt the waves of grief overwhelm her and, in the safety of Jasper's arms, Lydall allowed herself to fall apart.

…

Archer ducked as another spear of ice flew through the air and shattered against the cave wall. He grimaced as he looked up at the raging Sorceress, her eyes as cold as the ice she mercilessly flung in his direction.

Caillic had taken to fits of rage ever since Archer had returned from his failed attempt to lure Lydall to the darkness. He had hidden in the deep woods for several days, many miles from both the Catha stronghold and Caillic's mountain cave, and contemplated how he would tell the Sorceress he had failed. He knew exactly how she would react and feared what her anger would mean for him.

Over the past two days Caillic had unleashed her frustrations on her elf lover and captain of her army. She had refused to speak to Archer aside from the occasional hiss or snarl of fury as she gazed coldly in his direction. Today was no different.

"Caillic, my love, I've apologized. I don't know what else you want from me," said Archer desperately, dodging another one of her ice-spears as it shattered behind him.

"Your apologies are useless to me," seethed Caillic as she stalked back and forth across the cave like a cat, head low and snarling, "We needed Lydall. Her magic is the biggest threat to our future. You had one job, Archer! ONE!"

Archer cried out as he narrowly avoided another icy blast from Caillic, "Caillic! I tried! She was too powerful. I nearly had her, but she resisted. Her magic is strong…"

"Excuses!" screeched Caillic, her eyes bright, "Excuses! You could have just doomed us all with your insolence! I ask very little of you, Archer, and yet you still cannot manage to do even *that!*"

Archer growled in frustration as he side-stepped away from another blast of ice magic, moving steadily closer to Caillic.

"Listen to me," he said through clenched teeth, "You stand the best chance of stopping her. Thank about it Caillic! You have ice magic; she has fire magic. Fire and Ice. I wasn't prepared for the strength of her fire…but you have the very magic that is capable of quenching it."

Caillic hesitated for a moment, eyes narrowed as she weighed Archer's words, "Perhaps," she conceded, fury still glittering in her eyes, "I had hoped to eliminate that threat *before* the battle."

Archer moved forward swiftly, grabbing her arms in his large, strong hands as he looked down into Caillic's hateful eyes.

"Caillic, you know I would move worlds for you," he growled softly, "I tried. I gave it everything I had. She was trapped in my magic, but—something inside of her broke through it. I have never felt someone do that before—other than you. You are blood of my blood, Dark Sorceress, rightful Queen of Krekania. I may have failed this time, but I know that *you* will not fail. Please—please just know I will be by your side. We will win this, and you will take the throne. Together we will reshape Krekania and its magic for our doing. We will make it the world it was always meant to be. You will finally get your revenge on your sister, and I will finally be rid of my brother…then together we can rule this world."

Caillic's eyes softened slightly at Archer's words, "Krekanian magic must be destroyed. The Krekanian's obsession with love and light has weakened this world, the stupid fools," she hissed, "This land must be turned into something greater than it has ever been before."

"Yes," breathed Archer as he leaned down and brushed his lips against hers, "And you and I will fix that problem," he added as his hands released their grip on her arms and began to trace her body, "Allow me to show you my devotion to you, my Queen."

Caillic purred, her eyes taking on a hungry gleam as Archer's hands began to glide over her body, gently guiding her down to the cave floor.

…

Caillic woke up a few hours later, tangled in Archer's arms on the cold cave floor. She smiled when she saw that he had buried his face in her long, snow-white hair.

Caillic felt a rush of emotion as she sat up slowly, gazing down at the muscular, handsome elf. She remembered the day she had found him wandering alone in the woods. She had felt his rage, hatred, and fear as she approached him. The moment their eyes met, Caillic felt as if they had known each other for centuries. It was as if he could read her very soul. He alone had been capable of seeing beyond the bitterness that had shrouded her true self for so long.

Archer had a darkness in him that thrilled her and awakened her own in ways she had never thought possible. The longer they had been together, the stronger her magic became. She remembered leading him to the Pool and guiding him in the ritual as he gave himself over to the darkness, swearing an unbreakable oath to serve it for the remainder of his life.

The darkness, in turn, had felt the need to bestow upon him the power of manipulation and deceit so that he might help Caillic in her quest to recruit an army. That ability had served them well as their numbers quickly began to grow and their dark army strengthened.

That first night they lay together, Caillic felt the darkness take an even tighter grip on her heart and felt the power flow through her veins. It was as if the dark magic itself approved of their union and strengthened them as a reward. Soon, darkness became all that she and Archer knew. It became a very part of who they were.

Now, as she gazed down at the elf who had changed her world, Caillic felt ready. She snarled slightly as she thought about the Woman of Fire. Caillic was disappointed that this human girl had somehow evaded Archer's trap, but no matter. They had the numbers, they had the power, and they had each other. The time to destroy her sister was now. Woman of Fire be damned.

Caillic felt the years of hate and bitterness well up inside her as she thought of her sister. The favored one. The chosen one. The one who all of Krekania had fallen in love with. Her effortless beauty, perfect flowing dark hair, regal nature, cutesy magic ability to speak to animals—all of it combined to create the perfect little princess that they adored oh so much. Such weak, closed-minded simpletons. They had seen Caillic'smagic as dangerous, cold, and undesirable. Her unusual white hair was viewed as bizarre and ugly. They even criticized her demeanor as being hateful and unattractive.

And Fenelia had done nothing to contradict their hateful words. If anything, her perfect little sister's silence in the wake of their mockery had only made things far worse for Caillic— and the Sorceress had never forgotten that.

On the day she made her stand and slaughtered their parents, Caillic felt as if she were getting part of her soul back. She felt vindicated and renewed in her hardened heart—until Fenelia had banished her. Fenelia sent her own sister into the wilderness to die.

Caillic sneered slighty as a wicked grin creased her features. She had not died as her sister had hoped. Instead, she had flourished and taken the Captain of the Army of Spellbinders' brother as her partner. How poetic.

Destroying Fenelia and her pathetic magical creatures would fill her soul with joy. Taking over Krekania and making it into the land it was always meant to be would restore her. Leading a world full of creatures with real power and dark magic, while also ushering in a new age would make her a revolutionary. She would go down in history as one of the greatest rulers in all of the magical universe. Krekania would remember her name long after she was gone.

With her heart full of sudden hope and energy, Caillic leaned down and gently kissed her sleeping lover.

"Wake up, Archer. It's time.

The weeks following Effie's funeral had moved at a glacial pace. Lydall's days were filled with constant pain and anguish. Every waking moment served as a reminder that her best friend was lost to her forever. She spent the majority of her time laying in bed, her energy depleted and her resolve faltering with each passing day.

The fiery rage that had overtaken her had extinguished completely. All that was left was endless sorrow. The pain that kept crashing over her in waves would not cease. Nothing she did would ever fix the fact that Effie was gone and that part of her very soul had gone with her.

Jasper frowned as he glanced up at his tree house where Lydall had been hiding for several days now. Dionysus cawed softly in question as he glanced between the house and Jasper.

Jasper sighed as he pet his griffon, "I know," he murmured sadly, "I miss her too."

Triton stood off to one side of Catha with severalunicorns and pegasi as they grazed in one of the lush fields. His mane was limp and his stance dejected. He was also looking up at the tree house, ears flicking hopefully as he heard the door open.

Lydall blinked against the harsh morning light as she looked out at Catha. She glanced down and saw Dionysus and Jasper looking up at her. Jasper gave her a nervous wave while Dionysus flapped his wings and cawed up to her, urging Lydall to join them.

Triton whinnied, drawing her attention to the mixed herd of unicorns and pegasi. Her dark stallion, possessing both wings and a horn, stood in stark contrast to the bright white unicorns and pastel colors of the pegasi. He tossed his head impatiently and stomped a hoof, eager to have Lydall back with him.

Lydall felt her heart lift slightly at the sight and contemplated coming down to visit them. But when she gazed across the clearing and saw Syllus walking out of the armory, memories of Effie flashed through her mind. The young elf used to always be in the armory, working alongside Syllus, designing and creating leather clothing, her smiling face radiant with joy. That image nearly crippled Lydall with agony.

With a shuddering sigh she retreated back into the house and closed the door firmly behind her. She slumped down against the other side of it and gave into her despair. Her matted red hair nearly covered her completely as she drew her knees into her chest and wept.

Jasper frowned in frustration and tossed a stick across the clearing. Dionysus flapped his wings in confusion, not understanding why Lydall was remaining up in the house when it clearly bothered his bonded elf so deeply. Triton snorted irritably as he stomped off, his sadness and frustration evident in his gait.

"She has to come out of there," said Nyra as she walked up to Jasper, Zephyr hot on her heels, "It isn't healthy. Even Syllus is back to working on preparations for the final battle."

"I know," said Jasper, grinding his teeth in frustration, "But I don't know what it will take to get her to come back down. I can't force her. I already tried and that didn't end well," he added as he remembered the fury she had nearly unleashed on him as he tried to drag her from the house, "She still has horrible nightmares. She wakes up screaming and crying every night. I don't know…maybe we've lost her."

The despair in Jasper's voice made Nyra move forward and place a comforting hand on his shoulder, "I know she needs time, but time is not a luxury any of us have anymore. Caillic could unleash her army on us at any moment. Lydall has to get herself up and moving and help the rest of us prepare for this. We need her now more than ever."

Jasper sighed, his eyes full of sorrow as he gazed back up at the house.

"Perhaps you should try speaking with her?" he suggested, his eyes lighting up, "You seem to get through to her. Maybe she would actually listen to you."

Nyra smirked, "You mean because I'm mean and less sentimental and lovey-dovey than you?"

Jasper shot Nyra an annoyed glare, "Just try. Would you?"

"The captain is right," rumbled Corvus as the giant unicorn approached the elves, "Perhaps what the Woman of Fire needs now is someone like you, Nyra. She needs more than just a gentle push to get her back on her feet again."

Nyra sighed and glanced up at the tree house, "Fine. But if she fries my ass I can promise you I will come back and haunt you all for the rest of your lives," she said as she playfully punched Jasper in the arm and gave Corvus a withering glance, "Zephyr, stay here with Jasper and the unicorn. I need to talk to the Woman of Fire alone."

Zephyr whined in protest but flicked his ears in acknowledgement as he obediently sat back on his haunches. He, Jasper, and Corvus watched anxiously as Nyra began to climb up the ladder.

Nyra opened the door cautiously, her eyes flitting nervously around the room as she searched for Lydall. Shesaw a crumpled heap on the floor next to the door, covered in blankets with locks of red hair sticking out at odd angles. Nyra frowned as she approached slowly, careful to not startle the grieving young human.

"Lydall," she said quietly, "Come on you gotta pull yourself together."

Lydall's head emerged from the blankets to cast a baleful green glare in Nyra's direction, "What are *you* doing here?" she asked, her voice devoid of emotion.

"I'm here to get you up and moving," replied Nyra firmly as she put her hands on her hips, "You aren't the only one in mourning you know. You think Syllus is having a good old time down there working without her? Do you think it's easy on any of us having to accept that she's gone? Lydall, I know you two were close, but by all of magic we all knew each other for months before you even came here and none of us are holed up in our houses crying the days away!"

Lydall shoved the rest of the blankets off and stood abruptly, eyes blazing with fury.

"Don't stand there and pretend like you even understand how I feel!"

Nyra gaped in disbelief, "How selfish can you possibly be? It hurts every damn second, Lydall! You aren't the only one! But you *are* the only one sitting around doing nothing and wallowing in self-pity! You have to pull yourself together and start contributing to the cause again. You're the damn Woman of Fire for crying out loud! You're supposed to be the savior—the one who rescues Krekania! How do you suppose you're going to do that when you're in here moping from sunrise to sunset?"

Lydall looked away sharply as Nyra's words cut into her. She knew the black-haired elf was right. She just wasn't ready to admit it. Something inside of her was broken beyond repair and her desire to do anything about it was gone.

"Lydall."

Nyra and Lydall both jumped in surprise. Nyra whirled around, drawing her twin blades as she prepared to launch herself at whoever had managed to sneak up on them. Lydall simply stood still as a stone, staring over Nyra's shoulder with her mouth hanging open.

"What are you doing, Woman of Fire?" spoke the Seer as he emerged from the wall on the other side of the tree house.

"You know we have doors, right?" asked Nyra irritably as she sheathed her blades, "You could always knock. Or announce you're coming at least."

The Seer gave Nyra a kind look, "The magic controls my comings and goings, brave and fierce elf," he said with a respectful nod, "It beckoned me here and I simply complied. And here I stand. Although passing through walls is rather uncomfortable—I don't recommend that mode of magical transportation."

Nyra rolled her eyes in exasperation, "I like you and all, but the talking in that eloquent riddle-like gibberish does start to wear on an elf after a while, you know."

The Seer's eyes gleamed with laughter as he turned back to Lydall. The young woman stood still, leaning against the opposite wall. Her clothes were stained and unwashed and her hair matted and stringy from lack of bathing. Her eyes were full of deep sorrow with a touch of rebellion as she stared at the Seer.

"Lydall," he said as he took a step toward her, baubles glowing on his long antlers, "You have allowed your grief to control you. I know you are stronger than this."

Lydall scowled back and crossed her arms, "I am tired of being told how I should grieve. That is my issue to deal with and no one else's."

"It is everyone's issue to deal with when you are the Woman of Fire," retorted the Seer firmly.

Lydall looked away, her face growing hot with shame as she stubbornly refused to make eye contact with the Seer.

"Look inside yourself, Lydall," he urged, "Find the fire within you as you have done before. The day you unleashed your magic in the training field—that is what you are capable of. Do not fear it, do not repress it...*master* it. Control your emotions and you control your magic. Your despair is preventing you from channeling your warrior spirit and your fire, leaving you stuck in this state. You must remember who you are. Krekania is depending on you. Do not let Effie's death be in vain."

The Seer's final words struck Lydall like a shard of glass right into her chest. She clenched her eyes shut against the sudden mental image of Effie's broken body in the clearing. Her heart started racing and her breath came out in uneven gasps.

The Seer approached Lydall and stared into her eyes, "Look at me Lydall," he ordered, growling slightly, "Master it. Master your grief and your fear. Face it. Look inside yourself, find the source of your pain, and control it. Find yourself."

Lydall closed her eyes again and sought out the unending pain. She mentally traced it back to its very source and began to package the grief away neatly, as if packing a box. She placed each sharp stab of hurt away and began to seal the box, placing it away in her mind where she could access it at a later time. What she had lost was not to be forgotten, but to be remembered at another, more opportune moment—when the war for Krekaniawas over and there would be time for both mourning and healing.

Lydall's breathing slowed down as she felt herself regain control. She slowly opened her eyes and looked for the Seer, but he had vanished. She only saw Nyra staring back at her, eyes glowing with pride.

Lydall's grief-stricken gaze slowly converted into her fierce-warrior glare as she forced herself to remember who she was. She wrapped her mind around her purpose and latched onto the intensity and love she found there. She had been called to this place to save it and to save all of magic. Lydall was here to fight for more than just her own life. Her purpose was far greater than just that.

She was the Woman of Fire—and it was time for her to rise.

...

Caillic felt the rush of her magic like a comforting hug as it coursed through her body. She closed her eyes against the power and gave in to the darkness, giving it every part of her. In moments like this, when she paused to let her soul touch the darkness again, she felt everything inside her awaken. It was like renewing the vow she had made years ago, and it left her feeling powerful and reassured of her purpose.

Archer stood to the side and watched his mistress as a miniature blizzard swirled around her, whipping her white hair around her face with its force. The look of rapture on her face made Archer groan with longing. The Sorceress drove him wild. Her love of the darkness and her utter devotion to it, alongside with her passion for him made everything inside of Archer hum with life and energy.

Finding her was the best thing that had ever happened to him. He had felt complete from the moment they met, and now even more so as they prepared to launch their attack on the Castle. It was the culmination of everything they had been working toward and it felt utterly exhilarating.

The blizzard around Caillic slowly died down and she

opened her icy-colored eyes. She looked over at Archer and a smile, full of evil intent, graced her porcelain face. Archer returned the gesture and gave her a nod as he braced himself on the hilt of his sword.

"My love," crooned Caillic as she stalked toward him, "Prepare our army. We move tonight under the cover of darkness. I cannot wait a moment longer. It's time for the throne to be mine."

Archer growled as he leaned in close to Caillic and gently bit the side of her neck, causing her to gasp with pleasure.

"As you wish, my Queen," he whispered into her ear. He turned to face the horde of dark creatures who had gathered in the clearing below the entrance to the cave.

The manticores stomped their feet and lashed their long tails like whips, while the black winged-wolves snarled and snapped at each other, eager to unleash their unholy dark magic upon the Krekanians.

Archer raised his arms, calling for silence before he addressed them.

"My army!" he bellowed, loud enough for them all to hear, "We have trained a long time for this very moment. We have raided and defeated nearly every village in all of Krekania, reducing their forces and filling their hearts with fear. Even now Fenelia sits on her throne and trembles with trepidation as she awaits our arrival. She knows we are coming. She knows her days are numbered. She knows the reign of her sister is on the horizon and she fears what that means for her. Are you ready to prove to the False Queen that her fears are well-placed?"

Roars and howls of excitement answered Archer as the dark beasts clawed the ground, anticipating the moment they would dig them into the soft bodies of the Krekanians in the Castle.

"Are you ready to show Fenelia, and all of Krekania, the true power of dark magic?" snarled Archer, froth forming in his mouth as he rallied the troops, "To reveal to them why our magic should rule this land? To wipe their weak forces from this world forever and replace them with our own? Are you ready to make Krekania ours, now and forever?"

The dark creatures were worked up into a frenzy, snapping and clawing at each other as the dark magic within them began to surface.

Caillic looked on, her eyes alight with lust and the hunger for power as she watched her lover command their forces.

"To me dark ones!" shouted Archer, lifting his large sword high above his head, "Tonight is the night we begin our reign! All hail Queen Caillic, rightful ruler of Krekania! Onward! To the Castle!"

With cries and snarls of vengeful fury, Caillic and Archer's army surged forward, following their captain and the Dark Sorceress deep into the woods. They stalked quietly through the night, eyes gleaming with the desire for violence and death as they turned their eyes toward the Castle.

...

Lydall climbed down from the tree house and walked into the center of Catha, blinking against the sun's dying rays. She was beginning to feel more human again after bathing and combing her tangled hair, but her chest still ached. Some things, she thought, just could not be so easily washed away.

Lydall took a deep breath as she neared the massive fire pit, her heart hammering in her chest and her face flushed with shame as she prepared to meet the Spellbinders after days of hiding. The Seer and Nyra had helped her come to her senses, but she felt a deep sense of regret and embarrassment for how she had been acting.

Nyra was right—the others were mourning too, but unlike herself, they had been continuing on with the work necessary to prepare for the coming war. She had chosen to wallow in her own misery and self-pity rather than help the rest of the Army. The guilt made her cringe.

"Lydall!" said Jasper, as he glanced up from helping Syllus in the forge.

Lydall smiled sadly as she walked over to them, keeping her eyes carefully averted, "Hey," she said, quietly.

Without hesitating Jasper reached out and wrapped her in his arms. Lydall felt her body relax in his embrace and she let out a long, shaky sigh.

"It's good to have you back," breathed Jasper into her ear.

"I'm so sorry," said Lydall, emotion choking her, "I should have been here—helping."

Jasper shushed her, "You had to do what you had to do," he said, closing his eyes and breathing in her scent, "You've not experienced the things the rest of us have the past few years. We've all lost several people in our lives— Effie was your first. It's okay. We're all broken in our own ways."

"He's right," said Syllus, his voice strained.

Lydall pulled away from Jasper and gazed up at Syllus. The large elf's eyes had dark grey circles underneath andhe looked as if he had lost some of his muscular build over the past several days. Lydall felt another pang of regret as she realized Syllus had been suffering just as much, if not more, than she had.

"Syllus, I—"

Syllus held up a hand to stop Lydall and shook his head, "Don't apologize," he said quietly, "We all grieve in different ways. I—I just kept working in the forge and the armory. It keeps my mind busy."

Just then, a loud cry of distress from the gates of Catha

caused the elves and Lydall to draw their blades. They whirled around in a single, practiced maneuver, bracing for whatever was coming their way.

Nyra climbed down from the small home she shared with Zephyr, twin blades slicing the air menacingly as she landed on the ground. Zephyr's growl made the earth beneath them vibrate slightly as he tore off toward the entrance, hackles raised in alarm.

The wolf guardians opened the gates and let an injured phoenix, flying low and cawing in pain, land clumsily inside Catha. It sat up slowly, its fiery feathers askew and one wing hanging limply by its side.

Lydall felt a jolt as she realized the scene was oddly reminiscent of the injured winged-wolf who'd arrived in Catha following the dark wolves attack on Effie and her patrol. She moved quickly toward the phoenix, drawn to its magic. It's tail feathers still smoldered slightly as its magic weakened by the moment. It gazed up at Lydall, eyes full of terror.

"It's okay little one," said Lydall gently as she bent down on one knee, "You're safe now."

The phoenix gave another screech, eyes wide and imploring as it gazed up at Lydall's face. She suddenly felt an overwhelming sensation course through her. Lydall's vision began to blur and shift, colors circling around her wildly. She shut her eyes against the spinning images as she felt her stomach turn and her head began to ache.

When she opened her eyes again, Lydall saw she was at the Castle of Krekania. Several parts of the Castle appeared to be on fire and bricks were falling into the sea below, while the cries of the injured and dying emanated from deep inside. She felt her blood run cold as she saw an image of Caillic, white hair whipping around her face with a wicked grin, as the Dark Sorceress leapt off a manticore and lunged at the Queen.

How was this possible? Could this fire-creature

communicate with her in this way because of their shared fire magic? Lydall had no more time to contemplate the vision because as quickly as it appeared, she blinked, and it was over. The phoenix was before her once more and she was crouched on the green grass of Catha, her breath coming out in ragged gasps as she tried to orient herself.

Jasper frowned as he knelt down next to Lydall, "What is it? What's wrong?"

Lydall tried to calm the rising panic that threatened to choke her. Her eyes were filled with horror as she slowly turned and looked up at Jasper.

"It's the Castle. Caillic—Caillic is at the Castle."

26

Lydall felt her heart racing as waves of panic cascaded over her like a storm-tossed sea. She gripped Triton's mane as her destrier's wings pumped harder, giving it everything he had.

Lydall glanced around and saw the other members of the Army of Spellbinders, battle armor on and weapons drawn, flying and running as swiftly as possible toward the Castle.

Jasper's face was set in the same grim line Lydall remembered from the first time they had met. With his full battle armor on, Jasper looked more animal than elf. His face was creased with fierce pride and determination and his posture showed the promise of violence as he leaned forward on Dionysus. The white griffon was also decked out in battle armor made from the bones of the dark creatures they had defeated in previous battles. He donned a griffon-skull helmet that made his already-fierce appearance even more intimidating.

It had been Effie's idea to do that—to fashion the magical creatures' armor from the bones of Caillic's army.

Lydall remembered thinking it had been a rather morbid idea for the otherwise happy and gentle elf, but Effie had insisted that it would send a message to the dark army and to Caillic. It could be just enough to unnerve them and give the Army of Spellbinders an edge.

The bone armor would send a message to Caillic: although they fought for the good magic of Krekania, they were not weak and they would not be afraid to do what it took to save their land. Effie had felt that this message would be vital to their cause—so she and Syllus had created the deadly-looking armor, fastening the bones together with bits of metal in the forge. After Effie had been killed, Syllus finished her work in her honor, bringing her vision to life.

A loud clap of thunder overhead followed by a bright streak of lightning startled Triton. He tossed his head and whinnied in surprise at the unexpected shock, pumping his wings even harder. The destrier's legs churned beneath him as he tried to fly as fast as possible through the coming storm.

Lydall glanced around her. She was surrounded by pegasi, winged-wolves, griffons, and a couple of phoenixes, all wearing fierce expressions of rage and determination as they fought through the storm. Below her were a herd of unicorns, wood nymphs, firefoxes, and several sabretooth cats, running swiftly through the foliage, eager to play their part in saving Krekania.

The grey winged-wolves wore the bones of Caillic's dark wolves. While Caillic's beasts had been more powerful than the grey wolves in life, in death their bones provided protection for the Spellbinders. The irony had not been lost on the clever Effie as she had told Syllus exactly how to create these particular pieces of armor.

Corvus surged forward at the head of his small band of misfit creatures on the ground. His large head was held high, horn gleaming dangerously and his powerful chest puffed out in defiance as he snorted up at the storm.

Nyra rode atop Zephyr, the large alpha decked out in the most fierce-looking bone armor of them all, his face set into a snarl of rage under the skull of the former alpha of the dark wolf pack. Nyra gripped his fur with one hand, one of her blades swinging high over her head in the other, as they flew through the storm.

Syllus rode his gold-colored griffon, Augustine, who was also decked out in the same bone-armor as Dionysus. Armus flew on the back of his pegasus Mallen, the steed's large frame protected by the rib cage of a manticore and his white coat gleaming in contrast to the night sky.

A thrill of fear stabbed sharply in Lydall's chest as she thought of what she might lose tonight. She was surrounded by those she loved—and they were all racing right into the final battle for Krekania. Despite the fact they had all been training and preparing for such a long time, Lydall had not stopped to think about what it would feel like if she lost them all. What if Caillic took the other elves from her, just like her dark wolves took Effie? What if her beasts destroyed Triton? Or the two firefoxes she had saved and reunited? What if she lost everything and everyone tonight? And what if she failed and Caillic killed her as well? Krekania would be lost and everything and everyone she had come to know and love would be gone—forever. Krekanian magic would bedestroyed and replaced with something hideous and distorted. Even Histair would be forever changed with the absence of the powerful, good magic that flowed through this world. The entire universe would never be the same.

Lydall shook her head, trying to force the terrifying thoughts out of her mind. If she lost confidence in herself and her friends, she really would lose everything. That is what Caillic wanted her to think, feel, and believe. If Caillic could kill her spirit, then the battle was over before it even began.

Lydall closed her eyes and searched inside herself, trying to find the unquenchable rage that had filled her entire being the day of Effie's funeral. She imagined Effie, her body broken and bleeding in the grass; the bodies of innocent grey wolves slaughtered needlessly; the countless images of the injured and dying animals in the infirmary; the look of turmoil in Jasper's eyes as he retold the story of how he lost everything because of Caillic; and the image of the two firefoxes she had saved after they had been reduced to little more than ash.

Slowly, with each passing image, the fury grew. Anger for those who had suffered needlessly in the name of Caillic's desperate quest for revenge and power overtook Lydall's feelings of fear and uncertainty. If it were not for Caillic, Effie would be with them now, alive and well, laughing and dancing. But she was dead.

As the Castle of Krekania came into view, Lydall knew nothing but the fire inside of her, raging and rolling, burning and fighting to unleash its wrath upon the darkness.

…

Caillic sent shards of ice into the body of the white winged-wolf guardian, feeling a rush of satisfaction as she heard it cry out in agony. She threw back her head and laughed, giving in to the darkness and allowing it to control her. She looked over her shoulder and saw her partner, lover, and captain as he plunged his massive sword into the body of the other guardian wolf, snuffing out its life and sucking out its magic. He kicked the wolf's massive body down the Castle stairs, sneering in disgust as it landed in a broken heap.

Caillic smiled with pleasure as she launched herself back into the fray. The screams of the dying Krekanians filled her with life. She sucked their magic into her scepter, transforming it with the power of dark magic, and poured the tainted magic into members of her army. Her dark horde was growing stronger and stronger with each Krekanian death. It wouldn't be long before the Castle would be theirs. The Krekanian's pathetic excuse for defense was broken. Once they rid themselves of these weaker creatures, all that was left was what remained behind the doors of the Castle…and Fenelia.

Fenelia.

Caillic stalked forward in a cat-like fashion toward the doors that led into the Castle. The Krekanians who had desperately tried to keep them out had been slaughtered. Caillic stepped over their bodies as she pushed open the doors and strolled inside.

The throne room was a cacophony of sound as Caillic's army charged inside. Blood splattered the walls and began to cover the floors as creatures succumbed to the attack. Her massive fire-bull was charging through the various doorways in the Castle, destroying any semblance of protection the weaker magical creatures had.

But it was the figure in front of the throne, fighting fiercely with her longsword, that caught Caillic's attention.

Fenelia cried out with fear as another dark winged-wolf leapt for her throat. Moving swiftly, she dispatched the wolf with a single slice of her dagger and watched it collapse across the throne, dying as its blood spilled out onto the floor. Fenelia looked around and felt a thrill of terror as she realized how greatly outnumbered they were.

This was the end—this was the end of everything. And it would be written into history that she, the Final Queen of Krekania, was responsible for its downfall…all because she was not brave enough or strong enough to have ended her sister's reign of terror before it began. They would always remember her as the Weak Queen—the Queen who destroyed Krekania by her cowardice. The False Queen. The Doomed Queen. The Queen who ruined them all. The Queen who let magic be destroyed. The Coward Queen.

As Fenelia turned to plunge her blade into another dark wolf, she saw something that made her blood run cold: a lithe woman with flowing white hair stalking confidently toward the throne. Her shoulders were pulled back and her head held high as she strolled down the aisle, acting as if she already owned the Castle. With a heart full of ice, Fenelia felt the air rush from her lungs as she gazed upon the very woman who she knew would be her undoing.

"Caillic."

The Dark Sorceress sauntered toward the throne, her eyes never leaving Fenelia's as she slowly moved closer to her estranged sister. Caillic's tongue flicked out, licking her blue-hued lips as if she were already tasting her victory.

Fenelia felt as if Caillic had already used her ice magic on her. Her feet were frozen in front of the throne and her eyes were glued to the horrific sight of her sister at the Castle for the first time in years. The last time they had been in this room together, Caillic had killed their family and set Krekania on a path of destruction that had led them back here to this very moment.

"Its poetic isn't it?" purred Caillic as she stood before her sister, dark eyes glittering with cold pleasure, "To be back here—where it all began—together again, dear sister."

Fenelia swallowed the bile that rose up into her throat, her eyes flashing with fear as she forced herself to feign confidence before her sister's challenging stare, "I would call it inevitable, not poetic," she said, coolly, "I knew you would return one day. I knew you would try to take the crown from me. It was the reason you slaughtered our parents—jealousy. You were always so jealous, Caillic. And look where your jealousy has led you," she added as she spread her arms wide, pointing out the death and destruction that reigned down around them, "I just wish I had been strong enough to destroy you that day…then all of this would have been avoided."

Caillic smiled slightly, a laugh on her lips as she spoke, "Oh sweet, naïve sister," she crooned, as she took a step forward, "You are the one who has led us here today. It was always you. Always about you—everything," she said, her eyes glittering dangerously, "Everyone adored precious Fenelia and her cute little ability to speak to animals—and they were terrified of her strange sister who created ice. You were the pretty one, the perfect one in our parents' eyes. That is why they had to die."

Caillic had stated it so simply—as if killing their parents was just a logical solution to a problem she had to deal with. The cold, hard look in her eyes made Fenelia shudder inwardly. Her sister had become unrecognizable over the years. The day Caillic unleashed her rage on their parents and the guests at her naming ceremony, Fenelia thought she had witnessed true evil. But the woman standing before her today—she was the epitome of darkness. There was nothing but hate in Caillic's cruel eyes as she glared up at her.

"You would have ruled with me," said Fenelia, her heart cracking slightly as she thought of what had been lost, "We could have been true sisters—ruling side by side."

Caillic interrupted Fenelia with a loud cackle as she shook her head, "Like you would have ever allowed me to be onyour level, sister," she finished with a snarl, "Your selfish ways would never have permitted you to lower yourself enough to let me take over any aspect of Krekania. You were wonderful at pretending to our parents and making your followers fall in love with you. But the truth is, I knew what you were, even as a child. If you were not the center of attention, you would find a way to make it so. I knew, even then, what the future would look like for me if I chose to ride on the train of your cloak. I would be forgotten or cast aside eventually. My future was set in stone—until I changed it."

Fenelia shook her head, her eyes filling with tears, "No, Caillic. I would have never done that to you. I couldn't even kill you the day you murdered our parents!" she cried out, her voice taking on a desperate note as Caillic began to walk forward again, "I loved you! I always loved you—and I always will. Even now! Even after all you have done, you are still my sister! Stop this, Caillic," said Fenelia, as she tried to back away, "Please, for the love of magic, stop this. We can fix this. I won't let them kill you—we can get through this together. Please—let me help you."

Caillic's lips peeled back in an animalistic snarl as she laughed at her sister's empty words.

"Do not insult my intelligence, Fenelia," she seethed, raising her hands slowly, "Your love has made you weak. It has always made you weak—and stupid. Even now you won't kill me? After all I have done, yet you stand there willing to welcome me home? How pathetic of you. This is why you are unfit to be Queen. You were never meant to rule; you don't have what it takes to do the dirty work that a real leader must. Thankfully, I am here to relieve you of your duties—"

Just as Caillic prepared to unleash the full force of her ice magic into Fenelia, a loud crash and the sound of raging magical creatures startled the sisters out of their private battle.

Caillic whirled around, eyes flashing with fury as she watched the Army of Spellbinders pour into the throne room. Grey wolves launched themselves fearlessly onto the backs of the dark wolves, tearing and slashing with pent up fury. Unicorns unleashed their magic through their horns, aiming it full into the faces of the manticores, while the sabretooths launched themselves onto the great brutes' backs, long fangs drawing blood. The little firefoxes shot small flames from their tails, lighting several dark wolves on fire while the phoenixes dove on them from above.

But it was the woman riding atop a horned-pegasus, her eyes twin flames alight with the fire magic that raged inside her, that caused Caillic to falter.

For a moment, the Dark Sorceress saw her doom

reflected in the flash of fire that burst from the woman's hands, fully engulfing one of the manticores.

Caillic snarled, refusing to be cowed by the sudden arrival of the Army of Spellbinders and their precious Woman of Fire. The Dark Sorceress turned and glared over her shoulder at her sister. Fenelia was standing tall before the throne, smiling with pride and renewed confidence as she watched the tide of battle begin to shift in her favor.

"Your Woman of Fire is quite impressive," crooned Caillic, catching Fenelia's attention, "It's a shame she's too late to save *you*."

With a roar, Caillic released several large spears of ice from her palms, laughing manically as she watched her magic hit its mark.

With a gasp of shock, Fenelia's eyes widened in surprise as she slowly collapsed across her throne.

27

Lydall looked up just in time to see Caillic raise her hands toward Fenelia. She heard herself scream, tearing her throat to shreds as she tried in vain to warn the Queen. Lydall watched helplessly as the spears of ice went through Fenelia, sending her body sprawling across the throne.

Lydall slid off Triton and began to run. She saw nothing but the flames dancing in her eyes as she raced forward. The fire magic flowed through her veins and she could feel it beginning to pool in her hands, ready to be unleashed once more.

Caillic already knew what was coming for her the moment she shot the ice spears at her sister. The moment they sliced through Fenelia's body, Caillic moved. She leapt deftly off the steps that led to the throne and began to slide through the throng of fighting creatures. She could sense Lydall's rage as the Woman of Fire pursued her with deadly intent.

But Caillic also knew that, like her sister, Lydall's obsession with love would cause her to slow her pursuit and turn back to try and save the dying Queen. Caillic laughed wickedly at that thought. Not only would this allow her to move further from the Woman of Fire, but Lydall's attempt to save the Queen would be in vain. The Queen of Krekania would be pronounced dead in a few moments—and Caillic, as the rightful heir, would be declared their new ruler.

The Woman of Fire was too late.

...

Lydall felt her entire world spinning out of control as she raced toward the throne, watching as Fenelia's blood began to pour onto the floor.

They were too late. They should have moved faster. The Queen was dying and there was nothing they could do to save her.

"Fenelia!" screamed Lydall as she threw herself before the throne, desperately running her hands over the Queen's body as she tried to stop the flow of blood.

Fenelia's brown eyes flickered slightly in recognition as she numbly watched Lydall's hands begin to glow. The Woman of Fire was channeling her healing magic, desperately trying to save her.

"Enough," gargled Fenelia, her throat filling with blood, "Don't waste—your energy—"

"No!" shouted Lydall, eyes blazing with the power of her magic, "I won't give up on you. You're the Queen—we need you *here*, Fenelia!"

Fenelia smiled weakly as she reached out for Lydall's hands, "No—Krekania does not need me anymore," her eyes glimmering with sadness and regret, "I tried to serve them...the best that I could. But I failed. My reign ends today—and yours, Woman of Fire—your reign begins."

Lydall's eyes flashed with panic as she stared down at the Queen, "No! I'm not ready for that! You're going to be fine, hang on, just let me—"

"Lydall, enough," growled Fenelia, her hand tightening on Lydall's wrist, "Your time has come. This is what was prophesied. I always knew—that this is how I would die. I made my peace with it—a long time ago."

Lydall felt the tears beginning to well up in her eyes as the

Queen's grip faltered. Fenelia dropped her arm down to her side, the blood loss quickly weakening her.

"Be strong, Lydall," she murmured quietly, "Woman of Fire. The Chosen One. Lead them with love. Lead them with light—and always remember, power is not held by the darkness, but by those who control the light."

Fenelia closed her eyes and sighed, her body growing limp as her life blood steadily spilled out onto the throne room floor.

Lydall felt as if the world had completely upended. Her head felt light and her stomach clenched as she staggered to her feet, disoriented and in shock. The Queen was dead. The Queen of Krekania—was dead.

The Seer emerged from behind the throne, silent and black as a shadow, his eyes ablaze with magical light and his lips pulled back in an uncharacteristic snarl.

Lydall gazed at him as if she were in a fog. It felt as if she were watching the scene unfold in someone else's body. Surely this wasn't real? This wasn't happening to them. Fenelia couldn't be dead. This was a dream or a vision. She would wake up soon and the world would make sense again.

The Seer raised his head and unleashed a booming howl that rose above the cacophony of battle and seemed to pierce right through Lydall's ear drums. The magical creatures around her, dark and light, stopped fighting and cringed against the harsh sound, whimpering slightly in confusion as they sought out the source of the noise.

"Silence!" shouted Corvus as the massive unicorn reared up in the air, "The Seer has something to say!"

The Seer gave a quick nod to the unicorn, their eyes meeting briefly.

"Queen Fenelia of Krekania is dead!" snarled the Seer,

his eyes wide and glaring while all the ornaments and baubles on his giant antlers glowed as he summoned the ancient Krekanian magic.

Cries of dismay and horror echoed in the throne room while Caillic's dark army roared in victory at the news.

The Seer cried out again, silencing the creatures, "Krekania has chosen its new queen! It has called me forth to announce her name and crown her on this day!"

The announcement was met with a tense silence as everyone braced themselves for who their new ruler would be.

Caillic hovered along the edge of the throng, her eyes glittering with excitement. Of all the creatures and beings in Krekania, she was now the most powerful. Her sister's magic had always been stronger, and now that Fenelia was dead, Caillic would be the natural successor. Krekania always chose the most powerful beings to become its ruler. Knowing this, Caillic stepped forward and prepared to accept her new position—the one thing she had been working toward for so many years—the one she had sacrificed everything for.

"Krekania has chosen!" snarled the Seer, his eyes wild and froth beginning to form at the edges of his mouth as he turned to gaze down to the blood-soaked woman crouched before him.

"Lydall of Histair has been named the rightful Queen of Krekania!"

Caillic screeched in fury, ice flying from her hands and burying itself into the nearby creatures and the walls of the throne room.

"I am the rightful queen!" she snarled, stalking forward, "I killed Fenelia! I am the next in line! Who is *she* to claim such a title?"

Lydall was standing stock-still, her green eyes wide as she thought back to every conversation she'd ever had with

Fenelia and the Seer. Every prophecy, every vision, every prediction had led to this moment. She knew deep down that one day this would happen, but she had not prepared for it to be so soon. She still had not recovered from the shock of Fenelia dying across her own thrown before the Seer had appeared. Now, she was frozen with utter disbelief as she watched the Dark Sorceress rage in the center of the room.

The Seer snarled, his muzzle pulled back to reveal his sharp fangs, his eyes glaring wildly as he locked in on Caillic.

"You are questioning the very magic of Krekania!" he roared, his voice shaking the ground beneath them, "Magic has chosen Lydall. Magic chose the Woman of Fire long ago when you first destroyed the rightful King and Queen of the land. Magic decided when she would arrive here and magic has brought her to this place today. The Woman of Fire is fulfilling the destiny set forth by a power far above our own. To deny such a thing is to declare war on the ancient magic itself!"

Caillic laughed sadistically, her eyes glowing with power-lust and ice magic as she snarled up in Lydall and the Seer's faces, "Then I declare war on the ancient magic of Krekania! I declare war on the Woman of Fire and all who foolishly follow this child! I am the rightful heir to the throne; she is nothing more than a human child from a land without magic! Who is she to lead you all? I wield the most powerful magic in all of Krekania!"

Caillic turned to face the throng of Spellbinders and her own dark army, "I will make this land what it was always meant to be! Not this weak, pathetic excuse for a kingdom. Follow me and I will lead you all to greatness!" she screamed, gazing wildly around the room, hands raised above her head, as she tried to rally the creatures.

Lydall stared at Caillic as she slowly stood up from

Fenelia's cooling body. Her limbs felt numb and her mind felt detached from everything happening around her. Nothing felt real. It was like a living nightmare. She kept staring at Caillic, fixated as the Sorceress continued raging, looking more and more deranged by the moment.

"No," Lydall heard herself say. Something inside of her was speaking, urging her to stand up, to say something. She felt the fire inside of her begin to glow on its own, as if the ancient magic of Krekania itself was urging her to act.

Caillic whipped around, eyes narrowed as she hissed between her teeth, ice forming in the palm of her hands.

"You think you are strong because you kill those you see as a threat," said Lydall, the magic beginning to coil inside of her, "You thought Fenelia was your enemy—that your parents were the enemy. You believe anyone who may have slighted you is worthy of destruction. You take no responsibility for your actions, but instead blame and destroy everyone around you. Your power is fueled by darkness and that will always make you weak…weaker than me."

"Queen Lydall!" shouted Jasper from among the throng of watching creatures, his eyes alight with pride as he pumped his fist into the air and began to chant, "Queen Lydall! Queen Lydall! Queen Lydall!"

"Queen Lydall!" joined in Corvus as he reared up on his hind legs, urging the other creatures to voice their approval.

Syllus, Armus, and Nyra picked up the chant, voices raised and fists pumping. The Army of Spellbinders roared, howled, and voiced their agreement, drowning out Caillic's furious snarls.

Lydall raised a hand to silence the Army, her eyes never leaving Caillic's furiously cold stare.

"You're nothing," seethed Caillic as she put her foot on the first stair, edging closer to Lydall, "I was born into magic, raised by it, and strengthened by it. I am much more than you will ever be, child. You are foolish to stand against me. Relinquish your right to the throne and I'll spare your pathetic little existence."

A smile, that didn't quite reach Lydall's eyes, slowly spread across her face as she stared fully into the face of the woman who had already taken so much from her.

"You are a fool, Caillic," she said, laughing slightly, "You believe you are powerful because you sold your soul to the darkness, but the truth is…'power is not held by the darkness, but by those who control the light.'"

The Seer threw back his head and howled as Lydall recited the final words of the prophecy—Fenelia's final words. His baubles began to flare and swirls of magical power began to move around his body in golden, glittering coils as he gave himself over to the full power of the ancient Krekanian magic. The Seer laughed joyously as he felt the overwhelming intensity of it, knowing in that moment he was one with Krekania itself.

Opening his narrow jaw, the Seer spoke with a voice that was not his own. It was the voice of the long-dead, the most powerful beings to ever exist in Krekania, returning through the Seer. Their voices combined to create a powerful, booming sound that echoed loudly in the throne room: "Long live the Queen!"

The Krekanians roared in agreement while Caillic screamed, her white hair flying wildly around her face as she glared up at Lydall, hate filling her black eyes.

She opened her mouth to challenge the new Queen, but the Woman of Fire did not give the Dark Sorceress the chance. Feeling an overpowering rush of magic, Lydall unleashed the fire within, aiming for Caillic's heart.

The Dark Sorceress raised her hands and unleashed her ice magic to shield herself, screaming in fear and fury as the two forces collided together. A wave of magical force washed over the cavernous room, startling the creatures as they stared in awe at their leaders battling on the steps in front of the throne.

Lydall cried out as she felt the force of Caillic's ice magic pushing back against her fire. She growled as she fought back, willing the dark-fueled magic to falter. Caillic's magic felt similar to the way Archer's did, but significantly more powerful. It had a touch of temptation to it that beckoned her to give in, but Lydall was far removed from being able to be manipulated by the darkness. Her fire raged and increased its strength as the two streams of magic roared and sparked against one another.

Slipping through the distracted mass of creatures, Archer smiled to himself, pleased with his own cunning. He slunk along in the shadows, remaining largely unnoticed as he drew closer and closer to where his brother stood. It had been a long time since he had seen the elf responsible for the loss of Tiela. He hated Jasper for his continued existence in the world. If Jasper had just stayed away, Tiela would have been his. She would have never hesitated to be with him instead of his weak, cowardly sibling.

He remembered what it had felt like to take the young, pretty elf. He tempted her using his magic, using just enough to convince her to follow him into the woods that night. He remembered how he drew close to her, ready to kiss her, and how she had pulled away from him. She professed her love for Jasper and Archer had felt a rage unlike any he had ever felt in his life. Jasper. Of all elves. The favored brother. The brother who everyone loved and respected. The one that had caused him to always be forgotten.

He and Caillic had bonded over their hatred for their favored siblings and the things they had cost them both. How good it was going to feel to finally have them both dead, and to take back what he and Caillic had earned.

Archer smiled slightly as he paused, just a few feet away

from the Captain of the Army of Spellbinders. When Tiela had refused him, Archer had unleashed all of his magic on her. She didn't know how to refuse him after that. He had taken her, made her his, and then destroyed her. Nothing had ever felt so good or so satisfying. Perhaps killing his brother would make him feel just as happy. Then he could enjoy himself with Caillic when the battle was won and celebrate their victory together.

Archer nearly growled out loud at the thought of being with Caillic after all this bloodshed. Their best moments together had always been after the bloodiest of raids. And this union would top them all.

With a final grin full of madness and desire, Archer lunged forward…and plunged his dagger into Jasper's side.

28

Jasper felt the knife slice into his body. He cried out in surprise at the unexpected attack and fell to the ground hard, hand gripping his side as the blood began to flow. He moved deftly to the side, scrambling to quickly regain his footing. Whoever had attacked him was sure to do it again and he was determined not to let them catch him off guard a second time.

Jasper's cry of pain drew attention away from the throne as the mass of creatures turned to see what caused the disturbance. The moment the Spellbinders realized what had happened to their captain, they roared with rage and leapt upon the dark army, their fury lending them energy as the battle began to surge once more.

"Jasper!" screamed Nyra as she turned in time see the elf hit the ground.

Lydall felt a thrill of fear course through her as she heard Jasper's cry of pain and Nyra's scream through the blinding light and roar of the clashing magical forces. She forcedherself to take her eyes off Caillic for a moment to see what had happened. In the middle of the throne room, among the creatures wrestling in the throes of battle, stood Jasper, clutching his side as blood poured out of a fresh wound. In front of him stood a tall elf, muscles bunching as he prepared to attack again.

Lydall's panic fueled her rage. Jasper was about to be killed by Archer and she couldn't help him because of the Sorceress. Once again, Caillic was going to cost her someone that she loved. That realization sent Lydall's fury over the edge.

With a cry of outrage Lydall felt herself lose control. No longer did she possess fire magic; it possessed her. She became the fire, knowing nothing but the righteous, burning rage that overtook all her senses in an instant. She gave herself over to the magic, trusting in it and in Krekania's power alone.

When the fire finally began to recede from her vision, Lydall looked around her wildly. With a sinking feeling in her stomach, she caught a glimpse of the Dark Sorceress as the woman fled.

Caillic's face was contorted with pain and she held her hands protectively against her body. The Sorceress had evaded the explosion of fire from Lydall, but only after she had been thoroughly singed from the flames. Lydall's fire had overcome her ice magic and attacked the source of Caillic's—her hands.

Lydall snarled in frustration as she realized that she didn't have time to purse the Dark Sorceress. Part of her knew that she needed to follow the wicked woman and finish what she started, but her heart was screaming at her to get to Jasper. Lydall prayed that she was not too late and that Archer hadn't already finished what he'd started. Caillic would have to wait.

Racing down from the throne, Lydall charged into the fray, dodging battling creatures as she pushed forward to the place she had last seen Jasper.

She narrowly avoided running into Triton as her fearless destrier unleashed a stream of fire magic from his horn right into the face of Caillic's fiery bull. The huge beast cried out in pain as Triton pushed his attack. Corvus galloped to Triton's side, his horn alight with bright white magic as he unleashed the full force of his mighty power into the brute. Together, Corvus and Triton combined their streams of magic and pushed forward. The bull gave a great cry of distress as his body began to disintegrate, unable to maintain its form under the onslaught of the indomitable stallions' magic.

Nyra and Armus were back to back as they slashed viciously at a charging group of black wolves. Syllus was helping two sabretooth cats eliminate another group of dark wolves, while the two firefoxes, Aidan and Shula, were shooting flames from the ends of their tails. They cackled with pleasure as they sent a dark wolf running, tail tucked between his legs with half of his fur singed off his body. The Seer had also joined in the fight, frothing at the mouth with unhinged rage as he unleashed magic from the dangling bobbles on his antlers.

Dionysus clawed a manticore's face as he screeched out his battle cry, eyes blazing as he turned to face the next foe. Augustine and Mallen fought side by side, scratching and stomping on the dark wolves that leapt at them from all sides. Augustine's dangerous claws raked down across the muzzle of a black wolf who had leapt onto Mallen's back, while the pegasus kicked another in the head with his hooves, face contorted with anger.

A group of wood nymphs suddenly emerged from the woods. The shy, forest-made creatures looked uncharacteristically fierce as they summoned their magic. The little stick and leaf figures squeezed their eyes shut as they used their magic to throw logs, branches, and other forest debris into the faces of Caillic's dark army.

The phoenixes flew over the battle, shooting flames and launching attacks from above. The little owl-like strigs leapt down, slashing with their long claws before quickly retreating to the rafters before the dark wolves and manticores could retaliate.

The sound of battle echoed throughout the Castle. The merfolk heard the commotion from where they were swimming peacefully in the Lagoon and leapt onto the massive rock structure in the center of the pool. Together, they closed their eyes and clasped their hands together, focusing their magic and telepathically lending their strength to the Army battling the darkness in the throne room.

While the battle raged on, Lydall looked around the devastated throne room in a panic, desperate for any glimpse of Jasper. Finally, she caught sight of him. He was circling slowly across from Archer, the two brothers facing off with a lifetime of rage echoing between them.

Lydall moved swiftly as she pushed through the surging group of animals. She nearly slipped in a pool of blood as she desperately tried to reach the elf captain.

Jasper saw Lydall out of the corner of his eye and glanced over at her briefly, still circling his fiercebrother.

"Lydall, no!" he hissed through his teeth, "This ismy fight—my battle. Leave Archer to me."

Lydall felt her heart stutter in fear at his words. She knew what Jasper was capable of, but she also knew first-hand what Archer's dark abilities felt like. The years of deep-seeded hatred would only fuel his magic.

But as she made that brief eye-contact with the elf she had fallen in love with—she knew he was right. Lydall could feel the strength of her love for him in her very soul, making her chest ache with longing to stand by his side, but she knew this was something he had to do on his own—despite what it was costing her. To stand silent as he fought this final, deadly battle against his brother was tantamount to torture. She knew in her heart that one of them would not survive this day.

Lydall noticed the wound in Jasper's side and felt her stomach summersault. She studied it for a moment as Jasper circled back around closer to where she stood and gave a little sigh of relief. The dagger that Archer had used to try and stab Jasper had glanced off a piece of the metal armor Effie had designed. She sent a silent prayer of thanks to her friend, closing her eyes for a brief moment against the now-familiar stab of pain Effie's memory caused.

Archer lunged forward suddenly, startling Lydall as she watched with horror as the dark elf's blade narrowly missed Jasper's skull. Jasper snarled at his brother as he moved deftly to the side, his twin blades slicing through the air so fast that Lydall lost sight of them for a moment.

Archer cried out in pain and put a hand on his arm, cursing Jasper as he realized he was bleeding. Archer's eyes seemed to glow with hate as he darted in again and the brothers' swords slammed into each other with a loud clang and a shower of sparks. They moved with a speed that made Lydall's head spin, trading blow for blow.

Lydall felt sick as she realized that, although Jasper was wounding his brother several times, Archer was returning the favor. Their blood dripped onto the ground beneath them as the brothers began to pant with exhaustion.

"What's wrong, Jasper?" laughed Archer as he noticed how hard Jasper was breathing, "Not quite as strong as you thought, eh? You should reconsider your allegiance. The power of dark magic is tenfold the magic you weak Krekanians cling to. Wouldn't it feel so good to have real magic? Real power?"

Jasper cringed as he felt his brother send a silent wave of his manipulative magic over him. He felt the sudden desire to lay down his twin swords and swear allegiance to the darkness. Suddenly, the thought of walking away from his position as Captain of the Army of Spellbinders felt like the right thing to do.

Shaking his head Jasper growled and yelled in frustration, "Enough of your lies! You forget I know what you are! I know what you did to Tiela. You manipulated and used her! You took her innocence from her and then you killed her—all because she didn't love you like she loved me. Then you tried to do it to Lydall! You have used your deceitful magic to take away everything and everyone that ever mattered to me. It ends tonight."

Archer threw back his head and laughed at Jasper's threat, "You're truly pathetic, you know that?" he asked, circling slowly, "It would almost be sad if it were not so amusing. You honestly think you've made the right decision, standing where you stand now? You really think your little human girlfriend over there can actually rule Krekania better than Caillic? Perhaps brother, it is you who are deceived—and without the use of my magic. I'm only trying to show you the light."

"I found my own, thanks," sneered Jasper as he readied his blades, "Her name is Lydall—the Woman of Fire and the rightful Queen of Krekania."

Lyall felt the fire within her stir at Jasper's words. She smiled despite the chaos raging around them. In that moment Lydall had never felt more powerful. She turned around, momentarily distracted, as she heard the sound of a familiar wolf crying out in pain.

Zephyr was laying on the ground, wincing as a spear of ice pierced through his shoulder. Above him stood Caillic, laughing mercilessly as she spread her hands, preparing to unleash her ice magic onto the alpha of the grey winged-wolves.

"Caillic no!" roared Lydall as she felt the force of her fire magic welling up inside of her.

The Sorceress looked up briefly, hesitating just long enough for Lydall to gain ground as she raced across the room. Jasper would have to finish his battle completely on his own now. She was the Queen of Krekania—and her people needed her.

Lydall charged straight into the Sorceress, flinging her several feet away from Zephyr. She stood, chest heaving with effort and glared down at the woman below her.

Caillic scrambled to her feet, her eyes sparking with indignation and her face contorted in a snarl as she stalked forward, ice magic forming in her hands.

Lydall looked over at the injured alpha wolf and sent another grateful prayer to the magic of Krekania as she saw him limping steadily away. The wound looked painful, but not life-threatening, and Lydall knew he would survive.

The Seer caught sight of Zephyr and ran to his side, sniffing the wound gingerly as he helped guide the wolf to the far side of the room. He glanced at Lydall and gave her a quick nod, letting her know he would heal their injured friend with his ancient magic.

Lydall sighed with relief and turned her attention back to Caillic. She raised her hands as her fire magic began to form. She felt a twinge of guilt for not finishing the job earlier. Now, because of her choice to check on Jasper instead of go after Caillic, Zephyr was injured. Lydall would not make that mistake again. She snarled with fury at the Sorceress, fire encasing her hands as she stalked forward.

"Why don't you pick on somebody your own size, Caillic?"

Caillic laughed cruelly as she turned to Lydall, her eyes dark with fury, "Like you? Oh little Woman of Fire you know nothing of true power. Allow me to show you?"

Without warning, Caillic lashed out, ice shooting from her hands straight into Lydall's face. Lydall blocked the blast just in time with her flames and leapt to the side, eyes never leaving Caillic's.

"You can call me Queen now," she retorted, throwing a powerful jet of fire at the Sorceress.

Lydall's words seemed to enrage Caillic. The Sorceress began throwing ice-spears at Lydall, one after the other until she was bent over, gasping for breath after unleashing so much of her ice magic at once.

Lydall took the opportunity to attack, the fire hitting its mark and throwing the Sorceress to the ground. Caillic howled with pain as the fire burned through her long dark robes.

The Sorceress quickly used her ice magic to put out the flames, but the burning flesh on her stomach and arms made her cry out again. The burns across her stomach oozed blood and made Caillic hiss with pain. Furious, she rose to her feet, wincing as she threw ice at Lydall, slicing The Woman of Fire's arm open with a large sliver.

Lydall screamed with rage and pain, the injury only intensifying her magic. She had learned that the stronger her emotions became, the more powerful the magic inside her burned. Rushing forward, Lydall and Caillic locked in on each other, their magic colliding in a shower of sparks.

As Caillic and Lydall continued their fierce battle, a strangled cry resonated through the blood-soaked throne room. Caillic's eyes grew wide with disbelief as she tossed aside Lydall's stream of fire, causing the younger woman to stumble. Caillic hurried away from Lydall and peered over the bodies of the tussling creatures. The Sorceress knew that cry anywhere and her heart sank with dread as she scanned the blood-soaked room.

An unearthly scream suddenly came from Caillic's mouth, startling everyone in the Castle. The fighting stopped momentarily as all the creatures turned to see the cause of the Sorceress' cry.

An elf was lying in a pool of blood, unmoving. His features were almost indistinguishable with all the blood and injuries that covered his broken body.

Lydall let out a shaky breath of relief when she saw Jasper standing over him, blades drawn and dripping with blood—but alive. They made eye-contact and Lydall gave him a weak smile and a nod of acknowledgement.

Archer—Jasper's brother—was dead.

29

Caillic's cries of shock and despair echoed through the throne room. Her dark beasts froze, hesitating as they stared at their leader. They had never heard her make these sounds before—and their captain was lying dead in a pool of his own blood. A ripple of indecision and fear spread throughout the dark horde as the creatures began to glance at one another, doubt and uncertainty in their eyes.

Caillic looked around the room, her eyes wild and unseeing. Finally, after taking several deep breaths and trying to steady herself, Caillic looked up, her eyes finding Jasper's. An animalistic snarl contorted the Sorceress' face as she braced herself, preparing to attack the Captain of the Army of Spellbinders in a fit of vengeful rage.

"Caillic!" barked Lydall, streams of fire coiling around her arms and her eyes glowing like burning embers as she glowered at the Dark Sorceress.

Caillic glanced over her shoulder at Lydall, her eyes narrowed into tiny, dark slits as she bared her teeth, snarling back in defiance.

Lydall stalked forward quickly, deadly intent behind her fiery gaze as she lifted her hands.

"Now you know what it feels like to lose someone you love," she roared, "Your reign is over! Never again will anyone know pain at your hands. You'll take no more lives tonight, Caillic—it ends now."

Lydall shot forward, fire flaring out before her as she charged the Dark Sorceress, "For Effie!" she screamed as she gave herself over to the magic.

Lydall channeled all of her pent-up rage and pain into the magic, letting it fuel the flames as they burned brighter than ever before. A tidal wave of fire poured out of her, burning everything within sight.

When Lydall's vision returned, she realized she was on her hands and knees, gasping for air. She glanced around, looking for what had become of Caillic, and noticed that the remaining members of her dark horde were—fleeing.

The Krekanians and the Army of Spellbinders roared in triumph as they took down the dark beasts that tried to escape. The tide had turned. The death of Archer and the panic of their queen had shaken them to their core. What little remained of the dark army fled from the Castle, eyes wide with terror and disbelief at their own defeat.

"Where is she?" demanded Lydall as Jasper approached her, "Where did Caillic go? What happened?"

Jasper helped Lydall to her feet, wincing from his own wounds, "She's gone. You turned into fire—and the fire lashed out. You struck down several of her beasts," he added, pointing out several charred-looking animal forms, "Your magic targeted the darkness and destroyed it. It was like the magic was—alive," he added, eyes glowing in awe and pride as he gazed at Lydall, "Caillic disappeared into the crowd before the fire could consume her too. She's gone, but her army is destroyed. We've won."

Lydall's eyes flickered with doubt, "How can we have won while she still lives?"

"You burned her pretty bad," said Nyra as she and the other elves approached, "I'd say she's done for."

"We can send some of the uninjured wolves from Zephyr's pack to go track her down," suggested Armus, "Have them find her and kill her, or bring her back here for judgement."

Lydall nodded slowly, "Have them kill her. I never want to see her again and I don't care who does it—she can never come back. She can never do this to us again."

Nyra smiled in satisfaction and gave Lydall an approving nod, "You'll make a great Queen, Lydall."

Lydall gave the black-haired elf a quick smile before she turned to look at the destruction Caillic had left behind. Broken, dying, and dead bodies littered the once-beautiful throne room. Blood drenched the flora, or what was leftof it, and the light that had once shown so brightly had died out completely. She felt the absence of magic like a sharp pain in her chest. Every breath she took in this room full of death made her weary.

"Have Zephyr and his wolves go now," ordered Lydall, "The Seer should be done healing him. The rest of us need to repair what has been broken, bury our dead, and send those who survived to the infirmary to do what we can. We need to restore this sacred place as soon as possible. All of her darkness must be cast out and replaced with the light."

Syllus frowned slightly, "She's destroyed so much. How do we replace what's been taken? We've never found a way to create magic once it's been tainted with the darkness."

A voice inside Lydall's head told her the answer. She gasped in surprise as the thought came to her so clearly, as if someone had whispered it in her ear. She looked around in bewilderment, alarm sparking in her gaze as she tried to find the source of the information now running through her mind.

"Queen Lydall," spoke the Seer as he and Corvus walked over to the group of elves. The strange creature had a gleam of amusement and understanding in hisyellow eyes as he and Corvus walked alongside one another, "You are now as close to magic as I am—and as Fenelia once was. This is a gift Krekania has bestowed upon you. You have proven yourself worthy of the power and responsibility of being the true ruler of Krekania, and now the ancient magic is yours to wield."

Lydall gazed down at the Seer in awe as she slowly realized the voice she heard in her head—was the ancient magic of Krekania.

The Seer bowed his head low, his lithe body crisscrossed with claw marks from the many dark wolves he had fought. Corvus also bowed low, his pure-white coat now covered in dark masses of blood, some his own and some his enemies'.

"We would like to be your advisors as you repair Krekania and restore it to greatness," said Corvus as his intelligent eyes studied Lydall, "It would be an honor to serve and protect you, my Queen."

Lydall smiled as she felt warmth course through her. The power of the love and loyalty she felt from those around her lent energy to her weary body and soul.

"And I would be honored to have you both by my side," she said, choking slightly with emotion as her eyes filled with tears, "Let's begin our duty to our fallen friends," she added sadly, "Those who have fought and died for us—they deserve the utmost respect. There is a field right outside the Castle. We should bury them there and, once we are able to restore the Castle, we should plant the brightest flora full of the strongest magic to light their resting place. We'll make it a memorial to their bravery so that no one forgets what happened here today and what they did to save Krekania."

"I think that is a wonderful idea," murmured Jasper as he laid a hand on Lydall's shoulder, "I'll see to that right way."

The Captain of the Army of Spellbinders moved through the magical creatures, doling out orders and beginning to help with the difficult task of removing the bodies of their fallen friends.

Lydall watched as Jasper organized the members of his Army that had only suffered mild injuries, while the Seer and Zephyr began to organize a hunting party to track down Caillic. The Seer was murmuring in wolf-language to Zephyr, giving the alpha instructions based on his visions, before the wolf and his pack took off into the woods.

Lydall smiled to herself again. Despite the death and destruction around them, they were together. In her heart of hearts Lydall knew that they would recover from this, and not only would they recover…she knew they would also thrive.

She felt a sharp pain in her chest as an image of Fenelia crossed her mind. The former Queen knew all along that she would die in this battle and that Lydall would be named the new Queen. She wished Fenelia had trusted her with this knowledge. Perhaps she didn't want Lydall to feel the unnecessary pressure or the crushing weight of responsibility that came with being Queen until she was ready.

Lydall smiled slightly at the thought. Suddenly, she felt the power of the ancient magic coil and twist inside of her, burning her from the inside out with energy and strength. She may not have been ready for it then, but she felt more than prepared to take over as the rightful Queen of Krekania *now*.

Lydall walked over and laid her hand on a crushed magical fern. Its vibrant colors had been snuffed out by Caillic's dark magic and it lay crumpled and grey on the ground. She closed her eyes and felt her magic flow from inside her into the damaged plant. Almost immediately the plant straightened, its bright purple, pink, and green colors coming to life as it glowed full of Krekanian magic once again.

With a bright smile and green eyes sparkling, Lydall moved throughout the room, pouring her magic into the injured creatures and the crushed plants.

And for the first time—it did not make her weary.

…

Zephyr's pack moved swiftly through the woods, following the trail of dark magic that led in a straight line from the Castle to the heart of the Krekanian wilderness.

Snarling quietly, Zephyr led his wolves steadily forward, his eyes glowing with hate. This woman had destroyed half of his pack, injured him with her ice, and killed his sabretooth friend along with the small elf. The wolves had managed to destroy most of Caillic's horde, but the Dark Sorceress herself had escaped. That thought sent a thrill of rage through Zephyr. The villainous woman could not continue to live. No matter how tired he was, the alpha knew he would not be able to rest until the woman's blood stained his teeth.

His orders were clear. The Seer had translated Queen Lydall's words so that there would be no doubt: kill the Dark Sorceress. The new Queen had no use for bringing the foul creature back alive. The judgement had already been passed. Death would find the Sorceress today and it would be at his teeth.

Zephyr let his tongue loll out of his jaw as he thought about how good it would feel to taste her blood in his mouth—to watch it drain from her body—to give her a taste of the pain she had caused all of them for so long.

Stretching his wings wide, Zephyr made himself look even more massive as he slowed down. The trail was getting stronger and it tasted fresh as he drank in the morning air. He heard the anxious whines of his pack behind him as they also noticed how close they were drawing to the vile woman.

Zephyr folding his wings back in tight against his body as he indicated to the rest of his pack to move as silent as shadows. They slipped between the trees, heads low with deadly stares as they stalked forward. As they neared the edge of the wood line, Zephyr tilted his head in confusion. Just a few feet from the woods stood a massive rock, jutting straight out of the earth. It hummed with ancient magic and was covered in bizarre symbols.

It was here where the scent of dark magic disappeared.

…

Lydall felt her heart ache as she helped Nyra lift Fenelia's body off the throne. They gently closed her eyes and smoothed out her long black hair, trying to make her appear as elegant in death as she had in life. Laying her gently on a stretch of cloth, Lydall and Nyra carried Fenelia's body toward the large carriage where Triton stood waiting.

Lydall had a momentary flashback to when she, Nyra, and Triton had taken this same carriage to the Castle. They had been bringing back the injured creatures from the attack Caillic led on Catha and had reunited the two young firefoxes. That trip had been stressful, but significantly less sorrowful. At least most of the creatures they had transported had been able to be saved. This time, Triton would be transporting the dead to their final resting place.

Dionysus, Augustine, and Mallen helped organize the other creatures into two groups based on the severity of their injuries. Lydall quickly walked over to join them and began placing her hands on the broken creatures, slowly but surely restoring their magic and healing their wounds.

"How are you doing that?" asked Armus, raising an eyebrow in surprise, "I thought it drained you of your energy?"

"I—I'm not sure," said Lydall, smiling faintly, "I think something happened during the battle—when I became Queen. I think it may be part of the ancient magic

Krekania has given me. I feel stronger—and more capable. I just hope it lasts so I can heal them all."

"Fenelia's power increased when she was made Queen," said the Seer as he helped place another dead unicorn on the carriage, "She was able to understand animals and speak to them, but once she was made Queen she was able to communicate with them telepathically. It made her a great ruler who truly understood her people. Krekania has chosen to give you a fierce power to protect and heal. It most likely chose to increase the abilities you already had."

Lydall smiled a little as she closed her eyes and poured her magic into a struggling griffon. The young creature stood up, spreading his wings and squawking in surprise when he realized his broken limbs were restored. He screeched with joy and flapped them rapidly as he soared to the very top of the domed roof.

"I am glad they chose to give me this power," she said, smiling as the young griffon flew around with glee, "This is the most rewarding thing I have ever done."

Corvus nodded in acknowledgement, "Your heart is fierce and full of love. Those are two important qualities in a powerful leader. Both will serve you well in the days to come."

The hours went by quickly as the remaining creatures and elves worked to restore the throne room. The blood would take time to absorb into the earthen floor, but the flora glowed bright once again. Some of the inhabitants of the Castle even began to settle back into their old homes, the renewal of hope putting light back into their weary gazes.

Jasper and his crew finished digging the graves for the creatures who had died. The bodies of the dark horde were thrown into the fast-flowing river that bordered one side of the Castle grounds. Lydall wanted those abominations as far from their home as possible. Cleaning out the darkness was imperative to properly restoring the Krekanian magic to its former glory…and such creatures did not deserve the honor of a burial.

Lydall felt a weariness in her bones that she had never felt before. The ancient magic had strengthened her since she had been declared Queen, but even now she was beginning to tire. She glanced around at the other creatures and realized they were feeling the same level of exhaustion. Heads and tails drooping, the creatures kept moving, eager to finish their assignments and rest.

Just as they began to finish, Zephyr's booming howl interrupted their momentary peace.

"Have they found her?" asked Lydall as she turned to the Seer.

The Seer's face was grave and his eyes flashed with surprise and fury as he turned to face Lydall.

"Zephyr says the Sorceress' trail has disappeared," he growled.

"Disappeared? How is that possible?" asked Jasper, moving to stand next to Lydall, "Where could she have gone that the winged-wolves couldn't follow?"

The Seer frowned, lowering his head with exhaustion and despair.

"Caillic's trail disappeared into a large standing stone— An Chloch."

Lydall felt her world shift on its axis. She clutched her stomach and bent over as bile rose into her throat. Her eyes were wide with horror when she looked back up at Jasper.

"Caillic," she whispered, "Caillic—is in Histair.

30

"What do you mean she's in Histair?" asked Jasper, his face contorted in confusion and horror, "You mean—your home?"

Lydall was bent over, her breath coming out in ragged gasps as she tried to wrap her mind around what this meant for her—and her family.

"How...how did this happen?" she stammered, her heart and mind racing.

"An Chloch is only supposed to appear when Krekania has a great need of it," said Jasper, his temper flaring, "How can it be that it appeared for Caillic? What good could that possibly do?"

The Seer sighed, his ears hanging low in resignation, "For Krekania, Caillic leaving can do nothing but good," he explained, "For Lydall and her world in Histair, this could be devastating. But for Krekania—it means Caillic is truly gone. The magic would never allow An Chloch to bring her back."

Lydall slowly straightened back up, trying to regain control of her emotions. She gazed around the room. The elves looked shocked and stricken by the news and the other creatures were looking around in confusion, notunderstanding the sudden shift of emotions. Zephyr and his pack of winged-wolves stalked into the throne room, agitation coming off them in waves. They had been unable to unleash their fury in a final showdown against the Dark Sorceress and their frustrated energy filled the room as they snarled quietly among themselves.

Zephyr collapsed on the floor in an angry and tired huff, eyes still blazing in rage.

"So—what does this mean for Histair?" asked Jasper, glancing over at Lydall in concern.

"It means that Caillic gets a chance to start over," replied Corvus, his ears flicking angrily, "She will have the opportunity to have a new life, but one without the full force of her dark magic. For An Chloch does not allow the full power of magic to cross into the non-magical world. Her evil-spirited soul, however, will remain intact, so she can still cause a great deal of destruction and pain wherever she goes—and knowing Caillic that is exactly what she will do."

"She will still manipulate and lie to get her way," said Lydall quietly, her eyes glittering with rage and disbelief, "She'll do whatever it takes to get what she wants. Which means—my family is in serious danger."

Jasper turned to look at the Seer, "How do we know she's in Histair? There are dozens of other realms in the universe. What if it sent her to another one?"

The Seer sighed and looked at the ground, "Krekania lent me a vision of Caillic stepping out into the bright green grasslands on the outskirts of Lydall's land. There is no doubt. She is in Histair.

Jasper frowned, glancing between the Seer and Corvus as he moved closer to Lydall, "So what do we do? How do we find her and stop her?"

The Seer looked up and gave Lydall a steady, wise look from his ancient eyes, "You have passed through An Chloch once before now," he said, his voice gravelly and deep, "Perhaps you can pass through again. Caillic's ability to harm your former world would cause you great distress and affect your ability to lead Krekania properly…perhaps that is enough for the ancient magic to allow you to leave Krekania and return to Histair."

"Leave?" asked Jasper, looking to Lydall with bewilderment in his eyes, "But you were just named Queen of Krekania. We just buried Fenelia. There's no way Krekania will let you leave after all that!"

Corvus shook his massive head, his long white mane cascading down his neck, "You must trust the magic of Krekania, Captain—and you must trust your Queen."

Lydall gazed up into Jasper's anxious eyes, feeling her heart tear in half as she made her decision.

"They are my family," she whispered, "I left them to make my own way—I abandoned them so I could live in freedom. The least I can do is make sure that the world I have chosen as my home does not cause the destruction of theirs. Caillic escaped because I didn't go after her when she fled. I have to fix this…because it's my fault it even happened," added Lydall, hanging her head in shame.

She had allowed her heart to rule her head, just like Fenelia had once done long ago. And now Lydall felt the same guilt that the former Krekanian Queen had lived with for years. She refused to live the way Fenelia had. She had to correct her mistake.

"What about us? What about Krekania—and me?" asked Jasper, glancing away as his face turned red, a part of him feeling guilty for pressuring Lydall to stay, "We finally have peace in Krekania. We can finally be together—and now you're leaving."

"Will we ever truly have peace while Caillic still lives?" countered Lydall as she looked around the room, "Look at what her hatred has done to us. I need to finish this fight, then I will return to take my place on the throne."

Nyra nodded, stepping forward, "Then I will be coming

with you—myself and Zephyr. You'll need protection and Zephyr can track down anything. We'll leave one of his strongest wolves in charge of the pack while we're away."

The Seer nodded, "This is a wise decision. Nyra and the alpha wolf Zephyr shall accompany Queen Lydall on this journey."

Lydall smiled kindly at Nyra and gave the Seer a nod before she called out for her destrier.

"Triton will come as well. The only being here who knows Histair as well as I do is him," she said as her stallion trotted obediently to her side, nuzzling her affectionately.

Jasper signed in resignation, "I know you're making the right decision," he said as he ran his fingers through her long red hair, "It'll just be so hard to watch you leave—and who will rule Krekania in your stead?"

Lydall smiled, her eyes twinkling in amusement, "Do you really need to ask that question?"

Jasper raised an eyebrow, confused by what Lydall was trying to convey.

"Jasper, Captain of the Army of Spellbinders, you will rule as King of Krekania until I return," declared Lydall, raising her chin and gazing upon Jasper with pride, "Your Army has no need to continue living in our old training ground in Catha. Have them relocate their supplies and homes here, in the Castle. We'll make this our new home so you can run the Army and the business of the Castle while I'm away."

Jasper's eyes were wide with shock, "You want—you want *me* to be—to be *King?*"

Lydall laughed as she stood on her toes to kiss Jasper, "Not King…but my regent. I'll always be the Queen of Krekania, no matter where I go. But I'll need a trusted member of my court to rule in my place. And I can think of no one better to lead our subjects. You'll have Syllus and Armus to help you too."

Jasper smiled as he returned Lydall's kiss, pulling her in as close to him as he could get until he could feel every curve of her body pressing into him.

"You know we're all still standing here, right?" asked Armus as he rolled his eyes in exasperation.

"They're so dramatic," agreed Nyra as she kissed Armus, "Take care of my wolves while I'm away?"

"Always," growled Armus, giving Nyra another fierce kiss.

"Hypocrites," laughed Jasper as they watched the two elves embrace.

"Perhaps you all will escort us to An Chloch?" asked Lydall, gazing up at Jasper hopefully.

Jasper smiled, his eyes wet with emotion as he looked down at the woman who had become his entire world, "It would be an honor, Queen Lydall."

. . .

It was a solemn and quiet journey toward the place where Zephyr and his pack had seen An Chloch appear.

Lydall sent a silent prayer to the magic she had come to rely on, hoping above all hope that An Chloch would still be there and that it would allow her to pass through again. Although, part of her had no desire to leave the land that had become both her home and her responsibility, she knew deep down she also had a duty to the family she left behind.

Her family. That thought sent a thrill of fear and dread through Lydall's heart. She missed them dearly, especially her younger brother, but what kind of reception would she receive upon returning to the place she had abandoned? What if they didn't accept her? What if Caillic had already found them?

Lydall forced these thoughts out of her mind and focused on the trail ahead. Jasper, Syllus, Armus, Mallen, Augustine, Dionysus, and the wolf-pack had joined them on their journey to An Chloch. The wolves scouted ahead, making sure the way was clear and free from any threats. Lydall rode on top of Triton, feeling slightly more at ease knowing she would be returning with her best friend back to their homeland.

Nyra walked steadily next to Zephyr, her eyes glittering with excitement at the challenge and adventure ahead. Lydall wished she had the same courage and tenacity that the darker elf had always possessed. Nyra was meaner, stronger, and more fierce than any of the other elves. Armus found her personality charming and attractive, while the others found her rather intimidating and overbearing. Lydall smirked slightly at the thought. She would likely need Nyra's intense personality in the near future.

Soon they came to the edge of the woods where the field began—and where An Chloch stood.

Lydall felt her heart skip a beat in her chest when she caught a glimpse of the grey stone through the trees. An Chloch was still there.

The group stopped walking for a moment as they stood on the edge of the tree line. Nyra turned to Armus to give him a final farewell.

Lydall felt her heart clench a little as she slid off Triton's back, preparing to say goodbye to Jasper. She watched as he jumped off Dionysus and approached her hesitantly.

"I'll be okay," she whispered as she noticed the fear in Jasper's eyes, "We've been through so much already. We will make it through this too."

Jasper nodded, his throat closing up as emotion

threatened to choke him, "I know."

Dionysus moved to nuzzle Triton affectionately as the two creatures said their goodbyes, startling Jasper and Lydall.

"Well I suppose those two finally decided to be friendly with one another," she said with a laugh.

"Well, it's like I said when we first met. Lock them away in a room together long enough, or put them in a perilous situation and they'll find a way to get along," smirked Jasper as he gently ran his fingers down Lydall's cheek and looked into her eyes, "Worked out well for us too."

Lydall leaned forward to kiss Jasper again, her heart full of love for the elf captain.

Armus and Nyra finally separated from their embrace. Zephyr nudged Nyra forward and the pair stood facing Lydall, waiting for her order to pass through An Chloch.

"I suppose this is it," said Jasper, his eyes bright with sadness.

"I'll come home to you," said Lydall, her green eyes glowing with fierce determination, "I swear it."

Jasper nodded as he gave her a final hug, "I know you will. I found you once. I'll find you again."

Lydall bit her lip as tears threatened to spill from her eyes and pulled away from Jasper's arms. She turned to face the stone—the very thing that brought her here—and stepped forward.

Nyra, Zephyr and Triton followed Lydall as they walked up to An Chloch, their eyes wide as they felt the pulsating power of magic emanating from the large structure.

Taking a deep breath, Lydall reached out and placed her hand against the stone.

Epilogue

Caillic bent over, holding her stomach in a protective manner as she slipped through the trees. She growled low in her throat as she felt the pain of the burns on her stomach and arms—damn that Woman of Fire. She could hardly believe the Krekanians had destroyed her army. She especially could not believe that Archer was gone.

The thought of Archer made Caillic's pain considerably worse. She had not realized how much she cared for the dark elf until she watched his lifeblood spill out on the throne room floor. He had died too early—far too young. Archer would never get to know how deeply Caillic loved him—or the secret she never had the chance to reveal. She had planned to wait until they won the war, and now that chance would never come.

Caillic frowned as she glanced down at her singed clothes and the dark red burns on her stomach. She gave a silent thank you to the darkness for protecting her from further injury.

Caillic grimaced as she continued her long, painful journey. An Chloch had dumped her out into a field full of bright green grass in the middle of nowhere. Out of instinct she had fled to the edge of the distant woods and traveled in the shadow of the trees, eager to not be seen before she figured out where she was and what her next move would be.

She had noticed almost immediately that the land was void of any magic. Her ice magic was gone; she could not even feel its presence in her body anymore. A slight flickering of the darkness inside her eased her troubled mind. At least she had retained a small amount of her power.

After several days of wandering, Caillic saw something in the distance. She narrowed her eyes and peered through the foliage. It was a castle. Not nearly as large as the Castle of Krekania, but it was a castle nonetheless. And in castles were kings, queens, riches, and power.

A wicked grin crossed Caillic's features as she slipped out of the woods and into the daylight, her eyes fixated on the ornate structure ahead—and the future she began to form in her mind's eye for herself.

And for the unborn child inside of her.

THE END

Acknowledgements

Many people view the writing of a novel as a solitary venture, but a feat such as this requires an army…and I am very grateful to my own Army of Spellbinders for their support, love, and encouragement this past year.

First and foremost, thank you to my family. Your constant support of even my most fantastical dreams has culminated in all of my accomplishments, including the courage to publish a novel…the first of many, I hope.

To my phenomenal friends who not only spur on my outlandish ideas, but frequently ask if I've made any progress and push me to keep going even when I want to quit. Thank you for helping me extinguish my fears of releasing my work to the world.

To my beta readers who caught things that I completely missed, and helped bring Lydall into an even grander light. Her story is as vibrant as the flora of Krekania because of your help. Any errors that remain are mine and mine alone.

To the young people who read Lydall's story. I hope her journey has inspired you to overcome your fears and to take the plunge. Find what makes your heart race and pursueit with reckless abandon. Too many of us go through life not following what makes us the happiest. Never be afraid to recognize that you deserve more…and be willing to fight tooth and nail for it. Find that inner fire and stoke the flames. The world needs your light.

Last, but far from least, to my lovely Lydall…my soul brought forth onto paper…

Dearest Lydall,

We did it. We really did it.

Somehow we overcame our fears and pushed through our doubts and now our story is out there for the world to experience.

Perhaps the most beautiful thing about it is the fact that we did not have to do it alone. The friends we made along this journey will be with us again as we move into the next part of our story. The most valuable lesson we learned was that, while we are fully capable of doing things on our own, we should not *have* to. We now have our own Army of Spellbinders supporting our every move, and we will need to rely on that strength more than ever in the months to come.

There were so many times I wanted to give up on us...on our story...but you kept me from quitting. On the hardest days I would sit at my computer and dive into the parts of your story that were not so beautiful...those moments when you felt broken and defeated...and through those events I helped you find the warrior inside yourself, and you helped me find mine. I am not sure there is much that can stop either of us now.

But our demons will not be so easily quelled. The darkness is not done with us. We defeated our initial fears and destroyed the things that have always held us back, but such things have a way of seeking their vengeance.

As overwhelming as this next step seems, I know we can do this. After all, what is one more battle?

Now that we have become warriors, we must learn to be something else entirely.

We must become *Queens*.

Therefore, Lydall, I will ask you one more
time: Shall we begin?

Love,

Scarlet

My Writer's Playlist

Live Like Legends – Ruelle

Meet Me on the Battlefield – SVRCINA

Tomorrow We Fight – SVRCINA

You Should See Me in a Crown – Billie Eilish

Just Like Fire – PINK

Girl on Fire – Alicia Keys

This is Me – Keala Settle

Fight Song – Rachel Platten

Rise – Katy Perry

Spirit – Beyonce

Confident – Demi Lovato

Safe and Sound – Taylor Swift featuring The Civil Wars

Eyes Open – Taylor Swift

Speechless – Naomi Scott

Journey (Ready to Fly) – Natasha Blume

City of the Dead – Eurielle

Battle Cry – Beth Crowley

Warrior – Beth Crowley

When the Darkness Comes – Colbie Caillat

Open Your Eyes – Bea Miller

Heroes – Zayde Wolf

Awake and Alive - Skillet

Hero – Skillet

Indestructible – Disturbed

Bring Me to Life – Evanescence

Made in the USA
Columbia, SC
31 August 2019